The Healer

Allison Butler

16
EasyRead Large

RHYW

Copyright Page from the Original Book

ISBN: 9780857991911

Title: The Healer

TABLE OF CONTENTS

The Healer
Allison Butler

Curb your Outlander *cravings with Allison Butler's seriously sexy Scottish novel about an English woman, a Scottish Laird, a case of mistaken identity and a love that will surpass all barriers.*

An outcast in her own home for as long as she can remember, Lynelle Fenwick will do anything to earn her father's approval. Including exaggerating her healing skills, and setting off alone to rescue her stepbrother from a band of raiding Scots.

Living under a curse that has haunted the Closeburn Clan for years, Laird William Kirkpatrick, will do anything to save his sole surviving brother. He may not believe in curses, but his clan does, and the growing number of graves seems to support their side. Having banished all healers from the clan for trickery, he has no choice but to allow an Englishwoman, claiming to be a skilled healer, into his home and into the room of his wounded brother.

Enemies by birth and circumstance, they can only succeed together. But blood runs deep, and tensions high. What matters the desires of a heart?

About the Author

Allison Butler is an author of Scottish historical romance. She spent her early years in country New South Wales building pretend castles with hay bales and leaping white posts with her army of two older sisters and a younger brother. Many years later, with her mother's influence, she discovered a passion for words and history, read her first historical romance and was inspired to create her own. She writes by day and cares for the elderly by night. Her love of travel has given her the gift of many amazing sights but none more heart-stirring than the rugged beauty of Scotland. Allison lives in a small town in New South Wales, Australia, with her very own Scottish hero, two beautiful daughters and a Jack Russell named Wallace. She loves travelling, dancing like no-one's watching and seeing the sights from the back of her husband's motorcycle.

Acknowledgements

Many thanks to Romance Writers of Australia and Romance Writers of New Zealand for the ongoing support and guidance and all the amazing members I've met along the way. Huge thanks to Kate Cuthbert and the wonderful team at Escape Publishing. Thanks to the fabulous members of Claytons who were there when *The Healer* first came to life, especially my awesome writing buddy, Alissa Callen. I'd be lost without you. A special thank you to Mentor-Extraordinaire Anna Campbell, who taught me so much and is one of the most generous people I know. Super thanks to my friends and family, especially my two beautiful daughters for their constant encouragement and excitement. And finally, thank you to my gorgeous Scottish hero for believing in me, for still bringing me flowers and for providing constant inspiration by looking fantastic in a kilt.

To all the Healers out there

Chapter 1

Fenwick Keep
Northern Cumbria, April 1402

'Run!' Lynelle shouted from the far side of the field as the horn signalling danger blasted from the keep.

Men and women grabbed sickles and hoes before fleeing to safety. Lynelle clutched her burden, lifted her skirts and ran as if the devil were at her heels. Her chest burned with every indrawn breath as her leather-clad feet pounded the hard ground. Every footfall jarred her body, distorting the figures running toward the iron-studded gates ahead.

A blood-curdling cry erupted from the pack of mounted men spilling over the grassy ridge to the north. A noose of fear tightened around Lynelle's throat. Would she make it to the keep before they rode her down? She had to. She must!

Fenwick's people ran through the gates and were now safe within the stronghold. Cool shadows cast by the curtain wall fell about her as she neared the opening. She stopped at the threshold and searched for stragglers. Seeing none, she hurried inside.

'I am the last. Close the gates,' she said, hoping the guards would do her bidding despite who she was.

She pressed her bundle to her side to ease the ache there, as the giant beam was lowered into place. A faint lick of triumph sparked inside her. The barbarians would gain little this day.

Why were they attacking now? Raids usually took place between Lammas in August and Candlemas in February. It was now mid-April. They always came before dawn, or late at night, cloaked in darkness, yet the afternoon's sun still glowed brightly in the west.

The bailey was crowded. The air filled with tales of people running for their lives. Grasping her skirts, Lynelle raced up the uneven stairs to the battlements.

Straining for breath, knees weak as she reached the top, she forced herself to keep moving. She chose a section along the wall that granted the best view, and slipped between two of the sentries. They shifted away from her, as she expected.

She set her bundle down at her feet, gripped the cold stone before her and peered at the scene beyond the walls.

Sunlight blazed upon every drawn sword the invaders brandished high above their heads. This was her first real glimpse of the men her father often named savages. A whisper of fear swelled inside her, mingled with a strange sense of awe.

Did they know her father was away? It was Truce Day and as Warden of the English West March, Lord

Fenwick would spend his day dealing with crimes against the Border Laws – crimes committed by both the English and the Scots. Only a few men remained to guard the well-fortified keep. Once the gates were barred, those within were secure.

She watched the intruders, counted at least a dozen. The sound of galloping hooves filled her ears as they approached.

One of the Scots at the head of the pack stood out from the rest. His dark hair rose and fell about his shoulders with his horse's rhythmic stride. Lynelle lifted her hand to block the sun's brightness. The man looked up at her.

Lynelle's heart skipped a beat. Time slowed. Her body heated. The distance was too great to discern his features, but his gaze seared her like a brand.

He turned, severing the invisible bond. The sound of thundering hooves filled her ears. Suddenly, in tight formation, the riders veered to the right, away from the fortress. Lynelle cupped her hot cheeks with cold hands and sucked in a long breath.

The Scots rode to the far side of the open field where a thick line of trees marked the west wood. Why had they come? Were they searching for something or someone?

Who was he, the man with the scorching gaze?

'God o' mercy,' said one of the guards to her left.

Turning, she bumped into someone. She drew back and took in Bernard's kind features. Bernard was one of the older guards and was one of the few who didn't avoid her gaze or keep his distance from her. He even dared to touch her. He must have followed her to the battlements once the gates were closed.

'What is it, Bernard?'

'I do not know,' he said, moving to peer out through the next gap in the wall.

Lynelle joined him, and leaning forward she searched the ground below. Her heart lurched as she glimpsed a small figure outside, galloping away from the keep.

'Thomas,' she whispered.

No! It couldn't be. Had he escaped his personal guards again?

'We must help him,' she said, latching onto Bernard's sleeve. 'Bernard, you must tell the guards to open the gates.'

Bernard slowly shook his head. ''Tis too late, my lady.'

'It is never too late.' She'd never given in. She wouldn't now. But Bernard resisted her efforts to pull him along with her and continued staring out from the battlements.

Though part of her didn't want to know what was happening, she forced herself to look.

The wild men from the north surrounded Thomas. He was shouting and shaking his fist at the grown men who appeared enormous by comparison. They *were* enormous compared to her eight-year-old stepbrother.

'He is just a boy. Surely they won't harm him.'

'The master's age is not important to the Bloody Elliots,' Bernard said quietly.

A shudder ripped through Lynelle at the mention of the Elliots.

'I must go to him,' she said spinning away. A large hand grabbed her and spun her back around. She glanced at the weathered fingers holding her upper arm and then gazed into Bernard's beseeching brown eyes.

'No, mistress. They already have Thomas. Surrendering yourself will do the boy little good. You will only give the Scots another prize.'

'How can I do nothing?'

'You have no choice.'

'Look there,' one of the sentries called.

Bernard's hand fell from her arm as they both scanned the field beyond. Four mounted men emerged from the west wood. One looked to be struggling to stay upright in his saddle. The Scot with the fiery gaze rode among them.

'Who is the dark-haired man?' Lynelle asked.

'His colours and larger mount mark him as other than a Elliott,' Bernard said.

His horse was several hands taller than those his companions rode, and the garment draping his body was blue and green while the others wore blue. She'd been enthralled by his dark visage and hadn't noticed the obvious differences. Shame rushed through her. She must be wicked indeed to have found him or any of his kind fascinating.

The four joined the men who had formed a circle surrounding Thomas. One of the Scots caught and lowered her brother's raised fist, ending his show of defiance. He then tied Thomas' hands behind his back.

Lynelle clenched her hands and sealed her lips to silence her words of anger.

The same man secured the reins of Thomas' horse to his own mount. The Scots closed in around their young captive, stealing Thomas from sight.

The pounding hooves from more than a dozen retreating horses was deafening. Dread pooled in her belly for her young stepbrother. A sense of helplessness swamped her as she watched the Scots gallop north and disappear over the ridge in a cloud of dust. Thomas vanished along with them.

Sweet Mother of God. What would happen to him?

Were the Scots truly the savages the elders swore them to be? Were the longwinded tales of cruelty and barbaric deeds true?

Would they torture Thomas? Cut off his fingers and return them with a demand for ransom? Or bind his hands and feet, gag him and suspend his small body from a tree, taking turns to watch and laugh as the birds pecked his sweet blue eyes from his head and ripped the flesh from his little bones?

Lynelle shuddered as a cold hand of fear gripped her heart.

How she wished her father were here, for he would know what to do. Sweet Mary, if Thomas was hurt or killed, her father would be devastated. Furious. John Fenwick doted on his son. Thomas was her father's heir, his greatest source of pride and joy.

Lynelle's fingers turned white as she clutched the cold stone before her. But her father wasn't here, and Thomas' mother...

Dear God. Lady Fenwick.

In all the commotion Lynelle had forgotten Thomas' mother.

Spinning away from the view of the deserted field, she stumbled down the uneven stairs. She needed to tell Lady Fenwick what had happened, and gain her favour to rescue Thomas.

Chickens scattered and squawked as she rushed across the bailey. She climbed the few stairs to the tower-house entrance and stopped short as Bernard stepped out, blocking her path. Caught up in her grim thoughts, she hadn't noticed he'd left the battlements before her.

Regret deepened the lines of his aging features. She gave him a glance filled with gratitude to him for standing with her.

A hellish scream rent the air from inside the tower house, and then for a whisper of time, the world fell silent. Lady Fenwick must have learned of Thomas' fate.

Running footsteps echoed from inside the tower. Lynelle settled on the top step but didn't enter the tower house, and prepared to console the distraught woman. A chorus of murmurs filled the bailey. Shuffling footsteps moved closer behind her, though not too close. Word had spread and the people must be eager to witness their lady's reaction if they were willing to risk being near Lynelle.

Lady Fenwick suddenly filled the doorway, her gown of costly golden silk shimmering in the sunlight. Her chest heaved with every swift, audible breath. Lynelle's gaze lifted from the perfect silk-clad figure to the beautiful face, now twisted in fear.

Catherine Fenwick was her father's wife and Thomas' mother, and the woman Lynelle had once hoped would be like a mother to her.

Lynelle stared up into Catherine's cold eyes; pain and anguish clouded the blue depths.

Something struck one side of Lynelle's face and a stinging sensation tore through her left cheek. The force of the unexpected blow sent her tumbling down the tower-house steps.

Pain ripped through her hip as she landed on the hard packed earth. Dazed and shaken, Lynelle climbed to her knees. She cupped her burning cheek and witnessed Catherine's jewel-studded fingers curl into a fist and resettle by her side.

Lynelle clenched her jaw against the hot resentment bubbling inside her. The unfamiliar emotion dissolved as awareness took hold.

Merciful angels. After ten years of waiting, her stepmother had finally deigned to touch her.

Bernard stepped forward and reached for her. Lynelle gained her feet and saw the shocked expression on the older man's face.

'What a pair you make,' Catherine screeched. 'One as useless as the other.' Her stepmother's maids filled the doorway, hovering behind their mistress.

'You, Bernard, would defend this worthless strumpet rather than see to my son's safety.'

Lynelle's cheek throbbed and something warm and sticky coated the fingers she gingerly placed on the left side of her face. Blood. Her hand dropped to her side as her stepmother's eyes, blazing hatred, fixed on her.

'And you ... you vile creature,' Lady Fenwick said in a low, trembling voice. Lynelle stiffened, bracing herself for the insults she knew would follow. 'Your black heart is cursed and it is the innocent who suffer your evil.'

Each word plunged like a knife into her bleeding heart.

'They should have drowned you at birth,' Catherine spat before she collapsed in the arms of her maids.

Lynelle flinched but stood her ground and stared as the serving women aided a distraught Lady Fenwick back inside the tower house.

'Why my poor darling Thomas?' Catherine wailed. 'Why not take the devil's daughter instead?'

"Tis not your fault, Lady Lynelle,' Bernard said quietly.

Lynelle looked at the man who had been more of a father to her than her own.

'I was the last through the gates, and he is my brother.'

'Master Thomas did not leave through those gates,' he said firmly. 'And the boy ignores you, my lady.'

'Thomas is young, Bernard. He ignores me because others do. He is the only brother I have left.' She patted his hand. 'I must go.'

'Your wound needs tending. Let me help you.'

Gratitude swelled and threatened to choke her. 'I will go and tend to it now,' she managed to say. 'Thank you for your kindness, Bernard.' She gave his hand a final squeeze and slowly walked away.

She glanced to her left and right and found the eyes of Fenwick's people fixed on her. The shaking heads and condemning gazes came as no surprise. All blamed her for Thomas' plight. She was always to blame.

If the hens refused to lay it was her doing. When sickness ravaged the people of the keep, she was the cause. She'd always pretended indifference to their damning gazes, just as she would now.

She raised her chin and straightened her back. Clenching her teeth against the pain in her hip from her fall, she took slow, careful steps across the bailey.

Would her father blame her too?

Lynelle's hands clenched as despair filled her chest. Would he ever acknowledge her? Ever love her?

She rounded the far corner of the bakehouse, escaping the prying eyes of the castle folks. A gentle breeze touched her face as she paused in the alley between the bakehouse and the curtain wall. Her hip ached and her cheek stung. But her ailments were nothing compared to what Thomas might be suffering.

Pushing forward, she spared a glance at her herb garden, but didn't stop to caress either rosemary shrub or meadowsweet as she usually did in passing.

She entered the ramshackle hut she had shared with Ada since her birth, and breathed deeply of the familiar scent of mingled herbs. She bit down on her lip to still its sudden tremble. Her heart ached, for she desperately wished the old healing woman still lived. Ada would have offered comfort and guidance regarding her brother's capture.

She walked to the rickety, scarred table at the rear of the hut and gathered a bowl and cloths from the sagging shelf above. By the fading light filtering in through the single open shutter, she prepared a cleansing wash using sopewort.

Lynelle bathed her wound, gritting her teeth against the stinging pain, and tried to cut off the cruel visions of Thomas' torture before they fully formed.

Sweet God, please keep Thomas safe.

She wasn't sure if someone like her was fit to ask for help, but she had to try. Once a life was lost, it could never be restored. Lynelle knew this to be true, for she was guilty of stealing not one life but two.

She swallowed, knowing full well that prayers were not enough. If only she could rescue her brother herself.

Her fingers stilled.

Was it possible for her to rescue Thomas?

She clutched the cleansing cloth and slowly sat on the wooden pail that served as both bucket and stool. There was nothing to stop her from finding Thomas and bringing him home. She had nothing to lose, but much to gain.

If she rescued Thomas, her father would have to find favour with her, wouldn't he? How could he not? He'd finally acknowledge her as his daughter.

Excitement fluttered in the corner of her heart where she'd buried her greatest desire.

She *would* rescue Thomas.

Her spirits lifted as a sense of rightness flowed through her. She now had direction and a desperately needed purpose.

Latching on to her tattered hope, Lynelle finished tending her wound. The gash didn't seem to sting as much as it had before. As she tipped the unused wash into the slop bucket, she focused on what little she knew about her stepbrother's captors.

The Elliots were Scottish neighbours close to Fenwick. They lived beyond the north ridge, and were said to be a troublesome lot. Lynelle vowed to find them and set Thomas free.

Her feelings of helplessness eased as she gathered her scant belongings and waited for darkness to fall. She carefully wrapped small bundles of herbs and placed them within a worn leather pouch. If Thomas were injured, the herbs and Ada's teachings would prove necessary. She prayed the Scots who held him weren't the brutes most claimed they were.

A flicker of annoyance flashed through her at the ill timing of their raid. She'd finally begun to feel she belonged, had felt a part of something as she'd worked the soil. Though her small plot was separate from the rest, she'd turned and prepared the earth just as many of Fenwick's people had. She'd even had her own sprinkling of seeds to plant, though the bag of seed now rested atop the battlements.

Sighing, she glanced at the open doorway and saw that the day was almost done. Nervous anticipation coursed through her. It was almost dark. Almost time to go. Fenwick's people would soon file into the tower house for the evening meal. Lynelle's absence wouldn't be noticed, as she'd never dined inside the great hall.

Would things change once she rescued Thomas?

Lifting her small knife, she wrapped it inside her spare gown, and coiled a linen cloth about the half loaf from the day before. She stuffed them into a sack with the herb pouch and tied the top with a strip of leather cord. Finally, she closed the window's warped shutter, wincing as it creaked into place.

Taking up her cloak, she walked to the door and swept the hooded garment around her shoulders. She secured the ties at her throat, pretending her hands shook not at all. She peered outside and noted how the dusky shades of twilight smothered the alley running along the rear of the tower house.

She turned and drank in the dim interior of the hut, her home. Inhaling deeply, she snatched up her bundle and slipped out the door.

Crouching low, ignoring the ache in her hip, Lynelle clung to the rear of the bakehouse and crept on past the kitchens. At the gap between kitchen and tower house, she looked up at the curtain wall. Two guards walked the battlements, their figures little more than dark shapes floating across the dull grey of the evening sky. The flaming torches at either end of the stone edifice shed pitiful light at this hour.

Lynelle ran across the gap and stopped at the eastern corner of the tower house. Leaning against the cool stone wall, she closed her eyes and paused to catch her breath. The sound of her thudding heart filled her ears. She'd covered little ground, but her fear of discovery had her heart racing as if she'd run for miles.

Fenwick's people would not stop her due to concern for her wellbeing, but they might detain her, ending any chance of her rescuing Thomas.

The pounding in her chest slowed. She pushed away from the stone at her back and peeked around the next corner. With no one in sight, she dashed across to the little used postern gate, and found it ajar.

So this is how Thomas had made his escape.

Few knew the gate existed. Its dimensions were smaller than that of the average doorway. With the stonework so cleverly done, it could be seen only by a trained eye or someone who knew it was there – or a child who'd explored every inch of the keep to hold her loneliness at bay.

A cough sounded from somewhere behind. Lynelle flinched and glanced over her shoulder. Once certain she was alone, she opened the gate and stepped through the opening. She latched the door, clutched her sack tightly to her middle and turned around.

Full night was but a breath away and she suddenly felt very small and very alone. She held no fear of the dark, but a shiver rushed through her as she felt a thread of doubt at what she was about to do.

She must save Thomas. There would be no turning back. She was tired of living as an outcast. She wanted more.

She cast all misgivings from her mind, stretched to her full height and lifted her chin a notch. Cursed she might be, but a coward she was not.

Chapter 2

Castle Redheugh
Scots side of the border

William Kirkpatrick slipped into the dim, deserted corridor, and drew a deep, shuddering breath. Edan's wounds had been appraised and tended. Thanks to the draft given to the lad by Iona, the Elliot's aged and crippled healer, William's young brother now slept.

He'd dismissed Iona and the burning glare she gave him as she'd shuffled awkwardly from the room. She had been insulted by the terms he'd set for treating Edan. But William didn't care. Relief surged through him. His brother would live.

William rolled each aching shoulder, easing the tension caused by the day's unexpected events, and welcomed the moment of solitude. Closing his eyes, he sank against the hard, stone wall and dragged roughened hands over his face.

The memory of his brother's grey eyes dulled by pain and rounded with terror filled the blackness behind his lids. Edan's pain was due to his injuries. His terror stemmed from the blasted curse.

William's eyes snapped open. Bringing his brother with him to visit his friend, Lachlan Elliot, hadn't been worth the effort. He knew now it would take more than a day or two away from Closeburn Castle to eradicate his brother's fears. William was not a man led or controlled by foolish superstition. But many of his clan were, including his younger brother.

Four members of William's immediate family had died within the last year. William knew their deaths had nothing to do with the ancient curse and everything to do with the deceitful, inept tricksters who called themselves healers. He blamed himself too, for not recognizing the truth sooner.

Wiser now, he'd ensure Edan didn't suffer the same fate. He'd protect his only surviving kin with his life.

Straightening, he stretched and turned to stare at the stout oak door he'd closed a short time ago. He peered over his shoulder and looked through the arrow slit on the opposite wall, surprised to see it was completely dark outside. He would find Lachlan and let him know he and Edan would be leaving tomorrow. But first, he'd take one last look at his brother.

Cracking the door open, he blinked as heat bathed his face and the smell of herbs consumed his senses. His gaze immediately sought the bed across the small chamber and the still figure lying upon it.

The crackling flames in the hearth painted Edan's brown hair and pale face with splashes of red. His eyes were closed, his lips slightly parted. The bedclothes pulled up to his chest rose and fell with a steady rhythm.

The tightness in William's chest eased. Withdrawing from the room, he latched the door.

William strode toward the glow at the far end of the corridor, passing two closed doors on his left. Halting, he peered at the massive iron-studded door directly opposite the stairwell, wondering if Lachlan had retired for the night.

He had no clue as to what time it was. The bevy of snores floating up from the great hall at the bottom of the stairs proved it was later than he'd first thought. He could retire himself, but he wanted to be certain that Lachlan's brother had escaped the boys' foolish adventure unscathed.

As William descended the stairs, the faint smell of roasted meat lingered in the air. His belly rumbled, reminding him that he'd missed the evening meal.

'Ah, William,' a voice rose above the din of slumbering noises. 'Come sit and tell me how your brother fares.'

William searched the hall and found the Elliot laird lounging in his chair, booted feet crossed and propped on the table's top. Surprisingly, he was alone.

''Tis late. Why is it nae fair lass has lured you to your bed?' William teased, surprising both his target and himself. Drawing out the chair closest to where his handsome, fair-haired friend sprawled, he watched as a grin stole over Lachlan's features.

'I fear I've worn them all out.'

But William noted the smile didn't reach Lachlan's blue eyes, and he remembered no village woman vying for his attention the previous night either.

'Enough of me,' Lachlan said. 'How is young Edan?'

William sat and accepted the goblet of ale his friend slid toward him. He sipped, swirling the ale in his mouth to eradicate the bitter taste of the sleeping potion he'd sampled before it passed Edan's lips. He wondered if Iona had rinsed her mouth the moment he'd sent her from the chamber.

'Two, perhaps three ribs are broken,' he began.

He drank deeply before naming the rest of the injuries his brother sustained. Edan had fallen from his horse. He'd landed awkwardly on a pile of deadwood within the small forest they'd rescued him from.

'A small gash marks his face. His left arm is broken below the elbow and his body will soon rival the hue of a thundercloud.' William drained his goblet and made no protest when Lachlan refilled it. 'But it's the wound to his left leg that concerns me most.' He tried to erase the image of the rotted wood jutting out of Edan's bloodied thigh. 'What of Caelan?'

'Caelan is the luckier of the two.' Lachlan shifted and recrossed his booted feet. 'He told me the tale of their adventure, and now I suspect his banishment from the stables until summer and cleaning every stone of the curtain wall to the south will hurt more than the few scrapes he sustained.'

'He alone is not to blame for their foolishness.'

'You and your brother are *my* guests, Will. Your safety is *my* responsibility while you're here. Caelan knows the Borders are a dangerous place. Crossing into England is forbidden and the lad knows it. Being barred from the horses and a spot of cleaning is little to suffer for his crime.'

'Have you not led your men across the border a time or two?' Will asked with mock innocence.

'Aye. It is my duty as a Border laird to wreak havoc on the English scum. Bring some excitement into their dull, witless lives.' A frown replaced Lachlan's smile. 'But never were we ill prepared or outnumbered, as our brothers were today.'

William nodded and sipped his ale. Both lads bore injuries, but they had escaped with their lives. For that he was grateful. The lads, both fourteen, had not been seen since dawn when they'd fetched horses from the stable and ridden south toward the border. Lachlan had immediately rounded up ten of his men, he and William making their party twelve. They had ridden over the ridge to search for their brothers.

Caelan and Edan hadn't gone far into English territory. They'd even managed to avoid any confrontation with the English. But a startled rabbit had spooked their horses and unseated both young riders.

'How did you know where to find them?' William asked.

'Caelan believes the west wood is haunted. Tales of ghosties and goblins have kept him away until today. I heard Caelan telling Edan the very same stories last eve and suspect they found the courage to explore the wood together.'

William nodded in understanding. 'What of the lad you brought back? Who is he?'

'He claims to be Lord Fenwick's whelp.'

'Was it necessary to bring him along?'

A mischievous grin dawned on Lachlan's face, this one reaching his eyes. 'Nae, but it was too good an opportunity to pass. It has been months since we harassed our English neighbours and the lad *was* there for the taking.'

'What will you do with him?' William saw his younger brother as a lad, when at fourteen he was more a man. But the boy Lachlan had taken hostage was just that, a boy.

'Ah, the lad.' Lachlan took a swill of his ale and said, 'Torture comes to mind.'

William stared at Lachlan, trying to see beneath his friend's set features. 'You jest?'

Lachlan burst out laughing. 'Aye, Will,' he said between bouts of laughter. 'We will keep the lad for the night and release him, unharmed, come the morn.'

William slammed his goblet on the table and stood.

'Come now, Will. You've grown too severe over the years, man. Where's your sense of mirth?'

'I leave early for home. 'Tis time I sought my bed.'

'Is Edan well enough to make the journey?' Lachlan asked as he too got to his feet.

William ran a worried hand through his hair. His concern for Edan's health weighed heavily on his mind. He'd been gone from Closeburn for only two days, but the sudden need to return home swamped him.

'It is less than two days' ride from here. Your healer believes Edan will survive if the pace is slow and his wounds are constantly tended.'

Lachlan nodded. 'Iona knows what she's about. 'Tis a pity her aging, twisted bones make her unfit to accompany you home.'

'I believe she'd rather keep her distance from me.'

William glanced at his friend and found the man grinning widely.

'Have you offended the woman who has pieced me back together more times than I care to think?'

'Aye. Iona didn't like having to test each salve on her own skin and then mine before applying it to Edan's broken flesh. But I think it was tasting the sleeping potion that sealed her hatred of me.'

Lachlan laughed and shook his head. 'Take care while you're here then, Will. Iona has a long memory and will probably watch you bleed to death before raising a disfigured hand to aid you.'

William nodded and turned for the stairs. His visit with Lachlan hadn't been long, but he needed to look in on Edan again.

'I could always ransom the English lad,' Lachlan called out.

William ignored him, knowing his friend was goading him. Skirting the sleeping horde, he picked a path where no unsuspecting fingers would be crushed beneath his boots. Thoughts of treating his brother's injuries on the journey home filled his mind.

He'd almost reached the first step when Lachlan's next words stopped him in his tracks. 'You need a woman, Will.'

William turned and stared at his friend. 'Nae, I need a healer. One I can trust. I bid you good night.' Spinning about, he climbed the stairs two at a time.

William strode to the guest chamber he shared with his brother and quietly slipped inside. The pungent aroma of herbs filled the air. He searched Edan's face, relieved to see the lad still slept deeply.

He eyed his brother's pallet, now his bed for the night, but William knew he wouldn't sleep. The room suddenly seemed overcrowded, stifling.

He quietly left the chamber, leaving the door ajar. The cool air in the hallway brushed his heated skin and he drew several deep breaths to clear his senses. He crossed the corridor and peered at the night sky through the slit in the stone.

Lachlan's comment about needing a woman filled his thoughts, though this time a flash of remembrance came with it. The picture of a lone woman standing high on the English battlements blinded him to the twinkling stars outside. Her red-gold hair seemed to catch fire beneath the sun's warm rays. Her face had been hidden from view by the slender hand shading her eyes.

She'd been the perfect target for a bowman's arrow. Unexpected anger had bubbled inside him. He'd glared at her, willing her to move back and find shelter. The pack of mounted men he rode with had changed direction, veering away from the fortress. He and Lachlan continued riding straight for the west wood, while the others altered their course again. From then he had been consumed by Edan's welfare.

A commotion outside drew him back to the present. He tried to see what was happening in the darkness below, but found it impossible to view much at all. Heavy footfalls ran through the hall downstairs, then swiftly echoed up the stairway.

A fist pounded on the laird's door. William glanced in on his brother and closed the door on the gentle snores coming from the bed. His curiosity piqued, he made his way along the corridor to the top of the stairs and halted in the shadows, watching and waiting for Lachlan to answer the knock.

The door suddenly flew inward. 'What is it? Lachlan asked.

The guard mumbled something too softly for William to hear. But Lachlan's response was no doubt heard in the next glen.

'God curse the bloody English! Fetch me some ale while I dress,' he shouted before slamming the door. The day's unfortunate events had troubled Lachlan more than he'd admitted or allowed others to see.

William followed the guard down into the hall and slipped into the corner near the laird's table. Propping a shoulder against the wall, he waited for his friend to appear.

A sleepy-eyed servant dashed off to fetch the requested ale while others scurried about lighting torches. The rest of the castle-folk scrambled to line the hall's perimeter, blinking wearily as they dragged their pallets with them.

Lachlan had never been at his best when awoken from sleep. Apparently he hadn't changed and his people knew him well. It was the only time the man lacked a grin on his face. Witnessing his friend's bout of unusual annoyance made William smile. It also gave him something aside from his own worries to think about.

The servant dashed out of the kitchens and deposited a jug of ale and a goblet on the laird's table. Lachlan stormed down the steps, dressed but looking dishevelled.

William's smile widened.

Lachlan poured a measure of ale into his cup and took a long swallow before wiping the back of one hand across his mouth.

Deeming it safe to speak, William said, 'So they've come for the lad?'

Lachlan's head snapped to his left, searching the shadows. William moved a fraction, allowing his friend to see where he was before settling back against the wall.

'Aye, the inconsiderate curs,' Lachlan said. 'They must want him badly for they couldn't even wait till the bloody morn.'

'How did they know to come here to find him?'

'We are one of their closest neighbours across the border and it's usually we Elliots who cause the Fenwicks the most grief,' Lachlan said proudly before tilting the cup to his lips once more.

''Tis not they, laird, but a single woman,' announced the guard who'd woken his laird.

'What?' Lachlan demanded.

'Your reputation is fierce indeed if the English send a lone woman to rescue the heir,' William said.

Lachlan glared at him, obviously not sharing his sense of humour.

Turning back to the guard he asked, 'Where is this woman?'

'She awaits you in the bailey, laird,' his clansman said.

Lachlan slammed his cup down and stalked the length of the table. Reaching the far end, he said, 'Bring the wench to me.'

The guard ran from the hall to do his laird's bidding.

William's wide smile became a grin as he watched Lachlan's fumbling attempts to straighten his attire. 'Are you planning to interrogate the woman or bed her?'

Lachlan spared a glance William's way before muttering, 'I thought you needed your bed.'

William chuckled. 'And miss the mighty Elliot vanquish his enemy? I think not.'

Lachlan's chest swelled as he sucked in a breath. 'You may stay and learn, but only if you hold your tongue.'

William's quiet laughter trailed off as the double doors to the great hall opened. A gust of night air bent the flames in the wall sconces sideways, freshening the crowded chamber. A small, cloaked and hooded figure entered, surrounded by half a dozen Elliots.

William remained at ease, knowing the flickering torches did not penetrate the space he occupied. He could watch the drama unfold without detection.

With hesitant steps the English lad's saviour moved into the hall. Not a wisp of hair or flesh showed of the darkly clad form. William's curiosity lifted a notch. What kind of woman dared to enter an enemy's domain alone to rescue a boy?

She is either a fool, or foolishly brave.

The woman stopped an arm's length from the laird's table and William absently measured her height compared to his. The top of her head would barely reach his shoulder.

'Tell me your name and why you have come at such an ungodly hour,' Lachlan said in his best laird's voice.

William saw the cloaked figure start. Small, pale hands emerged from the confining cloak and pushed back the hood to reveal the woman.

'I am Lynelle,' she said in a tremulous voice. 'I have come for Thomas, Lord Fenwick's heir.'

The glowing light from the torches fell on the woman's hair, turning it red-gold. Recognition hit William like a blow to his gut. Anger swelled inside him.

He surged forward, away from the wall. For the first time in his twenty-six years, William Kirkpatrick was furious without actually knowing why.

Chapter 3

'Little fool.'

Lynelle flinched and looked to where the harsh whisper exploded. She gasped as blazing eyes fixed on her.

Dear God, it was *him.*

She would know the dark-haired man's burning gaze anywhere. It stole her breath and heated her body from inside out. A shiver ripped through her. Beneath her cloak she pressed clenched hands to her middle.

She'd been called many heinous things, but never in her life had she been named a fool. He did not know her, yet he branded her. How dare he!

The melting feeling disappeared. Her initial fear at confronting Thomas' kidnappers ebbed. Driving her fists deeper into her stomach, she drew strength from her building anger. She glared back at him.

'How do you know we have Fenwick's heir?' The fair-haired man behind the long trestle asked.

Lynelle dragged her eyes away from the source of her sudden ire and focused on the man who spoke. He was looking at her, but unlike the man standing half in the shadows, he radiated not an ounce of judgment, only curiosity.

Her fingers uncurled a fraction.

'Is this the home of the Elliots?' She was pleased her voice rang steady and clear.

'Aye. I am Lachlan Elliot, laird of Redheugh Castle.'

Relief flowed through her. She'd found her stepbrother's prison. A warm, jittery feeling sparked in her chest and trickled into her belly. She knew pride to be a sin, but she had so many other faults that a few moments of self-indulgence would make little difference to her doomed soul.

'I have come to the right place, then,' she said. 'Fenwick's guards recognized your people and named the Elliots as Thomas' kidnappers.'

Inquiring blue eyes studied her. 'What gift have you brought in payment for the lad's release?'

Her momentary pleasure curdled like goat's milk left to lie in the sun as she noted his severe expression. He was serious.

'I ... I have naught to give you in return for freeing Thomas,' she said in a small voice.

The crowded chamber remained still and quiet as every eye rested upon her. Their curiosity surrounded her like a living thing. Of all the appraising eyes, she was acutely aware of the pair continuing to blaze at her from the side of the room.

Why his opinion of her mattered so much she had no clue. Perhaps his naming her a fool drove her to prove she wasn't.

Her palms grew moist and her body again heated beneath her dusty cloak. She'd worn the garment as a barrier. Yet now the flimsy shield seemed to imprison her, stifling her.

She'd come ill prepared, not realizing Thomas' kidnappers required a gift to set him free. Inexperienced she might be, but she was definitely not a fool. As she did at Fenwick, she used the dark stranger's contempt to fuel her flagging courage.

On the opposite side of the long table, Lachlan Elliot paced back and forth. Head down, deep in thought, his booted steps echoed off the bare, stone walls.

Despair surged. Without a gift, she had nothing to offer, nothing to give, save herself.

She straightened and squared her shoulders as an inconceivable idea took hold. If she traded herself for Thomas for a short time, then surely she'd be welcomed home to Fenwick with open arms.

Having come this far, she couldn't leave, wouldn't leave, without doing all she could. Her father would have to acknowledge such a sacrifice on her part, leaving him no choice other than to acknowledge her.

Lynelle searched her mind for the right words to make her offer as tempting as possible. She needed to stretch the truth a little to snare Lachlan Elliot's interest. She drew a deep breath, licked her dry lips and tilted her chin.

'I have no coin or gift, but if you release Thomas, I am willing to offer my services in return.'

Resounding gasps erupted. The Elliot laird stood still as a rock, his pacing abandoned. Unblinking, he stared at her.

She didn't really know why her offer garnered such a reaction, but she took advantage of the resulting silence.

Swallowing the lump of nervousness in her throat, she moved a step closer to the table.

'My skills are well known and many seek–'

'Enough!'

Lynelle jumped as the bellowed command ripped through the hall from her right.

Wide-eyed, she watched as the savage strode toward the Elliot laird and stopped beside him. Darkest-brown, almost black, his hair skimmed his impressive shoulders. The creased material of his shirt drew taut across his chest as he placed powerful hands upon his lean hips and turned to Lachlan.

Over her pounding heartbeat, she could just make out their low words.

'God's teeth, Lachlan. I will not stand by and watch while the wretched lass offers to whore for you.'

'I did not suggest such a choice. I only asked what gift she had brought to trade.'

Fire filled her cheeks as the meaning of their heated exchange sank in. Stunned, she stared at the dark-haired man. He'd called her a fool and now a whore. A wave of shame and fury crashed over her.

'No!' she shouted in outrage.

Both men whipped around to look at her, their discussion forgotten. Her legs shook and she reached for the table to steady herself.

'You ... you mistake me,' she said. 'I am no man's ... you mistake me.'

As they continued to watch her, Lynelle's heart dropped into the pit of her belly.

She would do anything to gain her father's approval, but did anything include being Lachlan Elliot's whore?

Lachlan Elliot was a tall, handsome man. She tried to conjure images of him holding her, his mouth upon hers, but she failed.

As her gaze travelled to assess his silent companion, her sudden breathlessness shocked her. Lachlan may leave her unmoved, but the same could not be said for the man beside him.

His eyes were the colour of the sky on a cool, winter's day. An omen to all that snow was on its way. His square jaw avowed stubborn determination, his shapely lips...

Heat flooded her being as his sharp grey gaze skimmed her form. She felt skittish, like a newborn foal. Images of his mouth devouring the pounding point in her neck filled her strangely spinning head. Her pulse quickened.

'Lynelle, is it?' the Elliot laird asked quietly.

She tore her gaze from the fascinating, terrifying mouth and slowly nodded. The softness in Lachlan's eyes eased her fears.

'Tell me, Lynelle.' His gaze swept her length. 'If you weren't offering your body for the lad's release, what skills and services were you volunteering?'

This was her chance to free Thomas, her chance to change her life. She drew a deep breath. 'Once I know that Thomas is unscathed and set free, I promise to willingly, for an allotted time, use my skills to benefit your people.'

Lachlan nodded. 'Nae harm has befallen the lad, Lynelle. Despite the tales you may have heard, we do not torture, starve or eat small children.'

She wasn't certain if she felt better or worse at such a reminder. But she heard the conviction in his voice and decided he spoke the truth. The frowning man beside him muttered something but Lynelle ignored him.

'You still haven't named the skill you have *willingly* offered to benefit my clan,' Lachlan said.

'Oh.' Looking him squarely in the eye, she let the small, necessary lie slip off her tongue. 'I am a healer.'

A groan escaped the laird's companion, but Lynelle forced herself to concentrate on Lachlan's features. A slow-spreading, mischievous smile dawned on his pleasant face.

'Ah, Will.' The laird slapped the broad back of the man beside him. 'It appears all your wishes have been granted.'

'Aye, Lachlan. It seems good fortune has finally found me.' Sarcasm dripped from his words.

A sinking feeling started low in her stomach.

'What say you to a month, Lynelle?' Lachlan asked, snaring her attention.

Four weeks wasn't such a great space of time, but if she had to spend any length of it with the disapproving man named Will, it would seem never-ending.

'A sennight,' she countered.

'Three,' Lachlan said jovially, enjoying their bargaining.

'Two,' she said quickly, caught up in the play.

'Done,' Lachlan said, ending her chances to lessen her stay.

The single word echoed about the great hall. Lynelle's heart raced with excitement as she realized her accomplishment.

Despite all odds, she'd gained her stepbrother's release. And she'd also managed to halve the initial length of her stay.

Admittedly, there would be a delay in receiving her father's praise for rescuing Thomas, but she'd already waited a lifetime. Two weeks would flit by, if she kept herself busy tending the people of Redheugh Castle and avoided the brooding man called Will. She prayed no one suffered any serious illness during that time.

*** *

William stared at the woman standing so straight before him, her bargaining with his friend now concluded.

Was Lachlan right? Did he really need a woman? By the unwanted stirring of his body, he must.

Why this particular woman awakened his repressed desires was beyond him. She certainly wasn't without flaws.

Her red-gold hair was untidy and dull without the sun's light. Her round, sapphire eyes were too large in her delicate face. The gash on her cheek would likely leave a hideous scar. The thought of someone giving her such a wound burned low and hot in his gut. He pushed his unwanted, protective thoughts away but couldn't help noticing that the injury would detract from her otherwise unblemished complexion.

His gaze lowered as he studied her body. The cloak she wore was ill fitting and smeared with dirt. It hung in folds off her too slender form, hiding any shapely curves she might possess.

He suddenly wondered if she would have given herself to Lachlan if it were the only means to free the boy. Was she so self-sacrificing or was she the fool he'd named her? Would Lachlan have accepted her offering even after admitting he'd release the lad the next day? An unfamiliar knot tightened in his gut.

What did he care? Why had he interfered to begin with?

God's teeth, she is English.

'The lad will be returned to Fenwick come morn,' Lachlan announced.

William's hands clenched as a tremulous smile graced her generous lips, lighting her face. She looked ... beautiful. Heat pulsed through his veins.

'Lynelle,' Lachlan said, 'your allotted time will begin at dawn and end at dawn two weeks hence. Are we agreed?'

'Yes,' she said without hesitation.

William unfurled his fingers.

'Good,' Lachlan said. 'Now for the introductions. Lynelle, this is my good friend, William Kirkpatrick.'

Thick-lashed, enormous eyes briefly met his. William acknowledged her with a slow nod. She lowered her gaze to somewhere in the vicinity of his chest and he watched as one of her small hands skimmed her injured cheek.

The smooth skin beneath her chin rippled as she swallowed.

He clenched his hands again, fighting the urge to crawl over the table and bury his face in her neck. The impulse to know her scent was strong. He inhaled an uneven breath and felt his nostrils flare.

Someone coughed. With a silent curse, William forced the unwanted images from his mind and relaxed his stiff fingers.

Christ's blood. She is a healer.

He must be more tired than he thought for her presence to have such an effect on him. How could he have forgotten life's past lessons? A few hours of sleep would likely restore his judgment.

'William is returning to his castle at Closeburn tomorrow,' Lachlan said.

Was that relief in her eyes as she looked at him?

'I wish you well on your journey home,' she said, surprising him with her graciousness.

'Thank you for your kind words, though I believe they are given in haste,' William said.

Her lips barely moved as she breathed, 'Why?'

'I depart for Closeburn tomorrow,' he said, and he noticed a crease appear on her brow. 'And you, healer, will be leaving with me.'

Chapter 4

Knots of worry coiled in Lynelle's belly as she followed her burly escort down through the great hall and outside. She had paced a rut in the wooden floor of her assigned chamber for the rest of the night, and now she welcomed the faint breeze brushing her cheeks, cooling her skin.

She clutched the edges of her cloak together, her fingers aching from constantly wringing her hands. Thomas' release was all that mattered. Her fears for herself were of little importance.

Early-morning sunlight wrestled with the last of the night's shadows that bathed the outbuildings and the bustling occupants of the bailey in grey. The clanging of steel upon steel echoed from one of the huts to her left, and a young girl with fiery-red hair scattered feed for the chickens squawking about her feet.

Head down, Lynelle quickened her steps to keep up with the guard and almost collided with him when he suddenly stopped.

'Wait here,' he said, and entered the long structure before them.

Lynelle peered into the opening but could see less than a few feet inside the dim interior. The pungent odour of horse dung wafted out from the stable.

Surprised that she'd been left unattended, she turned and scanned the bailey. The massive gates she'd been ushered through hours earlier stood close by. Her heart thumped faster. Was escape possible? Could she don her hood and walk away from Redheugh Castle?

A vision of Thomas' stricken face formed in her mind and she cast the idea of leaving from her head. She couldn't forsake him now.

Staring across the way, she studied the people entering and exiting the large doors leading into the keep. They all appeared content as they headed off to begin their daily tasks.

It was the same here as it was at Fenwick. She stood alone, watching as the men, women and even the children actively participated in life. The only difference here was that curious eyes rested on her as people went about their chores. At Fenwick, everyone avoided looking at her. Lynelle swallowed the lump that rose in her throat.

Would her circumstances at Fenwick change once it became known she'd freed Thomas? It all depended on one man's approval. Lord Fenwick.

A woman singing a merry tune cut into her pensive thoughts. Now wasn't the time for wishful thinking. She pushed her hopes to the back of her mind and tucked her dreams safely away in her heart.

'If all else is ready, I'll fetch Edan.'

At the sound of the deep rumbling voice, a shiver skittered up her back.

'Aye, Will,' another said.

Lynelle stepped to one side of the stable entrance and stared wide-eyed at the empty doorway, waiting for William Kirkpatrick to appear. The man who'd melted her insides with his flaming gaze. The man whose injured brother she'd agreed to tend. The man who'd branded her a fool.

Gritting her teeth, she willed the brute to show himself.

Footsteps pounded on the hard earth. A tall figure emerged. Deep brown hair framed a sun-bronzed face. Dark stubble coated his square jaw, the whiskers proclaiming his manliness and adding a sense of danger to his appearance. Full lips softened the intensity of his face, complimenting his aquiline nose.

Blessed saints, he is beautiful.

Lynelle resisted the urge to turn and see if all the other women were staring too.

Her gaze flew upwards and collided with flint coloured eyes. She shuddered, glad her cloak hid her twisting fingers.

He'd halted at the stable entrance and she had no clue as to how long she'd spent exploring his features. Or how long he'd allowed her to.

Her cheeks heated as he slowly appraised her from head to toe. She wanted to move, but found her body had frozen. Gooseflesh erupted on every inch of her skin as his gaze climbed up to settle on her face. Though her body was totally covered, she felt as if he'd laid eyes on her bare flesh.

A shiver ripped through her at such a wicked thought.

'Donald,' he said, his gaze lingering on her scarred cheek. 'Stay with the healer. When I return, we leave for home.'

How dare he look his fill and then dismiss her without a word? Lynelle squared her shoulders, grateful her quaking limbs were finally responding to her will.

'Wait!' she said.

The man who triggered her ire and stole her senses stopped mid-stride and turned around to look at her. Impatience radiated from his powerful frame and his fists came to rest on his plaid-clad hips.

'What is it?'

'My br...' she bit down hard on her lower lip, furious with herself. The tanned skin showing through his unlaced shirt proved distracting, and she'd almost revealed Thomas was her brother. 'Fenwick's heir is to be released before we depart. The Elliot laird agreed. It was part of our barg...'

'The lad was taken south and turned loose, *unharmed,* at dawn.'

Lynelle looked up into his eyes. 'Thomas is gone?'

'Aye.'

'How do I know you speak the truth?'

His gaze darkened. 'You don't. You'll just have to take me at my word. Now all that remains is for you to uphold *your* part of the agreement.'

He turned, and Lynelle stared at the breadth of his shoulders as he headed for the keep. Emptiness welled inside her.

Thomas was gone! He was free! Even now was he wrapped in his mother's embrace, cramming sweetmeats into his mouth as he regaled his daring adventure?

She struggled to summon an ounce of delight. She'd wanted to speak with her stepbrother or at least have him see her. No one knew she'd left Fenwick, and with Thomas gone, not a soul would know what had become of her.

Her stomach churned at her selfishness. Looking about, her self-pity receded beneath mounting apprehension.

Being alone wasn't new to her, but nothing was familiar here. Not the surroundings, nor the people. They spoke with an odd burr and the men dressed in garments that exposed their legs. Even their hair was worn much longer than that of her countrymen. Everything was different.

'The laird doesn't tell falsehoods, Miss.'

Lynelle jumped and spun around at the sound of the voice behind her.

'And what of yourself?' she asked the man of middle years, before she could still her tongue.

'Oh, I've told a good number of untruths in my time,' he said, with what appeared to be an amused twinkle in his brown eyes. 'But only when necessary.'

Shocked at herself for speaking so freely with another person, Lynelle suddenly realized her confrontations inside the keep last night and outside this morning were the most she'd spoken with someone else besides Bernard and since Ada's death three years ago.

'What about you?' The man said.

'Me?'

'Don't look so worried, lass. I'm only foolin' with you.' He grinned. 'The name's Donald, and if you care to listen, I'll give you some advice for free.'

All traces of humour vanished from his weathered face, the transformation capturing her attention.

'Tend his brother's injuries well and you have naught to fear from the laird. Will's a good man, but he's had little to feel good about of late.'

Donald's kind eyes and gentle explanation eased her fears somewhat. She'd come here to gain freedom for Thomas, and she'd succeeded. The cost of her success was two weeks of her time. It wasn't such a vast interlude in her uneventful life. She believed she could uphold her end of the bargain with little fuss, so long as she avoided William Kirkpatrick as much as possible.

A commotion from inside the stable entrance interrupted her musing. She and Donald shifted to the side of the doorway as a horse was led through by the burly man who'd escorted her from her chamber.

'This is Keith,' Donald said. 'An ugly brute, but he has his uses.'

Keith grunted and Lynelle bobbed her head in greeting.

Attached to the horse was a flat contraption made from two long, slender tree trunks and stretched animal hides. The top end of both tree limbs were strapped to the saddle, leaving the bottom ends dragging in the dirt. The hides spanned the distance between the poles, forming a movable pallet. It would be comfortable, Lynelle decided, spying the numerous furs strewn atop the hides.

'A litter,' Donald informed her. 'Young Edan's means of travel.'

Lynelle tried to swallow, but her mouth had gone dry. Holy Mother of God. Were the boy's wounds so bad he couldn't walk or sit a horse? What had she done? She may have gained Thomas' freedom, but at what price? Her small lie could have grave consequences.

She'd vowed never again to be the cause of another's death.

'I've saddled the other mounts,' Keith said, and he disappeared inside the stable.

Panic surged. Her heart raced. She couldn't do this. She needed to tell the truth before it was too late. Tiny black dots invaded her vision. Blinking furiously, she tried to dispel them.

'Ah, just in time, Keith,' Donald said, as the other man appeared once more, towing four horses in his wake. 'Here comes Will with Edan.'

Lynelle turned quickly and fought to gain her balance. Her vision cleared and she focused on the entrance to the keep. William Kirkpatrick descended the stairs, carrying Edan. His long, graceful strides closed the distance and before she could gather her wits, he lowered his brother onto the litter.

A groan sounded and was cut short as the injured boy's weight settled onto the bedding. Lynelle battled to keep her mouth from falling open, as Will, the hard-eyed, scowling man knelt in the dirt at his brother's feet and adjusted the furs.

An invisible hand wrapped fingers of envy about her heart and squeezed. She missed her next two breaths, as William's sun-browned hands carefully bunched the coverings under the boy's head.

The brothers exchanged a few quiet words and then the elder brushed a lock of dark hair from his brother's brow and stood, wiping the dirt from his knees. Lynelle stared at him, confused by the harsh, frowning laird she'd dealt with and the concerned older sibling she'd just witnessed coddling his brother.

He looked up from the boy and his intense gaze met hers.

'Come.'

Lured by the gentle command, Lynelle walked forward on unsteady legs.

'This is my brother, Edan,' he said, pride and worry evident in his tone. 'Edan, this is the healer who promised to restore your health.'

He didn't use her name. A cold clamminess washed through her. She peered down at the young man, for now she could see him she realised he was past the age of being labelled a boy.

A fat bandage circled his upper left thigh and his left forearm lay in a splint, across his stomach. Though he was comfortably positioned, his body curled in on itself a fraction, as if he were protecting further hidden injuries. A small gash marked his right cheek and she almost stumbled back as clear, grey eyes, so like his brother's, looked up into hers.

Relief swept through her. His injuries weren't as dire as she'd imagined. Perhaps she could do this. Perhaps she could finally make use of Ada's teachings on someone other than herself.

'Do your wounds cause you much grief?' she asked softly.

'You're English,' he said, wide-eyed.

'Yes.'

'The pain is not so bad,' Edan said, though she noted his gaze darted to her right and back again.

The man beside her made a scoffing sound before saying, 'Iona has tended his *meagre* wounds already this morn. Your services are not needed, yet.'

Relief fluttered in her belly at her reprieve. She'd come to rescue her stepbrother, and though the event hadn't turned out exactly as she'd envisioned, she'd been successful.

Fate had seen fit to injure young Edan and she'd sworn to return him to good health. She was needed here, and had the chance to make a difference to someone else's life.

'Keith,' William said. 'You take the lead. Donald, you take charge of the horse pulling Edan. I'll ride at the rear.'

He retrieved two bundles from the ground at his feet and added them to the supplies on the horse that would drag his brother – a brown horse that for some reason appeared familiar to Lynelle. His task complete, he threw one last command over his shoulder. 'Donald, help the healer mount.'

'Come, lass. I'll get you into your saddle,' Donald said as he approached.

'But ... but I don't ride.'

'Ever?'

'Ever,' she said, shaking her head.

Donald scratched at his whiskered chin and then rubbed a hand along the back of his neck. 'Will,' he called. 'We have a wee problem.'

Will stood beside the largest of the four horses. His gleaming sword posed a brilliant contrast to the jet-black beast it was strapped to. 'What is it?' he said, stroking the steed's long, thick neck.

'Ah, the lass ... doesn't ride.'

The laird's head jerked up and Lynelle witnessed the thinning of his usually generous lips. 'Come.' He gestured her forward with his fingers, and then drew his sword. Her steps faltered. She relaxed as he sheathed his blade in the harness he wore on his back. 'It's past time we were gone.'

Lynelle halted before him and noticed the hue of his eyes change from pewter to pale silver as he said, 'You'll ride with me.'

'I can walk.'

'You'll ride with me.' His harsh tone brooked no further argument.

Large, warm hands spanned her waist, branding her flesh beneath her numerous layers of clothing. She gasped as he lifted her high in the air and set her atop his horse.

With her legs spread wide to accommodate the width of the massive beast, her skirt and cape rode high on her thighs, exposing her bare legs. She wanted to draw her garments down and cover herself, but she sat unmoving, clutching the front of the saddle for dear life.

Suddenly, the world tilted to one side and then righted itself as William mounted and sat flush against her back. Powerful legs wrapped about her own and daring to move only her eyes, she peered down at the dark hairs covering his lower thighs.

Heat flashed into her cheeks.

'Ready?' His voice rumbled through her back.

'God speed,' someone shouted from the vicinity of the keep.

'Farewell, Lachlan,' William called.

'Iona sends her best,' the Elliot laird yelled and then laughed.

'Always the jester,' Kirkpatrick mumbled.

Lynelle stiffened further as the body behind her pressed closer. Strong arms circled her, as he reached for the reins. Her heart drummed and her breaths came short and fast.

The enormous beast started forward, heading for the now open gates. The rest of their small travelling party passed through the opening, leaving Lynelle and William to bring up the rear.

Saint Jude, save me.

Just when Fate finally granted her a purpose by providing someone she could aid with her healing knowledge, it threw up more hurdles. If she didn't tumble to her death from so great a height, she feared she'd burst into flames from William Kirkpatrick's masculine heat.

Chapter 5

William stretched his aching neck and peered up at the sun as it crawled ever higher in the clear blue sky. Its mellow heat announced an end to bitter-cold winter days and offered a hint at the warmth to come.

He looked away, his eyes adjusting and settling on his brother's face. The lad slept on as he had for most of the morning, lulled by the sway of the litter and the constant clopping of unshod hooves.

Donald rode beside the laden horse, leading-rein in hand, as he held them at a steady pace and searched for the smoothest tracts of land to cross. Keith scouted ahead. His natural instinct for sensing trouble made his position in front, inevitable.

The small party followed the worn trail into a copse of silver birch. The branches angled sharply toward the sun, the tips curving downward as if all hope of reaching its brightness were lost.

The desperate need to return to Closeburn ate at William's soul like a festering wound. He could imagine the stricken faces of his clan as they crossed themselves and stared down at Edan stretched out upon his horse-drawn pallet. Sorrowful eyes and defeated whispers would abound.

If he hadn't whisked his brother away to escape the ill-fated murmurings, he was certain Edan would have avoided the horrible injuries he sustained. He should have eased the lad's fears by treating the superstitious babblings as the foolish ravings they were. But he hadn't, and the woman sitting as stiff as his blade before him was a vivid reminder.

Her rigid posture affected the joy that normally washed over him when he rode. His back and shoulders ached after only a few hours in the saddle. He lightly gripped the leather reins in his left hand, sure that his mount was content to follow the others for now. The fingers of his right hand bit into his leg.

The healer sat between his thighs, holding herself so ramrod straight to ensure none of her body touched his.

A small gust of wind wafted through the tree-enclosed passage, stealing a lock of red-gold hair from the tight knot on her head. It danced and tickled his cheek, teasing him with a faint smell of lavender.

He caught the long, stray strand and gently twined it around two fingers. The saddle creaked as his weight shifted forward. He leaned over her shoulder to murmur in her ear. 'If you don't relax, it's unlikely you'll survive the journey.'

She flinched, emitting a tiny gasp.

Tilting his head, he gazed at her gold-tipped, wide-eyed lashes and skimmed her profile with cool interest. The sprinkling of freckles on her nose and cheeks faded as her face reddened. He continued his perusal downward, past the line of her clenched jaw and skimmed the length of her slender neck.

Her pulse skipped wildly beneath her flushed skin, enchanting him. He longed to set his lips against her throbbing flesh and taste her with his tongue. His groin sprang to life under his plaid and his heart thumped erratically in his chest, keeping time with the swift beating of her throat.

Christ's blood.

He jerked away, but only as far as the saddle permitted. *Not nearly far enough.* He'd meant to warn her of the discomfort she'd suffer later if she didn't allow her body to move with Black's even gait, never knowing how badly his own composure would be shaken.

Curse her and the clean, flowery scent tormenting him still.

Releasing the hair wrapped about his fingers, he stifled a groan. He saw that Edan was awakening, and looked ahead through the tunnel of silvered trunks standing sentinel. Patches of sunlight glistened on the water of a narrow burn to the right. He often made use of the shaded curve in the stream whenever he traversed this route, but never before had he been in such dire need to feel the chill water on his heated body.

'Donald,' he called, startling the woman whose posture had become stone-like since he'd spoken to her. Why couldn't she have been an able rider? It would have saved her from the pain she'd experience during the next few days and him from the torture racking him now. 'Stop at the usual place.'

'Aye, Will,' Donald said.

The thought of having her ride with Donald had crossed his mind, but he'd dismissed the notion. In the unlikely event they were attacked, he knew the stalwart older man would protect Edan with his life. He and Keith were younger, more agile, and would swiftly dispatch anyone who dared to threaten them.

Will drew Black to a halt and threw himself from the saddle. He wanted to get away from her as fast as possible, but his conscience and the censorious stare creasing Donald's brow had him turning about and reaching for the healer. He cursed beneath his breath. He needed time to quell the urges tightening his body. But first he needed to help her dismount.

Spanning the healer's waist with ease, ignoring her fingers biting into his forearms, he lifted the woman to the ground. Her legs buckled, forcing him to continue holding her. God above, he doubted even a few days of constant eating would be enough to put some meat on her slender bones. He was surprised she hadn't snapped in two both times it had been necessary for him to put his roughened hands on her.

'Can you stand?'

'I ... I don't know,' she said with a slight shake of her bowed head. 'I can't feel my legs.'

Will peered down at the cloak concealing her lower limbs, but the memory of slim calves and the white flesh above her knees lingered all too clearly in his mind.

'Believe me, they're still there. Give them a moment to adjust to your weight.'

Her face tilted upward and he stared into shimmering, sapphire eyes. They reminded him of the loch surrounding Closeburn Castle on a bright summer's day. Alluring, yet dangerous to any who dared risk breaking the surface without knowing what lay beneath the treacherous depths.

Just like Jinny, the Kirkpatricks' wrinkled, sweet-faced healer who'd promised miracles with her herbs and simples and had delivered heartache instead.

Will straightened, abruptly releasing his hold on the woman who stood too closely before him, her eyes too wide, too innocent.

'Donald will see to you.' He broke free of her white-knuckled grasp, spun on his heel and strode to where Donald crouched by the litter.

'Donald, I'll take charge of Edan. You see to the healer.'

William hunkered down. 'How do you fare?' He laid a hand on his brother's brow. Cool. Thank God.

Edan brushed his hand aside.

'Don't worry yourself over me, Will. I'm fine. But you look as if you lost a sword fight with one of the village lasses.'

Will scowled at his brother's teasing smile and snatched the water-flask from Edan's hand. He took a long swallow and while the water soothed his dry throat, Edan's attempt at humour eased his brotherly concern.

'Watch yourself, lad,' he said, offering the vessel back. 'Remember who has to carry you about when you need privacy.'

Edan's smile slipped as comprehension dawned. The lad hated being coddled.

'Hungry?' William asked, pretending he hadn't noticed Donald escorting the healer into the trees to his right.

'Nae. But when Lynelle returns, I would appreciate your help in finding somewhere to relieve myself.'

Hearing the healer's name slip naturally from Edan's lips stunned Will. It sounded too familiar, as if his brother knew her well, trusted her.

'The woman is here to tend your wounds, Edan. Do not let her bonny face sway you. Once we reach Closeburn, she will be returned home.'

From his reclining position, Edan's grey-eyed gaze fixed on him. William knew he'd sounded harsh, but his warning was necessary.

For the last year, many of Closeburn's women had done their best to fill the gaping hole left by the deaths of their mother and sister. William feared Edan was easy prey for any woman fair of face.

'So, you think Lynelle is bonny?' Edan said.

'I think you must have knocked your head when you fell off your horse,' William said, turning away from his brother's perceptive gaze.

Donald and the healer emerged from the trees. The pair closed the distance with slow, measured steps, Donald halving his natural stride to keep pace with the awkward gait of the woman he escorted.

Aye, she is bonny, he admitted to himself. But there was something other than her outward beauty that intrigued him, called to him. Her allure was new to him, sharpened his senses. Part of him hungered to explore his fascination for her, to discover exactly what it was about her that made him want to slide his fingers over her skin, press his lips against her flesh.

Enough!

The sooner they reached Closeburn, the better. It suddenly became imperative rather than an inner, desperate longing.

Leaning over his brother, he gently scooped him into his arms. Edan held silent, but William noted the thinning of his lips. Even with his careful handling, he'd caused his brother pain.

'Hold tight, lad.' Cradling Edan to his chest, William carried him into the trees.

***

Lynelle hobbled along beside Donald as quickly as her stiff, aching legs allowed. The older man had offered his arm in support, but she'd declined the caring gesture. Having spent the morning atop the huge horse in such close proximity with William, she needed to distance herself from human contact for a time.

After giving her a moment alone, Donald had escorted her to the stream where she'd splashed her face with cool water to restore her muddled senses. But the skin about her middle still tingled with the heat William's hands had left behind.

She glanced up and watched him lift his injured brother into his arms. The strained look upon each of their faces told her of the younger one's physical pain and the elder's anguish.

Lynelle looked down as they passed by, her heart thrumming in her chest. It was time. Time for her to do what she'd promised in return for Thomas' release.

A wave of giddiness washed over her. She stumbled, but quickly righted her footing.

'A few days in the saddle and you'll become accustomed to it, lass.'

'Yes,' she said, glad Donald believed her misstep was due to riding for the first time and not from the fear threatening to send her to her knees.

Keith led the three horses to the water's edge to drink and came back the short distance with a bowl of water for the mount laden with the supplies and the litter.

She eyed the sack containing her belongings and the satchel of herbs she'd brought. A fit of panic would not aid her and it certainly wouldn't help ease Edan's suffering. With slow, deep breaths, she calmed her racing heart and searched her memory for everything she'd learned about healing from Ada.

This was her chance to make a difference and be part of the living, instead of sitting on the fringes and watching her life go by.

Saints above, please help me do it right.

'I need my things if I am to tend Edan,' she said, approaching the horse-drawn pallet.

'Sit yourself down, lass. I'll fetch what you need.'

Gritting her teeth, she gratefully sank to her knees beside the litter, not daring to touch the hard ground with her tender buttocks.

'Thank you,' she said as Donald delivered her sack to her. Untying the leather cord securing the top, she rummaged for the satchel of herbs and ran familiar fingers over the worn hide.

Guide me Ada, she silently prayed.

Lynelle opened the satchel and as she studied the dried stems, leaves and flowers, it was as if Ada sat nearby, reminding her of their uses.

Yarrow leaves pressed to a wound will slow the bleeding. Betony juice mixed with honey and gargled, eases an aching tooth. Wormwood aids unsettled stomachs. Sorrel leaves make a poultice for wounds and boils. Feverfew, with its strong, aromatic smell, could reduce inflammation and relieve an ache of the head. It also acted as a mild calmative.

Lost in her thoughts, Lynelle jumped as Edan was carefully deposited on the pallet next to her. His damp hair was brushed back from his pale face and she saw small furrows bracketing his mouth. Eyes closed, brow creased, he was clearly in pain.

She glanced up at the man towering over her. Dark hair, wet and mussed as if he'd dragged impatient fingers through it, hung about his face. Beads of water dotted his forehead and ran in rivulets along his unshaven jaw to pool and drop from his chin. His eyes, like a storm-tossed sky, rested on his brother, and then his gaze met hers.

'Help him.'

Lynelle looked away, unable to bear the intensity of his thunderous stare. 'I need water,' she said. 'And a vessel to prepare a potion.'

With a few steps he stood beside the packhorse and retrieved the remaining supplies from its back. Watching him, noting his confident stride and powerful size, a sense of conviction rushed through her.

She might lack confidence in many areas, but in this instance she had one thing he did not – the knowledge and the ability to heal his brother.

He approached and handed her one of the two bundles he carried. 'A gift from Iona.'

Stunned, she simply sat and stared at the cloth sack in her lap. She'd never received a gift in her life. She hardly knew what to do with it.

Guilt welled inside her and she bit into her lip at such an ungrateful thought. Ada had gifted her with a roof over her head and made sure she hadn't starved. She'd also seen to it she was garbed, pilfering discarded garments that Lynelle had mended and altered for herself.

'Open it. It contains an assortment of herbs from Lachlan's healer.'

The bundle seemed too heavy to hold only herbs. Unwinding the ties at the top, she loosened it and pulled numerous pouches from within. She tucked them back in, knowing her own collection would suffice for now, but promised to explore the contents thoroughly later.

Her fingers brushed over something cold and hard and with a firm grip she lifted the unknown item out. A solid, stone bowl sat cupped in her hand, its centre hollowed and smooth. A mortar! Lynelle dipped her hand back inside the sack, rummaging around until she found what she was looking for. She pulled the small club-shaped instrument into the light, awed by the miniature pestle. The mortar and pestle were perfect for grinding and pounding her herbs.

'Will this hold enough water?'

Lynelle's gaze leapt from the implements to the man crouching beside her, holding a carved wooden cup in his large hand.

'Yes,' she said.

He rose and strode to the stream. In the sack he'd drawn the cup from, she caught sight of something gleaming at the top. Peering closer, she spied a small blade with an ivory handle.

Her knife.

The urge to reach for it was strong, but when she looked about to see if anyone watched her, she found Edan's pain-glazed eyes resting on her.

'Forgive me, Edan,' she said, shamed by her wandering thoughts when he needed her attention.

'Why? You have naught to be sorry for. My own recklessness caused my injuries. Though I'd never say as much to Will.'

'Why ever not?'

Edan's brows lowered thoughtfully. 'If I admitted I was at fault, he'd lecture me 'til my ears rang and then he'd confine me indoors.'

'He is concerned for you.'

'I know he is trying to protect me, but sometimes he can be overbearing.'

Lynelle smiled at Edan's description of William and wondered how it must feel to have someone care enough to seem repressive.

'Besides, all will be well,' Edan said. 'I have you to care for me, Lynelle. I trust you.'

Lynelle's heart dropped and her smile slipped. Would he trust her if he knew she'd never used her healing skills on anyone save herself? Dear God, she was naught but a fraud.

A footfall drew her attention to William's approach. What would he do to her if she failed to heal his young brother? She shuddered.

She had a choice to make, and quickly. Either use what healing skills she possessed or admit her false claims and do nothing.

The moment she again peered into Edan's trusting eyes, she made her decision. A sense of purpose eased the churning in her stomach and lessened the trembling of her hands.

'Are you in terrible pain?' she asked, setting Iona's sack of herbs aside and reaching for her own.

'Not so much. My leg pains me most.'

William hunkered down near her and handed her the wooden cup full of water.

'Thank you,' she said, placing it on a flat section of ground before her. She withdrew the pouch containing the feverfew, dropping several dried leaves into the mortar.

'Do you have any wine?' she asked as she used the pestle to grind the light yellow-green leaves.

'Donald, bring the skin flask,' William said.

When the feverfew resembled a fine powder, she tipped most of the contents out of the cup and brushed the ground herb into the remaining water.

Glancing to her right, she found William watching all she did.

'The wine, please,' she said.

He removed the stopper and handed her the skin. She poured the wine into the cup, a little more than half way and then used the pestle to mix the ingredients.

Satisfied she'd done everything correctly, she lifted the drinking vessel and offered it to Edan. A tide of warmth ran through her. She was doing something good for another, finally putting her knowledge to use.

'You, first,' William said.

She looked at him and his gaze slid from the cup she held to meet hers.

'You will sample it first,' he said.

'I have no need–'

'Do you fear tasting your own mixture?'

Her confusion mounted. 'No, but–'

'Then do it,' he said.

Concealing an odd sense of hurt, she flicked a glance at Edan and found him watching the exchange in silence. She brought the wooden cup to her lips, her mind awhirl.

The herb's natural strong scent had diminished when combined with the water and wine. Tilting the cup, she sipped and was not displeased by the flavour. She swallowed and turned puzzled eyes to William.

He studied her face intensely, as if waiting for some kind of reaction. She stared at him with a calmness she didn't feel. And waited.

'Now, 'tis my turn,' he said, reaching for the cup.

Lynelle gasped as his fingers brushed hers. She released the vessel, surprised when it didn't fall to the earth. His hand already firmly wrapped about it.

'Ah, Will,' Edan said. 'You don't need to test it.'

William ignored his brother, looked at Lynelle and took a drink from the cup. His eyes never wavered from hers. Understanding swept through her.

He didn't trust her. Didn't believe in her. The burgeoning hope, so new, shrivelled inside her.

He passed the potion to Edan and she watched him swallow it down without hesitation.

'Any mixture or salve you make must first be sampled by you and then me before it touches my brother,' William said.

Feeling numb and weighted by a great sadness, Lynelle heard but didn't reply.

'Do you understand?'

She turned to face William. His steel-edged tone matched the determined look in his cold, grey eyes.

Her voice was lost to her. She nodded in answer and it was as if the movement displaced her dejection. Anger rushed in to take its place.

All her energy suddenly centred on Ada's teachings of herbs. Which one could bring on an ailment of the stomach? Unfortunately, having to taste the potion first, she'd have to suffer the illness too. But it would be worth it, just to see this man laid low for crushing her fledgling spirit.

Chapter 6

William ignored the desolation clouding the healer's expressive blue eyes. He'd expected the same insulted reaction Lachlan's healer, Iona, had displayed. Not sadness. But Edan's welfare took precedence over everything. If he happened to harm anyone's sensibilities in the process, so be it.

A glimmer of defiance suddenly flared in her gaze and relief filled him. Her hostility was easier to dismiss than her despair.

Rising, he gave the order to resume their journey and secured the sacks on the borrowed horse. Edan nodded in response to his questioning look and settled back into the furs. William mounted Black and looked down at the woman clutching the ill-fitting cloak around her.

She stood rigid, chin raised, staring off into the distance, her bearing almost regal. But her mouth, usually soft in appearance, looked uneven as she chewed her lower lip. She obviously wished to be anywhere but here. Why had she come alone to rescue Fenwick's heir?

'Come.' He held out his hand to her, cutting off the multitude of questions crowding his mind. Her healing skills were all that mattered. 'Place your right foot on top of mine and give me your right hand.'

Her tongue peeked out to tease her upper lip as she contemplated his foot and then his outstretched hand. Heat rushed to his loins at the innocent gesture. Or was she practiced in the arts of enticing a man as well as herbal lore?

'Your right foot is the one furthest away from Black.'

'I know the difference between left and right,' she said.

'Then keep your tongue in your mouth and do as I said.' His voice sounded gruff.

Her lips thinned. She stepped forward and flung up her hand, the folds of her cloak parting as she lifted her leg. The moment her foot touched his, he grabbed her hand and pulled her up, twisting her about so she sat across his thighs.

He ignored her muffled oath as she landed in his lap. Leaning forward, his arm brushed the soft mounds beneath her cloak as he grasped the reins. He heard her sudden indrawn breath, as heat burned his ears.

William straightened and glanced at Edan, who lay watching them with a faint smile on his face. He looked at Donald and found a similar expression on the older man's face. William scowled, giving Donald the signal to move, annoyed the woman made him appear the fool before his brother and clansman.

They resumed their journey, holding to the same steady pace. William concentrated on Edan and the land they traversed, doing his best to ignore the woman wriggling in his lap. Impossible.

'God's teeth, woman. Keep still.'

'I can't. I'm going to fall.'

'You won't fall,' he said, tightening his hold.

She jerked forward, and her weight slid from his left thigh to the saddle between his legs.

He stifled a groan, silently berating himself for his unwarranted concern. Riding astride had been painful for her and he'd draped her sideways to minimize her discomfort. He frowned. Why was her comfort so important to him? At least she'd stopped squirming.

Had he frightened her when he'd shifted his arm or had she reacted to his touch?

She sat stiff and unyielding, the delicate line of her throat exposed as she stared ahead. Her appearance was of a woman calm and confident in her situation, but William had noted the little contradictory signs. Her cloak had fallen open, revealing white fingers clasped tightly together in her lap.

Were false impressions a façade she used often? Or only when she traded herself to free an English heir and was forced to tend an injured young Scot?

'Why didn't Fenwick come for his heir?' William wanted to slice out his tongue the moment the words slipped free. It wasn't his habit to ask questions. He always weighed a situation, made a decision and then acted upon it.

'Why did you kidnap him in the first place?' she said.

'Do you always answer a question with a question?' William silently groaned. Another question. But his curiosity was roused.

'No. My ... Lord Fenwick wasn't there. He doesn't know his son was taken.'

'Where is the lad's father?'

'It was Truce Day.'

'At Rockcliffe?'

'Yes.'

William knew of Truce Day. In the future, he'd likely have to participate in the proceedings, now he was laird. As the second son, he'd been tutored in sword fighting and defence, not crime and politics as his older brother Roger had been.

But Roger was dead and the responsibilities of his clan now rested squarely on his shoulders.

'Why did you kidnap Thomas?'

Her soft-spoken enquiry broke into his thoughts.

'The boy was there for the taking,' he said, repeating Lachlan's response when he'd asked the same question. 'He was returned, unharmed, as promised,' he said, annoyed by the need to reassure her.

'So you said.'

Did she doubt his word? Her opinion of him shouldn't matter, but he found it did. William fought the anger swelling inside him. He'd no need to defend himself to this Englishwoman.

'Fenwick will no doubt reward you handsomely for rescuing his heir from the *savage Scots,*' he said unkindly.

'Yes,' she whispered.

Her response surprised him, again. It wasn't only how swiftly she'd admitted to anticipating a prize for rescuing Fenwick's heir, something many people would deny. It was the fervent hope she'd instilled in the single, softly spoken word.

William clamped his jaw and fought the need to ask what fee she'd demand, in return for telling him exactly what reward she hoped to gain.

***

He asked no more questions, for which Lynelle was infinitely grateful. Her father's approval was the reward she desired most, but William didn't need to know. She had no desire to share her secrets with him, didn't want to reveal *anything* about herself if she could help it.

William's muscled thighs flexed and tightened around her. She'd heard anger in his voice when he'd made his final statement about her gaining a reward.

She hadn't meant to anger him and was confused as to how she'd managed it. She'd said very little, really. She'd given him honest answers and asked only a single question in return.

She'd tried to hold her tongue, a trait she'd mastered over the years – until now. It was as if she'd become a different person since setting foot on Scottish soil, as if the real Lynelle, buried deep inside for so many years, had finally awakened. She discovered she wanted to be her true self immensely.

She was a prisoner, and yet ahead of her lay fourteen days of freedom. Freedom to ask questions, to speak her mind, and use her healing knowledge to aid the sick. Two weeks of living among strangers, people who knew her as Lynelle the healer, not Lynelle the cursed.

Two whole weeks with William Kirkpatrick.

Lynelle swallowed, forcing her thoughts away from him to study the landscape ahead. The beauty of the gentle rolling hills in the distance and the haunting cry of an osprey overhead failed to provide the distraction she hoped for. It was impossible with her bottom imprisoned in his lap and his body heat seeping through her clothes, warming her skin.

They stopped beside a trickling stream and Donald helped her to the ground. The older man's hands at her waist didn't cause the burning sensation she'd experienced when William had lifted her earlier. Why was it William's touch had such a profound and lingering effect when Donald's did not? She tucked the confusing thought away for later.

Slowly making her way to Edan's side, she marvelled at how her legs and buttocks were less sore this time.

'How is your leg?' she said, crouching down before Edan.

'Whatever you gave me has helped with the pain,' he said with a smile. 'Thank you, Lynelle.'

Lost for words, Lynelle returned the smile, as a feeling of warmth and wonder unfurled inside her. This must be the pleasure Ada had so often spoken of when she'd eased someone's suffering.

A shadow fell across Edan's form. She didn't need to look up to see who it was. Gooseflesh erupted on her skin and it suddenly seemed harder to breathe.

'Hungry, Edan?'

The sound of William's deep voice rained down around her.

'A little,' Edan said.

'Good. We'll eat now and then press on.'

William moved away and Lynelle drew a full breath. Glancing up, she watched him converse with Donald while he unpacked bundles of food from one of the sacks.

'My brother won't hurt you.'

Lynelle's eyes darted back to Edan's face. What expression must she have worn for him to make such a statement?

'Mother taught us to be gentle with women,' Edan said.

Lynelle noted the wistfulness in his voice. 'Your mother is dead?'

The young man nodded.

'And your father?'

Edan lowered his lashes, but not quickly enough to hide the flash of pain in his eyes.

'I never knew him,' he said softly. 'He died three months before I was born.'

Lynelle's heart clenched within her chest. Edan would never know his father. Yet she had the chance to know hers, if only her father would allow it.

'From what I've been told, father's ideas were the same as mother's. He was an honourable man and died a hero.'

'How did he die?' Lynelle couldn't help asking.

'He was struck down by some English dog at Otterburn. He didn't survive his wounds, but he fought bravely, just like the Earl of Douglas.'

Lynelle noted Edan's anger and distress. It might have been a Scottish victory, but not for this young man.

'Perhaps my being English is the reason your brother isn't fond of me,' she said.

'I believe it makes little difference to William where you come from. Being a healer is the reason my brother is wary of you.'

Lynelle stared into the serious grey eyes observing her. 'He doesn't trust healers?'

'Nae,' Edan said.

Before she could ask why, a footfall sounded. She glanced up to find the topic of their conversation striding toward them, carrying a platter of food.

Lynelle stood and looked down at the injured young man. 'I will leave you to your meal. I need to wash.'

She headed to the stream and knelt to splash her face and hands with the cold water. Satisfied she'd removed the dust from her face and the smell of horse from her hands, she walked back and sat on a grassy mound a slight distance away from the others.

Donald brought her a wooden cup of wine and a platter piled with bread, a chunk of cheese and several slices of smoked ham. She thanked him and he returned to sit with Edan and William to eat his repast.

As she nibbled brown, grainy bread, she watched the others. It was a pastime on which she'd spent hundreds of hours during the course of her life.

Keith sat a little way downstream, where the horses lazily drank the cool, running water and rested. He seemed more comfortable with the four-legged creatures than with the two-legged kind.

Her gaze wandered to the three men sitting together. Donald chewed and chatted with his mouth full, his lined face breaking into a grin at something he'd said. She watched Edan, pleased his wounds hadn't interfered with his appetite.

Soon she'd have to unravel and remove Iona's dressings and see to Edan's wounds herself. A knot of apprehension blossomed low in her stomach. It would be the first real test of her healing knowledge, and one she prayed she wouldn't fail.

She tried to avoid looking at the third man in the group, but her traitorous eyes settled on him despite her efforts. Even sitting on the ground consuming slices of ham, the man exuded power. He sat side on to her, his dark, shoulder-length hair hiding most of his handsome face. His back remained straight, his every movement one of purpose.

He was a leader, as was her father, but as she observed William's gestures and manner, she realized the similarities ended there.

She couldn't envision her father, or any of the lords who visited Fenwick, perched on the ground sharing a meal and banter with their men. And never would her father share his saddle with another, as William had done for her, unwilling or not.

The idea of tainting a potion to make him ill suddenly soured her stomach.

She glanced down at her trencher, surprised to find it empty. Worry for Thomas had overridden hunger when the maid had delivered a tray to her room at dawn. She hadn't touched a single morsel then.

Thoughts of her stepbrother loomed, but he was far away at this moment and she had more important matters to focus on. She needed to survive the coming days by pretending to be an accomplished healer.

Sipping from the drinking vessel, she drank only a little. She needed to keep her wits about her here among these strangers.

Why did William mistrust healers? Edan's revelation snared her curiosity and she desperately wanted to learn the cause of his wariness. Discovering his reasons might help her understand the man better.

Or it could lead her into further trouble.

Chapter 7

Relieved the meal was over, William gave the order to move on. His agitation had nothing to do with the company he shared or the food he consumed. It had everything to do with his sudden urge to watch the healer to ensure she ate well. He'd won the initial skirmish, but knew he'd lost the battle when he'd asked Donald to report how much the woman had eaten.

Everything, he'd been informed.

He called another halt during the afternoon, giving them all a chance to stretch their legs, but mostly to give himself a respite from the woman nestled in his lap. Though she sat rigid and silent throughout the journey, he couldn't ignore her feminine presence. He almost wished she'd grumble so he could justify tossing her from his horse and making her walk.

She didn't utter a single word of complaint. Her meek acceptance of the situation after he'd witnessed the flash of defiance in her eyes fuelled his thirst to know more about her.

'Is there another at Fenwick who will tend the people in your absence?'

She stiffened and kept her face averted.

'No.'

'You will be sorely missed, then.'

William peered down and noticed her fingers twisting together. Before he'd spoken, her hands had been calmly folded and unmoving.

'A healing woman lives in the village to the east. She will be called upon if her skills are needed.'

'Have you saved many with your skills?' William anxiously awaited her response, not realizing how important her answer was until he'd asked the question.

'Wouldn't you rather know how many have died after I've tended them?'

She turned her head a fraction and stared down at her fidgeting hands. Her new position allowed him to see her face in profile. She appeared pale and drawn. Again she'd answered his question with one of her own.

'Aye,' he finally said.

Her slender shoulders lifted as she drew a deep breath and William held his own at her lingering silence.

'None I have treated have died under my care.'

William exhaled slowly and looked away. His worry eased, but he couldn't understand why she seemed displeased by her flawless record.

Looking to the west, he found the sun creeping slowly toward the horizon. A few hours of daylight remained and he wanted to establish a makeshift camp for the night before full darkness fell.

Ahead, a cluster of alder trees huddled together, protected by an outcropping of rock protruding from the hill.

'Donald,' he called. 'We'll rest here for the night.'

'Aye, Will.'

William's eyes strayed to the bandages wrapped about his brother's limbs.

'Pray to God your healing success remains unblemished,' he said softly.

***

The moment Donald lifted her to the ground, Lynelle dashed toward the clump of trees as fast as her unsteady legs allowed. She used the excuse that she was easing a full bladder, when truthfully she needed distance between herself and William's probing questions and soft-spoken threats.

Twisting his words had saved her from revealing the fraud she was. But how long would it be before he asked a question she couldn't alter?

Knowing she couldn't hide within the foliage forever, she emerged from the trees and found the three men making preparations for the night.

Edan lay on the litter, but it had been disconnected from the horse and placed beneath a sheltering rock formation. Donald gathered their belongings and placed the sacks under nature's stone roof for protection. Keith saw to the horses and William crouched nearby, building a fire. They all appeared engrossed in their tasks, but as Lynelle made her way to Edan she was aware her every move was being observed.

Extracting her sack from the pile, she removed her herb satchel and sat beside Edan.

'I'd like to look at your wounds while there is still natural light to see by.'

Edan's eyes widened a fraction and she heard him swallow.

'My aim is to ease your suffering, not increase it,' she said. 'I promise to be gentle with you.'

Edan rewarded her with a nod and a tremulous smile. She prayed she could uphold her promise.

'I'll start with your leg,' she said, and shifted to her knees beside the pallet.

Deep-voiced conversation sounded nearby, but she closed her ears to its content and focused solely on her task. With fingers that trembled only slightly, she began removing the strips of linen Iona had wrapped around Edan's left thigh, all the while glancing at Edan to ensure she wasn't causing him undue discomfort.

She paused after unrolling half the dressing and drew a fortifying breath. Edan peered up at her and her stomach clenched. She managed a reassuring smile despite knowing this was the easy part. He frowned and focused on his lower limb.

Sweat beaded between her breasts as she continued unravelling the linen discoloured by the salve the Elliot's healer had applied to the wound. Finally, she peeled the last of the dressing away and stared at the ointment-smeared wound.

'I need to wash away the salve and apply fresh ointment before I redress it.' The words slipped out as she spoke her thoughts aloud.

'The water is almost boiled.'

Lynelle jumped. William stood close behind her, looking intently at his brother's injury.

'I witnessed Iona's healing methods when Edan was first injured,' he said. 'She bathed his injuries before applying the stitches and the salve.' His gaze slid to her. 'I believe she included a pot of the ointment and fresh linens for the journey,' he finished, setting Iona's sack down beside her, before making his way back to the fire.

Lynelle blinked and reached for the sack, relieved she hadn't known he'd been watching her work. She rummaged and found a small earthen jar wrapped among fresh linen strips, all neatly housed within two wooden bowls.

She set aside what she needed and withdrew the crushed sopewort from her own assortment of herbs, placing a pinch of the herb into each of the bowls. Following Ada's adamant advice, she'd wash her own hands before touching Edan's open wound.

William returned carrying an iron pot, the steam from the boiled water wafting into the air. Lynelle held both wooden bowls, while he poured hot liquid into each and she set them aside to cool.

'Tell me of your other injuries,' she said to Edan.

'A bone in my arm is broken,' he replied, looking at the splinted limb.

'Is any of the skin broken on your arm?'

Edan looked puzzled and peered up at his older brother who stood watching over him.

'Nae,' William answered for him.

'Then I will leave it untouched for now,' she said, leaning closer to appraise the small gash on his face. She would wash the scratch and apply some ointment to it also. 'Anything else I should know of?'

'He might have broken a rib or two in the fall,' William informed her.

'May I take a look?' she asked Edan.

He nodded, and using his uninjured hand he drew his shirt up for her to see. Lynelle examined his bound middle and spied the purplish discolouration above the dressing on his chest and below his lower abdomen.

'You were certainly lucky to have Iona tend to your injuries. She is obviously a skilled and practiced healer.'

Gratitude for the learned healer welled inside Lynelle. Edan's ongoing care had been made much easier because of Iona's expert initial care.

'I will leave these dressings intact until we reach your home,' she explained, lowering his shirt back into place. 'Now to your leg.'

Dipping the tips of her fingers into one of the bowls, she tested the temperature of the water. Satisfied, she washed her hands as best she could and dried them thoroughly on a piece of clean linen. She lifted the used bowl and placed it before William.

'If you wish to test the cleansing wash, I ask that you use this one.'

William didn't hesitate.

While she waited for his consent, she hid her irritation by retrieving a fresh cloth and dipped it into the second bowl, squeezing out the excess moisture.

'Go on,' he finally said.

Licking her dry lips, she looked into Edan's wide eyes and explained what she meant to do. 'It's important to keep wounds clean. I'm going to bathe your wounds and then apply more ointment.'

Lynelle washed the gash on his cheek first and using a different cloth carefully began wiping all traces of the salve from his thigh. The flesh surrounding the wound looked slightly pink, but appeared free of infection. A neat line of dark stitches held the broken skin together and she stared in awe at Iona's handiwork.

'Where did you learn your healing methods?'

Lynelle glanced up at William before quickly looking back at the wound. 'My knowledge comes from Fenwick's previous healer, Ada. She taught me everything I know.'

About life as well as healing.

Swallowing past the lump that formed in her throat, she gently patted both wounds dry and grasped the crock of salve. Releasing the stopper, she scooped a little onto her finger and rubbed it into the back of her hand. She knew what William expected of her and would rather do it without his command.

The hog fat she believed Iona used to make the ointment made its application smooth and slippery. Not having prepared the salve, she didn't know the precise ingredients Iona had used.

She waited, half expecting some strange reaction to unfold when a large masculine hand was thrust into her line of sight. The offending limb slowly turned, revealing a hairless wrist, the skin a shade paler than the bronzed upper side.

Her mouth suddenly turned as dry as the leaves in her herb satchel. For most of the day she'd endured him touching her by necessity, avoiding it whenever and however she could. Now, she was expected to touch him. The thought of doing so terrified her.

You freely touched Edan.

But he is wounded, less dangerous.

Two weeks, Lynelle. Get used to it.

'Is there a problem?'

'No.' She answered too quickly, her voice too loud. 'No, there is no problem,' she said more calmly.

She coated the tip of her finger with salve, resolved to have it done. Carefully bunching her remaining fingers so they wouldn't brush against him, she aimed her extended finger at the centre of his inner wrist.

Heat shot through her finger on contact, but she forced herself to hold still and not snatch her hand away. With slow, even strokes, she painted an inch of his flesh with the salve. It was like caressing hot steel.

'Enough!'

She jerked at his low growl and the mesmerizing moment was broken. Her cheeks warmed and she gazed intently at Edan's bared wound to cover her embarrassment.

'You may apply the salve and bandage the wound,' William said. 'I'd like to eat and have all settled before nightfall.'

Lynelle glimpsed the fading daylight and set to work. She smoothed a small amount of ointment to the scratch on Edan's face and left it uncovered. As she applied a thick coating to the leg wound, she didn't bother telling William she was capable of tending to Edan if he had other things to do. She knew he wouldn't leave.

She wrapped fresh linens about his leg until a thick protective bandage covered the wound. Dropping back on her haunches, she inspected her work. Fierce pride filled her chest and a shimmer of moisture blurred her vision.

'Thank you, Lynelle.'

Lynelle blinked and smiled into Edan's young face. 'You're welcome, Edan. I'll leave you to rest now.'

Standing, she waited for the blood to rush back into her lower legs and then bundled the bandages together to be boiled for re-use later. Gathering the used bowls, she wandered to the stream in the fading light and washed them clean. Once done, she set them on the grassy bank and sat back, wrapping her arms about her bent knees and stared into the darkening sky.

She wanted to jump up and down and shout and laugh with delight. She wanted to dance and cheer and let everyone know she wasn't the blight on the world all believed her to be. Her body thrummed with repressed joy and her heart and breathing raced with excitement.

Nothing could erase her happiness. Not her predicament, or William's mistrust, or even the scorching memory of touching him.

Eyes closed, restraining her legs with shaking hands, Lynelle rejoiced in trembling silence.

'Keith has trapped and cooked several grouse if you're hungry, lass.'

Lynelle's eyes snapped open at the sound of Donald's voice. He stood a few feet away from where she sat, as if he hadn't wanted to disturb her.

'Thank you, Donald.' She couldn't see his expression in the darkness, but knew he waited for her. Rising, she picked up the wooden bowls and followed him back to the others.

The aroma of roasting meat filled the air, but failed to entice her appetite. She was pleasantly full on her sense of accomplishment. Keith ate alone by the fire, and when she peered to her right she could just make out two shadowy figures nearby.

She sank to the ground opposite Keith and set the bowls beside her. Accepting the platter Donald handed her, she nibbled on the succulent meat but ate very little. The heat from the flames warmed her, soothed her. Exhaustion seeped through her.

Stretching out beside the fire, she stared into the flickering flames. One whole day away from Fenwick, absent from all she'd ever known, and she'd achieved so much. She was a prisoner of sorts, but had never experienced such a sense of freedom.

Sleep beckoned and, oddly content, she had no will to fight it. Her last ounce of energy was spent on a single thought.

What would tomorrow bring?

Chapter 8

Dawn's dark and gloomy arrival did nothing to dampen William's determination to reach home before nightfall. If anything, it spurred him on. He'd made his wishes known to Keith and Donald as they'd downed bread and cheese to break their fast. After testing the tonic the healer prepared to ease Edan's pain, they'd set out.

The woman sharing his saddle was one of the main influences driving his resolution.

Even from the escarpment where he'd spent the night with his younger brother, the secret smile hovering about her lips as she'd settled by the fire had made him wary. And curious. He needed distance from her, an interim where she wasn't within sight, or reach.

Impossible at the moment, with her body against his, warming his flesh. Tormenting his mind and body.

The sun hadn't penetrated the brooding clouds in the hours since they'd begun riding. The blackening sky and the heaviness in the air matched his sombre mood to perfection.

William had permitted one stop, where he'd concentrated on Edan's comfort and given the lad an oiled hide in advance of the impending downpour. Though it wasn't cold, he'd flung his mantle about his own shoulders, knowing the woollen garment would keep him and the woman relatively dry.

Praise to God she'd refrained from speaking during the course of the day. William didn't want to hear her soft, musical voice. Her silence helped him keep his, though the unfamiliar need to question her played havoc with his thoughts.

Why had she risked herself to rescue Fenwick's heir? She'd never really answered him when he'd asked. Surely there must have been others eager to please their absent lord, either out of duty or concern for the young lad's safety.

Was there no one to forbid or talk sense into this woman who risked her life, her reputation and her virtue? Did she have no father or mother to advise her? No brothers or sisters to caution her impulses? No husband?

A fat raindrop splashed his cheek, drawing him from the unending questions spinning about in his mind. Edan appeared as nothing but a lump beneath the protective hide, as the ominous clouds hanging from heaven's rafters suddenly broke.

The path they followed through the valley between small rolling hills soon resembled a shallow, running burn. But the cluster of willow trees drooping under the weight of the deluge to William's right, and the smooth granite boulder growing out of a hillock to his left, announced they were on his land – Kirkpatrick land.

Ignoring the water soaking his exposed head and face, William caught the woman in front of him about the waist and tucked her more securely into the shelter of his body. She squirmed, but he held firm. Her wet hair cooled his neck but failed to douse the ever-present desire simmering in his blood. He closed his eyes, losing himself in the sensations and then shifting in the saddle, cursed his momentary weakness.

Thank the saints they were almost home.

The lay of the land rose to a slight incline and Black tugged on the reins, sensing a dry stall and fresh oats close by. William held him back. There would be no galloping the last short distance today, even if he shared his mount's eagerness to be home.

Instead, William studied the gait of the borrowed horse dragging his brother's litter. The end of each pole scored the rain-softened earth, but did little to slow their progress.

The slope levelled out and the woman shifted. William's body stirred at the heat they created between them. He tipped his head back and welcomed the stinging raindrops beating against his face.

William straightened in the saddle and peered through the curtain of water at the sight that always filled his heart with pride.

His castle. Home.

Closeburn Castle stood on an island in the middle of the loch; the curtain wall surrounding the grey-stoned keep was an added measure of defence.

Even on such a dull and dreary day as this, Closeburn inspired strength and warmth. It was a haven. Within its walls, William had experienced love and laughter, as well as tremendous pain and loss. But since he'd become laird half a year ago, he'd removed the cause of Closeburn's suffering. He'd banished the clan's healer.

His arm involuntarily tightened about the woman, the healer, in his lap. He loathed the thought of allowing her to cross Closeburn's threshold. But he'd given her strict instructions for tending Edan. Although his mistrust had saddened and then angered her, she'd done as he bid, so far. Her stay would be brief. Only twelve days of her allotted time remained. Once William was ensured of Edan's recovery, he'd cheerfully let her go.

The woman in his arms leaned forward as they rode down the gentle slope. Drawing Black to a halt, William dismounted and plucked the healer down from the saddle. She squirmed as he carried her the few feet to where Donald stood with Geordie the boatman.

'Here.' Almost carelessly, he deposited the woman into Donald's outstretched hands and turned to the young man beside him. 'Is all ready, Ian?'

'Aye, laird. Welcome back.'

'Thanks, lad. I'll fetch Edan.'

William strode across the slick grass toward the barge nudging one side of the pier, and gave a shrill whistle. Black trotted up and Keith stepped away from Edan's litter to lead the stallion onto the flat-bottomed boat. The barge was used for transporting horses, and any goods too large for the rowboat, across the loch.

'It's good to be home.'

William peered down into Edan's face peeking out from beneath the hide. With a smile at his brother's relieved tone he said, 'Aye, lad. You'll be warm and dry soon enough.'

Keith returned, having left Black and the other mounts in Geordie's capable hands. He scooped up the borrowed horse's reins and gave a nod.

William bent low to lift his brother from the litter. 'Time to go, Edan.'

Donald, Ian and the English woman were waiting in the rowboat, heads bowed against the relentless rain. William carefully climbed into the small, rocking craft and sat on one of the cross planks, using his upper body to shield his brother.

But Edan struggled up with a grimace, pushing the hide away from his face to search the water surrounding them. 'Are there any swans about, Will?' he said softly.

William's gut tightened. He studied Castle Loch, the body of water encircling Closeburn Castle, knowing he wouldn't see any swans. The dark, murky water appeared pockmarked by the driving rain.

'Nae swans, Edan,' he said. 'It is a foolish superstition, lad. One you'd be wise to ignore.'

'But–'

'Enough, lad,' William cut in, keeping his mounting anger from his tone.

Edan's lips thinned, holding back the words William knew he longed to say. Looking up from his brother's tight expression, William's gaze collided with the healer's.

Pools of blue stared at him from the opposite end of the boat. He glared at her, daring her to voice the questions lurking in her moist, wide eyes. She blinked rapidly and turned away.

She looked as if she'd fallen into the loch. Three times. Her wet, red-gold hair hung dark and lifeless, plastered to her head. The only colours in her oval face were her pink lips, rain-washed and full, and the sapphire eyes that now refused to meet his. She shouldn't be so appealing in such a dishevelled state but, much to his disgust, he found she was.

God save him from swans and curses and a foolish Englishwoman, whose claims as a healer should be enough to drive any thoughts of desire from his thick head and cool his unruly body.

With a gentle bump, they reached the jetty on the inner side of Castle Loch. Ian downed the oars, and with practiced ease he scrambled ashore to steady the craft so its passengers could alight. Once Donald and his charge climbed out, William followed. His brother's weight was no hardship.

He headed for the iron-studded gates with long strides, swiftly passing his clansman and the healer. One of the massive gates swung inward at his approach. As he stepped through into the walled courtyard, the downpour doubled its force and became a deafening torrent. Hunching over Edan, he absorbed most of the water teeming from the wretched sky above.

As they neared the first-floor entrance to the tower, Closeburn's steward held open the iron yett, the defensive gate of metal bars, allowing him entrance. Just inside the doorway William paused, and felt his mantle, wet and heavy, lifted from his shoulders.

"Tis good to see you home and whole, laird,' the steward said.

'My thanks, Malcolm.'

Edan shifted in his arms, pushing the hide away from his face to offer the aging steward a weary smile.

'And you too, master Edan.'

'The others will follow soon,' William said. 'Is all prepared above stairs?'

'Mary—'

'Is right here to escort you, laird.'

The plump older woman sailed into view. William hadn't missed the subtle grace of her hand as she'd approached, making the sign of the cross. She then clucked and fussed over Edan, showing no outward concern at seeing the lad in his brother's arms instead of standing on his own two feet.

'Everything is ready as you requested,' Mary finally said.

'I did not doubt it.'

'Then why did you bother asking?'

William hid his smile. Her familiar, gentle chiding felt so ... normal. After three days of constant mayhem, he welcomed it.

He strode through the archway leading into the hall and swept the occupants with his gaze. Preparations for the evening meal clattered to a stop, as men and women turned to stare wide-eyed at him carrying his brother. He gave a brisk nod in acknowledgement and turned toward the stairs, fighting to retain the brief sense of peace Mary's scolding had granted.

But it disappeared beneath growing frustration. The dread he had seen in the eyes of his clan folks settled heavily in his mind. He took the stairs two at a time.

Damn his ancestor to hell for supposedly shooting the swan in the chest with a crossbow bolt.

Edan gasped.

Peering into his brother's face, William eased his hold. 'Forgive me, lad.'

'Nae, Will. It's my own fault I need to be carted about like a bairn.'

'Aye, it is. But as long as you know it, I've nae reason to lecture you.'

'Really?'

An unbidden smile curved William's lips. 'Aye. Really.' His chest tightened as his brother relaxed in his arms.

Dear God. He'd do anything to see Edan dashing about, creating mischief again. Anything. Including swallowing his pride, for a time, to allow a healer within Closeburn's walls.

Leaving the stairway at the third level, William marched along the torch-lit corridor and swung right into Edan's chamber. Thankfully, the room stood empty of maids or servants with superstitious dread clouding their eyes. One of the two large wooden tubs Closeburn boasted sat before the flaming hearth, steam rising from its centre.

Gently depositing his brother upon the cushioned chair nearby, William inspected the water level, pleased to see it was shallow enough not to cover Edan's injuries, but deep enough to chase the chill and mud from his body. Several pails of water, some hot, some cold, stood ready for use.

Mary came into the room, huffing and puffing from scaling the stairs and carrying the extra load of fresh drying cloths in her arms. She dumped them on the wooden stool beside the tub, and rested her hands on her ample hips.

William approached his brother and carefully removed the hide draping Edan's form before dropping it to the floor. He turned back to Mary. 'There is an English woman accompanying Donald.' Mary's eyes flared with curiosity. William ignored it. 'I trust the chamber across the way has been as efficiently prepared as this one?' The older woman gave a curt nod and William continued. 'Good. Please take her there. She is wet, cold and no doubt hungry and will appreciate your aid. I'll see to Edan.'

He turned back to his brother, dismissing Mary. But she was an inquisitive woman and her years of faithful service allowed her some latitude. She held her place.

'Please close the door as you leave, Mary.'

Commanding Mary in such a way was discourteous, but William was tired and wet through and he didn't care to relive all the happenings of the last few days.

Not right now. He needed to tend his brother to ensure his haste to reach home hadn't caused Edan more suffering. God knew guilt for not protecting his sole surviving brother from harm ate at his heart relentlessly.

Edan's eyes reproached him for his ungentle treatment of Mary, but thankfully the lad held his tongue. At this moment, the last thing he needed was a fourteen-year-old abrading him for his ill manners. He'd mentally castigate himself for it later. After he'd seen to his brother.

Chapter 9

The slashing rain ceased battering Lynelle's head and shoulders as her escort tugged her into the lighted entrance. Her ears buzzed and her upper body felt numbed from the incessant downpour. A muddy puddle stained the flagstones where she stood, and as she adjusted to the rain's absence she watched the pool of water grow, her dripping garments adding to its size.

Voices penetrated her soggy thoughts. She heard Donald's and another she didn't recognize. Pushing strands of her sodden hair from her face, she spied a short, elderly man, his large brown eyes flicking from Donald to her.

She couldn't hear their softly spoken words, but it was obvious they were discussing her. Clutching the moist fabric of her cloak tighter, she pretended indifference and studied the stone walls of the entranceway.

'Lynelle,' Donald said, coaxing her forward with a wave of his hand. 'This is Malcolm, Closeburn's steward.'

She swallowed, took a small step closer and bobbed her head in acknowledgement. The steward returned the favour.

'Malcolm's wife will be along soon to see you settled,' Donald said. 'I must go.'

Lynelle didn't want him to leave her alone with the steward, but refused to beg him to stay. 'Thank you, Donald,' she said.

'I'll deliver your belongings soon.' Donald gently squeezed her shoulder. 'You'll be fine, lass.'

Surprised by the reassuring touch to her shoulder, Lynelle watched him walk back out into the unwelcoming night.

She soon lost sight of him, but through the driving rain she could see Closeburn's looming high curtain wall, so similar to Fenwick's. Both embraced the occupants with safekeeping, but she knew she wasn't happily accepted inside either.

Would that not change when she returned to Fenwick? After securing Thomas' safety, would her father open his arms and heart to her and finally call her daughter?

Pray to God your healing success remains unblemished.

William's softly spoken threat loomed in her mind.

Before she discovered how her father might greet her, she had to fulfil her part of the bargain here. There was no doubt William would blame her if Edan's condition took a turn for the worse. She shuddered.

'Here, lass. You'll catch your death if you stand there any longer in those sodden clothes.'

Lynelle spun about to find Malcolm offering her a blanket.

'Give me your cloak,' he said.

She stared warily. It was the only one she had.

Steady brown eyes met hers. 'I'll see it's returned to you when it's dry.' His tone rang with kindness.

She fumbled with the ties at her throat and passed over the dripping, threadbare garment in exchange for the dry woollen blanket. 'Thank you.'

He accepted her gratitude with a small smile. 'My Mary shouldn't be far away now. She's seeing to the laird and young Edan.'

Before he'd finished speaking, a short, round woman bustled into the alcove.

'If only the laird would allow me to do my duty. But nae, the stubborn man has to tend wee Edan himself.'

Lynelle stared in shock at how the older woman spoke of her laird. Her father would never tolerate being called stubborn, or anything else.

'Now Mary, it'll do your heart nae good to be fretting over the laird,' Malcolm said. 'He knows what he's about.'

'I know, Malcolm. But the young lad is injured and with Jinny gone...' Concern rang in the woman's voice. 'Who's to tend his wounds?'

'I am.'

Two sets of eyes, one brown, and one grey, fixed on her.

Fine white brows rose above the grey eyes. 'You're a healer?'

Shock laced Mary's tone. Did she not look as a healer should? The woman couldn't know Lynelle wasn't a true healer, could she?

Lynelle straightened and answered 'Yes' with as much confidence as she could muster.

'And you're English?' The older woman's brow shot impossibly higher.

Lynelle clamped her jaw and answered with a slow nod.

Grey eyes stared into hers. 'Never mind. You can't help where you were born, lass.'

Lynelle blinked.

'Come, then,' Mary said, beckoning Lynelle forward with a pudgy hand. 'I'll have you dry, warm and fed before you know it.'

Lynelle hesitated for a moment more, but she knew she couldn't continue standing here dripping wet. She caught the folds of the now damp blanket in front of her and crossed them closed before bobbing farewell to Malcolm and following his wife inside.

Warmth brushed her cheeks as she entered a huge chamber. The haze of smoke hovering overhead tickled her nose as a sea of faces turned to stare at her.

These were William Kirkpatrick's clan. She was inside his castle, a fortress filled with his people, Scots people, and she was pretending to be a skilled healer. She ducked her head as a feeling of aloneness swamped her. Is this how a mouse would feel among a pack of wolves?

Keeping her eyes on Mary's generous curves, she climbed the stairs at her heels. Her legs were trembling by the time she made her way up the third flight of thick stone steps. Two days on horseback, a short ride in a boat and her struggle against the drenching elements had sucked her dry. She wanted to lie down and simply stop all movement just for a while.

As if sensing Lynelle's physical strain, Mary turned and said, 'Not far now, lass.' The encouragement proved enough to get her to the next landing.

Padding her way along a torch-lit corridor, Mary ushered her into a room on the left. The heat from the blazing hearth instantly touched her cheeks, but the sight of the chamber's interior brought her to an abrupt halt.

Never had she seen such a glorious room. It wasn't surprising, since she'd never set foot inside Fenwick's keep.

A high bed strewn with cushions hugged the wall to her left. Stone walls were decorated with tapestries of wildflowers and animals of the forest. The thick hides thrown on the floor looked soft, inviting and far too lovely to walk upon. The huge, steaming tub positioned in front of the fire stole her very breath.

'If you don't hurry, the water will be too cold to warm your bones.'

Lynelle blinked and drew in a rush of lavender-filled air. 'This is for me?'

'Nae. It's for William's bad-tempered horse.' Lynelle's gaze rounded on the portly woman's face and found her studying her intently. A small frown puckered Mary's brow. 'That was a jest. Of course it's for you. Come now,' she said, coaxing Lynelle forward. 'And just so you know, I wouldn't allow that beast to set one hoof inside these walls.'

Still feeling a little uncertain about Mary and of where she was, Lynelle carefully walked around the perimeter of the room to avoid muddying the furs with her boots. She stopped beside the round tub and peered into its depths. The scent of lavender was stronger here and the dancing flames licking high in the grate teased her with warmth.

'I can help you with your bath, lass, or leave you,' Mary said. 'The choice is yours.'

Lynelle clutched the borrowed blanket more firmly. 'I will manage on my own.' She always had. 'Thank you.'

'If you're sure, then?'

'I am.'

'Then I'll fetch you something to wear for when you're done and bring you a tray.'

Mary strode to the door, but paused before leaving. 'I'm a good listener if you need an ear to bend, lass.' With those puzzling words and a direct look, the woman departed.

Lynelle stared at the closed door. All day she'd wondered about finally arriving at William's home and what it would mean for her. Since the crack of the dreary dawn, she hadn't doubted they'd reach his castle today. Even the horses had seemed to display a restlessness, a heightened edge of expectation.

As the day wore on, she'd resigned herself to expect the worse. Expecting the worse saved one from grave disappointment. Did Closeburn have a dungeon complete with rats and oozing moss-covered walls? Would she be dragged into the bowels of the fortress, permitted above only to tend Edan, never to see the light of day again?

But then the rain had tumbled down and William Kirkpatrick had pressed her against him, sheltering her from the downpour.

His caring manner had mystified her.

A log crackled in the hearth, drawing her back from the unfamiliar warmth and security his embrace had offered. She peered into the clear, still water and saw her lips were curved in a smile. Her eyes lifted to the graze marring her left cheek. Memories of her stepmother's fury flooded her mind and her smile fell. A droplet from her wet hair broke the water's stillness, distorting her features, shattering illusions.

She vividly recalled the hostile glare William bestowed upon her in the boat. The man didn't trust her. He didn't even like her. Gifting her with a bath hadn't changed anything. She'd been brought here to heal Edan, nothing more. She must remain wary and be prepared for the worst.

Lynelle quickly discarded the blanket and peeled off her sodden gown and shift, along with her sorry boots and hose. She threw nervous glances toward the door as she placed her clothes on the bare floor by the wall. Then on white, wrinkled toes, she used the wooden footstool and climbed into the tub.

A delicious shiver rippled through her as she sank down into the hot, scented water. A sigh slipped free and her skin prickled. Closing her eyes, she basked in the glorious feel of restored warmth, surprised how swiftly the chill left her.

William's dark, rain-swept visage loomed behind her closed lids. Her eyes snapped open. If the laird was wet through, how had Edan faired?

Worry spurred her on. She dunked her head beneath the fragrant water and made quick use of the pot of soap resting on the tub's edge. Hair and body scrubbed and rinsed as well as she could manage, she climbed out, dried her body and wrapped her long tresses in a towel.

Standing in front of the blazing hearth, she searched the chamber for something other than the drying cloth to cover her nakedness. She was eager to see to Edan's wounds, but could hardly tend him without a stitch on.

The image of William's stormy eyes assessing her unclad form rushed in from nowhere, sending a flash of blinding heat into her cheeks, a scorching so intense that no bath or flame could compete with its fierceness.

She tightened the linen cloth about her and moved closer to the fire. Freeing her hair, she clawed her fingers through the tangled mass, staring at the pile of sodden clothes she'd recently discarded.

Her spare gown was inside her sack of belongings, but it could well be as wet as the one she'd dispensed. Donald said he would deliver her things to her, but how long would she have to wait?

She frowned at the muddied garments. Why hadn't she thought to wring them out and hang them before the fire? A spare gown was one thing, but she only had one pair of hose and a single shift, as thin and worn as they were. Her boots were in an even sorrier state.

There was nothing else for it. Unless she wanted to parade around with only her waist-length hair adorning her body, she'd just have to dress in the cold, dirt-streaked clothes she'd lived and slept in for the past two days.

She imagined herself walking these halls naked and smiled. She could see the horrified stares from the women and the rounded eyes of every Scotsman watching her sail about the fortress with her shoulders back and her head held high. They'd think her mad.

She pressed her fingers to her lips to stifled the giggle building in her throat.

The memory of Edan's trusting gaze killed her urge to laugh. William's burning glare, hot enough to turn her flesh into a smouldering pile of cinders, wiped her smile clean. Then a sharp knock at the door had her reaching for her filthy attire.

***

William closed his ears to Edan's constant chant that he wasn't a babe and finished drying his ill-tempered brother. He laid him on the bed, threw the coverlet over his bruised and stitched body and plumped the bolster to annoy the lad further.

'I'd prefer one of your drawn-out lectures to your mothering.'

William hid his smile and strode back to the tub and began topping it up with the unused pails of hot water. If complaints spelled good health, then Edan's condition hadn't worsened. He mentally sighed with relief.

A soft knock sounded. 'Enter,' William called.

Mary came in. Her inquisitive eyes studied Edan's prostrate form and then settled on him. Why was she back so soon?

As if reading his thoughts she said. 'The lass has bathed and dresses in a borrowed gown as we speak.' William nodded and tested the temperature of the water.

'Have you discovered all her secrets while settling her?' Mary's innate curiosity kept her abreast of even the smallest changes within the castle. It was a great help to a busy laird.

'She refused my assistance, so I've had little chance to learn anything.' A note of disappointment crept into the older woman's voice. 'When I returned to her assigned chamber, with a tray and the clothes one of the kitchen maids kindly offered, I found she'd already finished bathing and stood by the fire clutching her wet clothes.'

An image of the Englishwoman, dressed in nothing but pink flushed skin, rose to the forefront of William's mind. As tired as he was, his body stirred to life.

'She looks as lost as a frightened lamb and holds her secrets close,' Mary continued. 'But given time, I shall find out all there is to know about her.'

'Good.' William didn't doubt it.

'Donald fetched her scant belongings,' Mary went on, 'but they were in poor shape. She has her healing herbs and is eager to see Edan.'

Though he wanted to rid himself of his sodden attire, William said, 'Bring her eagerness here, then. I doubt Edan will whine over her coddling, as he does mine.'

'A woman is meant to coddle the sick and injured,' Edan pointed out from the bed. 'And she is much prettier to look upon than you.'

Aye, she was, even travel-worn and soaked through. How would she appear freshly bathed and free of the sorry cloak she'd worn like armour for the last two days?

'Why don't you tell me everything you know about her, laird?'

William turned and looked into Mary's keen gaze. 'There is little to tell, Mary. Edan needed a healer. The woman volunteered.'

'Ah, blether. She's English and there's more to how she came to be here,' she muttered and headed for the door.

'One more thing, Mary,' William said. 'I expect you to pass on all you learn about the healer.'

Mary's eyes narrowed. 'Now I ken you're hiding something.' With a sharp nod of her head, Mary left the room.

William resumed filling the tub and sighed when a sharp rap sounded on the thick oak panel. Mary obviously wasn't pleased with him. 'Come.'

The portal opened and a scowling Mary trudged back in, followed by the healer carrying her herbs.

'Thank you, Mary. You can find your rest now.'

She threw him a glare and turned on her heel. 'Don't let them keep you long, lass,' she said to the healer. 'After sharing their company on your journey here, you'll be in need of a good night's rest. I'll come for you in the morning.' She marched from the room, slamming the heavy door behind her.

The healer flinched and lifted blue eyes full of uncertainty to his. Clad in a white gown, a nightgown, laced high on her throat, she looked as innocent and as lost as Mary had described.

Her hair was fashioned in a single plait that draped over one shoulder and shone red-gold in the flaming torchlight. His gaze travelled down the length of the garment and he spied bare toes peeking out from under the hem. The small toes curled inward as he watched.

'I've come to see to Edan.'

Her voice held remarkably steady, considering the nervousness emanating from her. She had a right to feel nervous, for in his tired and uncomfortable state a sense of wickedness had swelled in his blood. He held it in check.

'My brother awaits.' He gestured to the bed, where Edan lay quietly, and then poured the last pail of the now warm water into the tub. If he didn't make use of the cooling water soon, he might as well strip naked and wash outside in the rain.

Placing the empty vessel beside the others, William wandered to the unoccupied side of the bed as Edan finished telling the healer he hadn't suffered any ill effects from his drenching.

She mixed a potion using the water and wine set on the bedside table and sipped. William then tasted it before passing it to his brother. Her hands trembled slightly as she scooped the salve from the pot and painted it onto his proffered wrist. She used gentle strokes to coat Edan's thigh wound, wrapped his leg with thick bandages and then re-splinted his broken arm.

William aided her in binding Edan's bruised torso, her fingers brushing his as they passed the long strips of linen back and forth. Her breathing hitched with each feather-like touch and the control he mustered to tame his sinful thoughts slipped a notch every time she gasped. The scent of lavender wafting from her silky hair and skin only heightened his sense of wickedness.

She swiftly gathered her herbs, gently ordered Edan to rest before bidding the lad a good night and walked to the door. William reached for the latch and hesitated. Her gaze slowly travelled the length of his arm, burned a path over his shoulder and up along his neck, until her eyes met his.

A sinful thought broke free. 'Have you no commands or wishes for me?'

Her gaze dropped to his chest and skittered away. 'I suggest you rid yourself of your wet clothes...' She stopped speaking and looked at him with shock in her wide eyes.

The urge to smile tugged at his lips. He suppressed it. 'Are you offering to help me?

'No.'

His mouth curved faintly as her pale cheeks turned scarlet and she clutched her satchel closely to her chest.

"Tis as well I can see to myself then.' He opened the door and watched her hastily cross the hall, shutting herself inside her chamber.

Fixing the latch in place, he studied Edan's sleeping form for a moment, before he finally stripped out of his sodden clothes.

He stepped into the tub and sank down into the lukewarm water, relieved it had cooled. Though bone-weary from lack of sleep and mind-weary from his constant worry over Edan, the part of him that proved him male stood proud and tall, craving attention.

Thank the saints he'd asked Mary to uncover the healer's secrets for him. He could then learn all he wanted to know about her but only need suffer her unsettling presence each time she tended Edan. It would be safer this way, safer for him and for her.

William groaned and slipped beneath the tepid water.

Chapter 10

Lynelle woke as Mary entered her room with a laden tray the next morning. She dragged herself up in the bed. Despite spending the night in such a luxurious bed, she hadn't slept well. Her dreams had been tormented by images of a damp shirt, clinging to the muscled contours of a powerful chest, and dark eyes full of mischief.

'Morn, lass.'

Pushing her mussed hair from her face, she watched the older woman potter about, fussing with the hide draping the arrow-slit window and checking Lynelle's boots drying before the dying hearth. The tub had been removed while she'd tended Edan the night before. 'Have you seen Edan this morn? Is he well?'

'Aye. He slept the full night and is resting in his chamber.'

Lynelle slid her feet to the cold, wooden floor and crossed to the small round table where Mary had left the tray. 'You should not be serving me.'

The older woman turned and looked at her. 'Ach! Sit and eat, lass. Start with the bowl of oats. They taste better warm.'

Perching on the stool, Lynelle scooped up the oats with a spoon made of bone. Combined with goat's milk, the oats were delicious.

'If I didn't bring you something to break your fast, you'd waste away to naught.' Lynelle paused from eating the next spoonful. 'The laird has commanded you to stay within this chamber.'

Lynelle's stomach tightened at hearing the truth of what she was. Although she was confined to a beautifully decorated room instead of the cold, slimy dungeon she'd imagined, she was a prisoner.

She'd known what to expect, had believed she'd prepared for the worse. But still. Lowering her lashes to hide the disappointment she shouldn't be feeling, she took another mouthful. The oats now tasted like ashes. She pushed the tray away, leaving the bread and cheese untouched, and sipped from her cup, swilling the cool water around in her mouth.

She mustn't let disappointment find her again.

'Whose chamber is this?'

Mary ceased tidying the bed. Three heartbeats later she resumed smoothing the covers. 'This was sweet Rhona's room. She was sister to William and Edan.'

Lynelle's disappointment lessened as her gaze wandered about the feminine chamber. 'What happened to her?'

Mary stopped rearranging the pillows and stared down at the rose-hued cushion she held. 'The ague.' Squeezing the bolster to her chest, she sniffed and gently laid it on the bed with the others. 'Such a bonny wee lass and far too young to leave us.'

A knot of sorrow filled Lynelle's chest as she watched the older woman struggle to bring her grief under control. 'Forgive me. I ... I didn't...'

''Tis good to speak of Rhona,' Mary said, cutting off her apology. ''Tis nice to have a lass of similar age to fuss over.' She gave Lynelle a small, watery smile and walked to the door. 'I'll return with your attire soon.'

Left alone, Lynelle padded on bare feet to the window and peered out at the new day. With the hour still early, the sky appeared to struggle between blue and grey. Meek sunlight filtered in from the east, and each ray of pale gold seemed to point out the puddles and wet spots from the deluge last evening.

Had Rhona looked out her window each day and gloried at the gently rolling hills to the south? Was her hair as black as her brothers' hair and her eyes the same silver-grey? Had William wept when his sister passed on?

He was extremely protective of his younger brother, an honourable trait. Had he been as vigilant a guardian with Rhona? Had a healer tended Rhona? If so, what had happened to the healer?

Squeezing her eyes shut, she tried to clear her mind of her unwanted thoughts.

Hearing Ada talk about the joy of aiding the ill and easing another's pain had been the one bright spot in her cursed existence. Now Lynelle's small experience with healing had given her the first real feeling of accomplishment in what she sometimes saw as her wasted life.

It saddened her greatly to think anyone doubted the good of healing. Healing was a gift, a knowledge that needed nurturing. It must be, for if it wasn't she had nothing else to believe in.

Mary returned with her spare gown, and a young woman with bright red hair carried in a basin of water. Although the younger woman's time in the room was brief, she sent numerous fleeting glances Lynelle's way, before leaving along with Mary.

After washing, Lynelle dressed and welcomed the small measure of normalcy wearing her own clothes afforded her. She then spent the better part of the day sorting what remained of her herbs and studying the contents of the sack the Elliots' healer had given her.

Other than the pot of salve, mortar, pestle, bowls and clean linens, the gifted sack contained only a small pouch of yarrow leaves used to stem bleeding. Lynelle's own supply of feverfew was dangerously low, as she'd used the herb each day to make Edan comfortable and prevent a fever taking hold. She'd need to find a way to replenish her stock.

How was she to do this while confined to her room? Her answer came late in the day with a knock on the door and a summons, not from Mary but from the laird himself.

'Edan's leg pains him,' William said.

Lynelle jumped to her feet and tore her gaze from the broad shoulders filling the doorway.

'I will come immediately.'

She retrieved all she needed and kept her gaze averted as she walked toward the door, expecting him to move. Instead, he turned sideways. Her eyes lifted, assessing his carved profile. Did he see her as nothing other than a healer, a prisoner?

She sucked in a deep breath and fought the frustration heating her cheeks. Edging past him, his masculine scent teased her nostrils, and her breasts brushed his broad chest. She froze. Her breath caught. She darted through the doorway, crossed the dimly lit corridor and stopped in front of Edan's chamber. William halted beside her. His size made her feel tiny, fragile. Her sudden vulnerability annoyed her and excited her in an unfamiliar way.

She looked up into his dark, watchful eyes. 'To prevent Edan pain, it would be best for me to tend him each morning and night.'

William's gaze bore into hers before skimming her features. She willed her legs not to buckle, forced herself to stand her ground.

'Whatever is best for Edan,' he said, his voice deep and low.

He reached past her, his arm almost touching her shoulder as he opened the door.

Lynelle clutched her herbs to her fluttering stomach and entered the room. She conjured up a smile for the injured young man lying on the bed. 'Good eve, Edan.'

His smile was lost in a pain-filled grimace. Guilt rose in her belly, turning the recent fluttering to nausea. She should have spoken sooner about tending Edan more often.

She quickly prepared the same tonic she'd used from the outset, noticing the wine and water already sitting on the bedside table. 'This will stem your pain.'

Lynelle sipped the concoction and passed it to William, who drank, paused and offered the cup to Edan. Placing a knee on the bed, William propped his young brother up, as Edan drained every drop. He then gently lowered Edan back onto the bed.

Knowing it would take time for the tonic to take effect, Lynelle distracted Edan by asking of his other injuries. As they spoke, his body relaxed and his eyelids grew heavy. 'Rest now. Your leg wound needs redressing, but I will tend to it later tonight.'

A faint smile curved Edan's lips as his lashes dipped and closed.

Relief trickled through Lynelle and she looked across Edan's sleeping form to William. He peered down at his brother and his wide chest expanded and released, as if drawing a huge sigh.

'Do not worry. Edan's sleep is a peaceful one.'

William's troubled eyes caught hers and she glanced away from the open concern glinting in the charcoal depths. She gathered her herbs and strode from the room.

Pausing outside her chamber, she turned to face the man whose presence she felt like a touch.

'My stock of feverfew grows low.'

One dark brow lifted as he peered down at her.

'I must find more if I'm to continue aiding your brother.'

He folded large arms across his broad chest and leaned a muscular shoulder on the wall. He appeared relaxed, now Edan was asleep. Faint noises from the great hall below broke the quietness of the dim corridor where they stood alone. His lips looked full, having lost the tightness around his mouth. A shiver whispered along her skin and her heartbeat danced more swiftly in her chest.

Why did she feel hot and cold all at once when he was near? How could she feel safe, yet in danger at the same time?

Why did he not say something?

'I will see your herbs do not run out.'

Finally. 'Thank you.' She turned to the door. Fingering the latch, she sank her teeth into her bottom lip and turned back to face him. 'I am sorry about your sister, Rhona.'

William surged away from the wall. His powerful arms dropped to his sides, stiff, rigid. His large hands curled into fists.

'What do you know of Rhona?' His tone rang with menace. His expression spoke of hurt and anger.

Lynelle pressed back against the oak panel behind her. 'Only that she died.'

'My sister is not your concern.'

'Was there no one to care for her?'

'You dare too much, healer.'

His arm shot toward her and she ducked her head, prepared for the blow. It never came. Instead, the solid mass supporting her weight from behind, gave way.

She stumbled backwards through the opened door of her room. With flailing arms she tried to catch her balance. Strong, warm hands spanned her waist, sending streaks of lightning through her body. The world righted itself.

Gasping for breath, she stared into silver, narrowed eyes that studied her too closely. She felt the pulsing warmth of bare skin beneath her palms. She glanced down at her small white hands clutching his sun-bronzed forearms. William's arms, dusted with dark silky hair, and her hands, clinging for dear life.

Snatching them away, she stepped back and wrapped her arms about her quivering middle. Dear Lord. She didn't know where to look. So she settled her gaze on the toes of his boots.

Why didn't he leave? Was he waiting for her to thank him for preventing her fall? She should, but her voice seemed trapped in her throat. She struggled just to breathe.

The leather boots left her sight and she heard the sound of the door-latch sinking into place. He'd gone. She didn't need to search the room to know. While his presence disturbed her, the loss of it filled her with a strange ache. Why? She had no clue. She only knew she must learn to ignore it.

***

William stared at the closed wooden panel, his thoughts consumed by the woman inside the room. Lifting his hands, he pressed his open-palms to the cold stone on either side of the door. Had she thought he'd moved to strike her? Had someone beaten her before? The gash on her cheek was still fresh.

Straightening, William thrust his fingers through his hair and stared up at the shadowed ceiling. His hands still burned from when he'd clutched her narrow waist. The scent of her skin was imbedded in his mind. *God's teeth. She was a healer.*

Not a single complaint about her confinement had passed her rose-coloured lips. Every word she'd spoken had concerned Edan and his treatment. She'd even tried to reassure *him* about his brother, her large sapphire eyes staring at him with sympathy and understanding.

Then she'd mentioned Rhona.

Mentally burying the pain and guilt back into the pit of his soul, he turned and glanced in on Edan. Satisfied his brother would be safe for a moment or two, and glad to stretch his legs after spending the day in the chamber entertaining the lad, he slipped down the stairway in search of the woman who often became his eyes and ears. Mary could see to replenishing the healer's simples.

The Englishwoman unsettled him and intrigued him in ways no other living soul ever had. He didn't want her pity. He shouldn't want to know everything about her. He wanted her to heal Edan.

Then, he wanted her gone.

Chapter 11

Delicious smells floated up to greet Lynelle as she followed Mary down the stairs. She had no idea where the older woman was taking her, but she was still shaken by her recent encounter with William, and had leapt at the chance to escape her chamber.

'I've something to show you,' was the only clue Mary had given.

Voices grew louder as they descended and finally stopped at the foot of the stairway at the edge of the great hall. The chamber was abuzz with activity. A group of male servants strained with effort as they lugged long trestle tables from along the walls to the centre of the room. Women's laughter drowned out the grunts and groans. Was this what Fenwick's great hall was like before a meal?

Lynelle stretched her neck to see what the women found so amusing. As she searched, a faint tingling crept up her spine. She was being watched.

She discovered the source hovering beside the wall further into the room. The woman with the cloud of red hair, the one who'd delivered her water this morning, was staring at her now.

Lynelle smiled at the familiar face. The woman continued to stare for a few moments, before disappearing through an archway to the chamber's right. A twinge of disappointment caused Lynelle's smile to slip.

'Come, lass,' Mary said. 'You're keeping them from their chores, the nosey lot they are.'

Mary was right. Many of the servants had stopped their preparations and were looking at her. Uncomfortable at the attention from so many, Lynelle searched for Mary and found the older woman had already made her way down another flight of stairs. With a tiny hitch of her breath, Lynelle quickly moved to catch up.

Slowing her step part way down the dimly lit stairwell, she listened to Mary's footfalls echoing from below and shivered as the cooler air washed over her.

She reached a landing where a single torch burned and discovered another line of steps leading down into the deepest recesses of the fortress. Throwing a longing glance at the welcoming light above, she turned away, drew a cold breath and crept down the final flight of stairs.

A short, narrow passageway stood dark and uninviting, the cold stone walls seeming to close in about her. A flare of light winked from inside the tunnel. 'This way, Lynelle. We haven't got all day, lass.' Mary's musical voice echoed off the stonework, bringing with it a sense of brightness. With haste, she crossed the gloomy passageway and came to an abrupt halt as she burst out the other end.

A vaulted ceiling gave spacious depth to the area she now stood in. Shadows danced on the walls from the numerous torches, but did little to chase the chill from the air. Two closed doors appeared like mismatched eyes in the wall before her. The one on the left was iron-studded and centred to its half of the wall. A small barred grill, positioned high in the thick wood, allowed persons to see in or out.

The second door had no grilled opening, was smaller and sat far to the right of the stonework. Lynelle followed Mary to the second door.

'What is this place?' she said.

'Come and see.' The thin panel groaned as Mary pushed it open and entered.

Lynelle stood in the entrance as the older woman set about touching flame to unlit torches. Her jaw dropped wide as, with each flare of light, the slim chamber's secrets were slowly revealed.

The high arched roof outside the room continued inside. She sniffed the air, savouring the rush of mingled scents of meadowsweet and lavender and the strong presence of cloves. But it was the rows of cluttered shelves and clusters of drying herbs dangling from above that held Lynelle in wonder.

Moving into the room, she ran a trembling finger along one of the dust-covered shelves crowded with earthen jars, clay pots and glass vials. She inhaled deeply, breathing in the aroma of countless herbs – and neglect.

'The laird said you needed certain herbs to help with Edan's recovery. I'm certain you'll find what you're looking for among this lot.'

'Yes.' She heard the awe in her own voice.

'I'll leave you to search and will return when the evening meal has been served.'

Caught up in the wonder of the room, it took a few moments for Mary's words to register. 'Who created such a wondrous room?'

Mary paused in the doorway and turned back to look at her. 'This was Jinny's place. She was Closeburn's healer for nigh on forty years.'

Forty years! How much knowledge must the woman have gathered over such a long period of time?

'When did she die?'

'Oh, Jinny isn't dead. She moved to Thornhill village in the north half a year ago.'

'Why did she leave?'

'Jinny didn't leave.' Mary's tone turned serious. 'She was banished.'

Lynelle's blood ran cold. She knew what it was like to be outcast. She'd suffered it her entire life and knew nothing different. Forty years of caring for

Closeburn's people hadn't saved the healer from being cast out.

'Why?' She had to know.

Mary turned away, seeming to search for the answer among the herb-strewn shelves. 'Her healing skills failed to save those she tended,' she said quietly.

Jinny had most likely done all in her power to treat the people struck down by illness and she had forty years of practice. An unwelcome prickle of fear arose inside Lynelle at her own experience, which was near to none.

Dear God! Poor Jinny. Who would be callous enough to banish her for what must have been God's wish? She had an idea, but needed to know for sure.

'Was it your laird William who banished Jinny?'

Mary peered at her for a few silent moments. 'Have you ever lost someone you loved, Lynelle?'

A stabbing pain pierced Lynelle's chest.

Murderer!

She clutched the corner of the worn workbench and drew slow breaths past the agony of guilt and despair.

'Ah, I see you have,' Mary said softly. 'Then you must understand the pain and anger suffered by those left behind.'

She understood the hurt of being to blame. Lynelle swallowed past the gorge rising in her throat.

'Collect what you need and I'll return for you soon.' Leaving the door open, Mary disappeared.

Lynelle squeezed her eyes shut and prayed for heat to chase away the ice chilling her blood. The past was the past and she could do nothing to change it. She must concentrate on the present and keep the ugliness that had shaped her life buried deep inside her. She'd been brought to this room to find herbs to aid in Edan's recovery. It was this task that gave her a purpose to cling to.

Forcing her legs to move, she began searching for the feverfew. Half a year had gone by and none of the herbs would be fresh. She wasn't discouraged. Dried feverfew was just as effective as the newly picked plant.

A portion of her mind was filled with anticipation of studying every corner of the room and its contents. Her remaining thoughts were of sadness for Jinny, and the determination to prove that healers were good and caring people.

William must have been the one to cast Jinny aside. He needed his trust in healers to be restored and Lynelle was the one to do it.

Had no one at Closeburn been sick for the last half year? Were the Kirkpatricks a healthy lot or were they suffering in silence? Once she'd gained William's trust, she could then gain the trust of his people.

Removing a stopper from another jar, she sniffed the wrinkled leaves within. The scent was less pungent now, but still unmistakably feverfew. She replaced the stopper and carried the earthen jar to the entry. Leaning against the doorframe to wait for Mary, she looked back into the chamber, absorbing the air of the past, someone else's past, now enhanced by grime and cobwebs. She would ask to return here, to clean and to explore and perhaps make use of such abundance.

A footfall from the passageway drew her attention and she turned, expecting to see Mary. As she peered into the shadows, she caught a glimpse of red hair, then nothing. Had the young woman who'd watched her in the great hall come looking for her? Lynelle sensed the woman wanted something from her, but what? She'd do her best to find out.

Moments later, Mary came and escorted her back to her room, where she found a tray with steaming pheasant and an assortment of greens smothered in garlic. Lynelle's mouth watered at the sight and smell of such lavish food and she almost forgot to ask about the red-haired woman.

'Her name is Keita,' Mary said as Lynelle sat down before her evening meal. 'Why do you ask?'

Lynelle shrugged. 'I am curious.' She took great care in rearranging the food on her trencher, fully aware of Mary's intense regard.

'I will see all is ready in Edan's chamber,' Mary finally said before leaving.

Once alone, Lynelle savoured the delicious food, all the while planning a way to restore William's faith in healers. She could simply tell him how good healers were, recounting several of Ada's experiences to justify her claims. But would William fully understand? She didn't think so. It would take something stronger than old tales to convince him. William needed to be included, to play a hands-on role in aiding the sick.

If she pretended to be indisposed, she could ask for his assistance. Would he help? There was only one way to find out. Could she play him false? Yes, she believed she could if it meant renewing his trust in healers. What if he discovered her ruse? Lynelle shivered. She'd just have to make certain he didn't.

After a drink of water to wash down the most glorious meal she'd ever eaten, Lynelle wrapped her left hand in a bandage. To hide her supposed injury from Mary, she draped it with the clean bandages she'd use on Edan. She picked up her sack with her right hand and waited. Her belly churned with a mixture of fear at being caught out and excitement at the thought of sharing her world with William.

Mary came and delivered her to Edan's chamber. William opened the door and Lynelle's stomach clenched at the sight of his serious expression. Her bound hand began to throb. She hastened into the room and halted at Edan's side, as William bid Mary farewell and closed the door.

'Good evening, Edan.' She focused on the young man sitting upright against the pillows.

'Good eve, Lynelle,' Edan said. 'You've come to change my bandages.'

'Yes, and to make certain you haven't lost your appetite.'

'Not likely.' His accompanying smile told her he'd enjoyed the meal as much as she had.

'Mary tells me you found what you needed in the room below.'

The sound of William's deep voice shivered through her as she placed her sack on the end of the bed and withdrew its contents. 'Yes.' She paused after setting the mortar and pestle on the small table and finally looked at William. 'I would like to return there, if permitted to do so.'

His dark-lashed eyes narrowed. 'Why?'

She'd expected the question, but her courage dwindled a fraction beneath the intensity of his gaze. She resumed her unpacking and said, 'I could make great use of the chamber's contents. There is an abundance of herbs going to waste.'

'Also a fair amount of dust, if I'm correct.'

Lynelle looked up at William, wondering why he'd made such a comment. 'Nothing that cannot be fixed with some care and cleaning.'

She turned, busying herself with preparations.

'You may visit the healing room, as long as someone is free to escort you.'

Her eyes met his and her heart fluttered with excitement. 'Thank you.' She couldn't believe he'd granted her wish without her having to beg.

This time, William looked away first.

She smiled down at Edan, with hope filling her chest. He smiled back.

'What have you done?'

William's voice, almost a growl, made her flinch. His drawn eyebrows and dark flashing eyes caused her smile to slip. She followed his line of sight and realized he was staring at her bound left hand. In her budding excitement, she'd forgotten her plan.

''Tis nothing.'

'Are you injured?'

''Tis nothing. Truly.'

A bubble of guilt blossomed inside her. To play him false after he'd been so unexpectedly kind to her made her feel ill. But she remembered the reason for her deception, and the sharp reminder burst the tiny bubble and renewed her strength of purpose.

'It will not hinder me while tending to Edan. But ... I may need your assistance.'

Lynelle imagined herself melting under his burning gaze.

'My assistance? How?'

She swallowed and pushed forward with her ruse. 'If you could perhaps grind the herbs using the pestle ... it would be a great help.'

He stared.

She felt herself wilting.

'Show me.'

She did.

The pestle looked tiny when grasped in his large, powerful hand and the herb gave way beneath his ministrations with ease. She made the brew and sipped, then passed it on to William and then Edan to drink.

When she began unravelling the bandages from Edan's thigh and chest, her efforts made awkward by her bound hand, William helped her with the task. After she bathed the wound, testing the salve on her own flesh and then William's, before finally smearing it on the intended injury, the laird aided her in redressing Edan's leg.

They worked in silence, heads bent close as they checked Edan's other injuries. Heat radiated from William and she had to mask her altered breathing with every accidental brush of their fingers. An air of shared purpose permeated the room and she wondered if William felt it too. When all was done, Lynelle stood peering down at Edan, a flush of satisfaction warming her cheeks.

'I bid you a good night, Edan.'

'And I you, Lynelle. Thank you,' Edan said.

'It is not only I who has given you ease this night.' She flicked a glance to the other side of the bed where William stood studying their handiwork.

'Thank you, too, Will.'

The laird appeared mildly distracted, but managed a slight nod.

Lynelle gathered her things, bundled them into the sack and walked to the door. William appeared at her side and opened the door.

Peering up into his handsome face she said, 'Thank you for your help.'

'For Edan's sake.'

A tiny jab of disappointment pricked her heart. Had she really thought he'd done it for her? 'I will return in the morning, once you've broken your fast.'

'I'll be expecting you.'

She turned and quickly crossed the hall into her room and closed the door. Leaning back against the thick oak panel, she tried to think of the good that had just happened and not dwell on her disappointment.

She'd asked for William's help and he'd given it. It was a start in her quest to renew his faith in healers.

What more had she expected? That William had also felt the connection she had as they'd worked together. That he too had experienced the quiet sense of achievement with each passing moment. That he had the feeling of being an important part, a vital part of something special. With her.

Not since Ada had she shared anything with another. But this was different.

For Edan's sake.

He'd done what was necessary for his brother, that was all. She should be content.

Then why did it feel as if a shadow blanketed her heart?

***

William closed the door and wandered to one of the windows in the north-facing wall of the chamber. He stared out into the night, desperately trying to rid his mind of the Englishwoman's face.

'Lynelle is rather pretty, despite having dirt on her nose and cheek.' It seemed his brother's thoughts matched his.

Aye. The smudge on the tip of her nose and the streak of dust high on her cheek, the cheek without the gash, gave her pretty face a new quality. With her wide, anxious eyes, she'd looked ... sweet.

'I thought of telling her,' Edan went on, 'but I didn't want to upset her.'

William had held his tongue for the very same reason. When he'd granted her leave to explore the room below stairs, the gratitude sparkling in her sapphire eyes had caused something warm to unfurl in his chest. He hadn't liked the feeling.

Then he'd spied her bandaged hand and a chill had dispelled the unwanted warmth. Her attempt to reassure him she was still able to care for Edan and then her request for him to help her had left him numb.

What if he'd done something wrong?

But he hadn't. They hadn't, and for the first time in his life he'd wondered if self-doubt ever travelled through a healer's mind as they cared for the ill and injured.

'Your leg is healing well,' William said as he turned from the window. Soft snoring sounds greeted him. He walked to the bed and stared down at his brother. He looked so much younger while asleep. Clenching his fists against the tide of protective emotions surging through him, he praised God for Edan's continued good health and silently thanked the healer for her skills.

Mary had discovered little about the Englishwoman and the life she'd led before coming to Closeburn. He now knew the healer had lost someone dear to her, but didn't know who the person was or how they'd died. The need to know everything about her grew stronger with each passing day, and although he fought against it and tried to pretend he wasn't interested, he knew he was only fooling himself.

Who or what had marked her cheek?

Perhaps if he found out all about her, he'd be satisfied and could concentrate on other, more important things.

He wandered back to the window, preparing for another long sleepless night, and peered out at the darkening sky. He'd granted her wish to explore the room below stairs. In return, he'd ask her a question about herself.

A boon for a boon, and to his mind a fair exchange.

Chapter 12

After breaking her fast the following morning, Lynelle almost forgot to bandage her hand and hide it from Mary before she returned to take her to Edan. She didn't like the deception, but she must now follow it through. It was the only way she could see to continue William's involvement in his brother's recovery, and hopefully open his eyes to the greater good of healing.

Edan's spirits were high, a sign of much improvement. Once again, William ground the herb for her and they went through the ritual of testing the prepared potion. Edan's dressings wouldn't need changing again until nightfall.

Gathering her belongings, fully aware the laird watched her with a heightened intensity that she tried to ignore, she walked to the door. But he barred her way, resting an open palm against the wood.

Her heart jumped about in her chest at his nearness, but mostly because of his silent regard. Her fingers tightened about the sack in her unbound hand. She fixed her eyes on the lacings of his leather vest, doing her utmost to appear calm.

'What happened to your face?'

The low-voiced enquiry surprised her. A large hand lifted toward her, and as she closed her eyes she silently begged him not to touch her. A warm tingling erupted inside her every time she relived the accidental brushing of their fingers the night before.

How would she react if he were to touch her cheek?

But he didn't.

Tamping down the shadow of disappointment, she opened her eyes to find him watching her, his hand hanging in a fist at his side.

'I have permitted you to explore the chamber below,' he said quietly. 'For this favour, I would ask a simple question in return. What happened to your face?'

Dear God. Would he recant his permission if she refused to answer? How to respond and not give anything away?

'I am ungainly at times. I fell,' she said, not quite meeting his eyes. She had fallen, if only after her stepmother had slapped her, slicing open her cheek with bejewelled fingers. She lifted her bound hand and covered the healing wound.

'You seem far from ungainly to me.'

A whisper of warmth flittered through her chest at his remark. 'Your words are kind.' She held up her bandaged hand. 'But see, I am awkward.'

He held her with the power of his gaze, causing heat to fire her cheeks. She struggled to find enough air to draw a full breath. He wanted to say more, she could tell, but instead he looked past her and opened the door.

She wanted to run but fought hard and held her pace to a walk from Edan's chamber to hers. She gently shut the door instead of slamming it closed, as was her urge.

Shivers rippled through her. Pressing her forehead against the cool wood, she waited for her body to stop shaking.

There'd been wariness in his silver eyes, a mistrust not only of her as a healer, but of who she was as a person. If these people should discover who she was...

Lynelle closed her eyes. It didn't bear thinking about. Revealing her past frightened her more than anything.

Though she was a prisoner of sorts here, she'd experienced freedoms she'd never known before. Simply talking with people, asking questions, giving voice to her beliefs, her thoughts, made her feel – dare she think it? – as if she belonged.

But if William and his clansmen were to learn who she was and how her own people shunned her, she feared their natural curiosity and wariness would disappear. She could imagine their expressions altering to mirror the disdain upon the faces of those at Fenwick – those who deigned to look at her at all.

William wanted to know all her secrets and truth to tell, she yearned to discover his.

A knock shuddered through the door. Lynelle flinched and stepped back, trying to pull her thoughts into order.

It must be Mary coming to take her to the healing chamber.

She set the sack down and reached for the latch, her eyes widening when she noted the bandage still wrapped about her hand. With haste she unravelled it, stuffing the linen into the sack's opening. Flexing her fingers, she again reached for the door.

Mary's kind face beamed at her. 'Ach, I started to think you were still caring for the lad.'

'No. I have already seen to Edan.' She tried to smile, but her lips trembled as she struggled to banish the unnerving allure William cast over her even now.

'Are you well, lass? You look flushed.'

'I'm fine.' Flushed was good, as she'd thought all her colour had rushed from her face to her toes. 'Just eager to explore the room down the stairs.'

Mary nodded. 'Ah, well. Let's be on our way, then.'

Lynelle glanced at the door opposite as she passed, half expecting it to swing open and the laird to pounce on her with more questions. Thankfully, the door remained closed.

She must be careful what she asked for in the future, if the consequences were William delving into her life.

A flutter of anticipation built inside her as they descended the stairs to the hall. Mary stopped, seemingly to search the large room. Malcolm waved to his wife from across the vast chamber and Mary returned the gesture.

'Ah, my dear husband.' Mary turned to face her, a smile lighting her face. 'Are you wed, Lynelle?'

Lynelle's heart skipped a beat. The warmth filling her heart at Mary and Malcolm's obvious affection disappeared. It may only be a friendly enquiry, but it came so soon after William's question that wariness seeped in.

'No.'

'Nae?' Mary's white brows shot up, almost reaching her hairline. 'Well, I am surprised.'

Mary's response puzzled her. 'Why?'

'You're a pretty lass, Lynelle. I imagined you had numerous men fighting to claim you as a wife.'

Stunned, Lynelle stared at Mary. The woman had called her pretty. She'd never really thought about her appearance before, for she looked as she did and there was nothing she could do to change it.

'Now it is you who acts surprised,' Mary said, studying her.

Lynelle's discomfort grew beneath Mary's steady regard.

Mary's thick white brows lowered over soft grey eyes. 'Has nae one ever called you pretty?'

Lynelle had been told she was many things, but pretty was never one of them. 'No.'

A fleeting sadness clouded Mary's eyes, before the usual sparkle returned. 'Then I am blessed to be the first.' Her hand stretched forward and gently patted Lynelle's arm.

A sense of wonder flooded Lynelle. 'Why have you been so good to me, Mary?'

'Are there reasons I should not be?' She said it with a smile, but more than simple curiosity glistened in the older woman's gaze.

Oh yes, many reasons, Lynelle thought, but she held her tongue. She hated deceiving these people, mostly because of their warm welcome and innate kindness. She was only here for a short while and so desperately wanted to be treated as a normal person.

'Kindness is a gift one can easily bestow on another,' Mary said. 'Everyone deserves to know such a gift. Even you, Lynelle,' she finished softly.

Something clattered to the floor nearby, saving Lynelle from responding. She might have given herself away if the girl named Keita hadn't dropped the broom she'd been carrying. She seemed to be struggling to keep hold of the pail of water and rags she still held.

Mary introduced them, informing Lynelle that Keita had volunteered to assist her in the room below. The young red-haired woman kept her gaze averted. Lynelle had guessed right. Keita wanted something. Why else would the woman be inclined to spend time in her company, cleaning?

After sharing out Keita's load, they descended the stairs and passed along the dark passage to the healing room. Musty smells and cobwebs greeted them, and once again all the chamber's secrets were slowly revealed as Mary lit the three torches mounted in iron-brackets high on the walls. With a smile, Mary left Lynelle and Keita to clean.

They worked in silence for a little while, clearing half the workbench and shelves, wiping them clean and replacing each item. Pent-up curiosity floated in the air alongside the dust moats, but Lynelle wasn't certain how to initiate conversation.

Her mind buzzed with thoughts of William and the probing questions she feared him asking. She'd have to ensure she asked no further favours of him. His handsome face appeared in her mind's eye. The memory of his hand reaching for her sent a frightening tingle up her spine. She could still feel the imprint of his fingers on her waist, when he'd lunged forward to steady her.

She scrubbed harder with her cloth, trying desperately to erase his image from her mind. But her imagination took flight and she could almost feel his fingers brushing against her cheek. She wanted him to touch her again, but not because she'd lost her footing.

The realization terrified her.

'You're a healer.'

Lynelle stilled, staring at her hands clutching a dirty cloth. Her breaths came shallow and fast and her heart pounded in her chest.

'Are you a healer?'

Releasing the rag, Lynelle turned to face Keita. The young woman stared back, a look of uncertainty on her pretty face. Lynelle welcomed the intrusion and Keita's pale, soft features soon overshadowed the image of the harsh, tanned face constantly stealing into her mind. She slowed her breaths and licked her dry lips. 'Yes. I am a healer.'

Keita's shoulders appeared to relax and her furrowed brow smoothed.

'Do you live here, in the castle?' Lynelle asked, keen to further their acquaintance.

'Nae. I have a cottage in Closeburn village.'

Lynelle threw questions at Keita, knowing it was safer to talk to the pretty young woman than allow her thoughts to wander on their own. Keita answered swiftly and willingly as they continued their labours, and Lynelle discovered a certain joy in speaking with a woman close to her own age.

She soon learned Keita was sixteen, two years younger than Lynelle. Her father was dead and she shared a cottage with her mother and Carney, her three-year-old brother. She worked in the castle's kitchens each day until the noon meal was served then spent her two free hours in the afternoon checking on her ill mother and young brother before returning to the keep to help with the evening meal.

With no healer in the vicinity, the sores on her mother's legs, caused by bites from some sort of vermin and irritated by her mother's constant scratching, had worsened. The pain had become so severe that her mother barely managed to walk, a dire problem due to Carney's three-year-old antics and a tendency to get into mischief.

'I will look at the sores on your mother's legs if she'll allow it.' Lynelle held her breath awaiting Keita's response.

'Would you?' A hopeful expression lit Keita's face.

Relieved, Lynelle nodded, though she didn't know how she'd manage to leave the castle. But she'd find a way.

They resumed cleaning and a companionable silence fell about them as they worked. Lynelle's thoughts were now awhirl with schemes to escape the confines of the fortress.

She dismissed the idea of asking for William's permission the instant it popped into her head. She feared the cost of the request too much.

A plan began to form. It wasn't perfect, but she was prepared to take a chance. Turning to Keita she said, 'I will go with you to the cottage when you have delivered the noon meal.'

'How?'

'Return here when your chores are done,' Lynelle said, finding it difficult to contain her nervous excitement. 'Do you have a cloak?' At Keita's vigorous nod she said, 'Be sure to bring it with you.'

Keita nodded again, although this time, a smile shaped her lips and her amber eyes brightened.

Lynelle went on. 'Do you know the boatman?'

'Aye. His name is Ian.' Colour suffused Keita's cheeks as she spoke the young boatman's name.

Good, Lynelle thought with a small inward smile.

'Can you describe the sores on your mother's legs, so I know which salves and herbs to bring?'

Just as Keita finished telling of the yellow pus that sometimes oozed from the sores, Mary entered.

Lynelle watched the older woman measure the progress of their work.

'There is still much to be done,' Lynelle said. 'I would like to return and continue after the noon meal.' She did her best to sound calm, hoping not to arouse Mary's suspicion.

'I too am happy to finish what we have started,' Keita said.

Mary's speculative gaze settled on each of them. 'I will speak to the laird, but I see no reason for him to deny your request.'

Trepidation rippled through Lynelle. Agreeing to her request granted William the right to ask her a question. There was little she could do to avoid it, if she wanted to help Keita's mother. Shrugging off her disquiet, she decided she would face the problem when it arose.

'Come then.' Mary motioned them toward the door. 'You must be hungry after all your toiling.'

They climbed the stairs and with a private glance, Keita headed for the kitchens as Lynelle followed Mary to her assigned chamber above. She flicked a cautious look at the door opposite her room, fearing the laird somehow knew of her plan and would storm out to stop her. Again, thankfully, the door remained closed.

Lynelle barely touched the food on her tray, her belly too full of anxious knots. She emptied the contents of her sack, repacking it with only the necessary herbs for treating Keita's mother, including a generous amount of Iona's ointment scraped onto a fresh piece of linen.

After wrapping the sack in her cloak, she bundled it beneath one arm and paced the length of the chamber.

When Mary returned, she eyed the cloak tucked tightly under Lynelle's arm.

'The air is cooler in the healing chamber,' Lynelle quickly explained.

'Aye,' Mary agreed. 'The sun hasn't shown its bonny face today. Too many clouds, though there's nae a whiff of rain in the air.'

She hoped Mary's assessment of the weather held true.

'William has granted your wish and says he will speak with you later.'

Lynelle nodded, sure that he would. She ignored the clenching of her stomach. She'd deal with the laird and his questions when she had to.

At this moment, she was too busy preparing to steal out of his castle.

Chapter 13

Keita entered the healing room soon after Lynelle, and Mary left to collect the trays from the chambers above. Once Lynelle and Keita were sure the older woman wouldn't return, they donned their cloaks and crept up the stairs. They paused at the top to make certain the clansmen in the hall were too distracted by the meal in progress to notice them.

'Malcolm has just returned from delivering the guards their meal,' Keita whispered. 'He will now join Mary in the hall to eat.'

Lynelle remained hidden as Keita slipped into the alcove – the only means of entering or leaving the fortress – and waited for the signal to move. Keita beckoned with a wave of her hand and Lynelle lifted the hood to cover her head. With a show of calm she was far from feeling, she walked out of the shadows and joined Keita in the recessed entrance.

Pressing a hand to her chest, Lynelle tried to quell her racing heart. Impossible. They still had a way to go before they were free.

They each gave a nod of readiness and then Keita donned her hood. The outer door made of metal bars swung noiselessly inward. They stepped out into the courtyard and Keita carefully closed it behind them. Walking quickly, they crossed the grounds to the massive timber gates and passed through the one propped open.

'Two guards remain at all times, but they will be busy stuffing their faces with food,' Keita whispered.

A sense of mischief flowed through Lynelle. She tamped down her growing excitement and kept pace with her accomplice as they hurried down to the pier. They still needed to cross the loch to the other side.

When they reached the structure that offered the boatman shelter from the elements, Lynelle stepped to the side out of sight and Keita ducked her head inside the opening. Voices sounded but the words were too muffled to hear what was being said. She pulled her cloak tighter about her and swallowed.

Keita straightened and moved away from the doorway. Lynelle's heart raced. This was the moment their plan either succeeded or failed. It all depended on Ian's reaction to her presence.

'How is your mother?' Ian asked as he stepped out into view.

'Not well, I fear. 'Tis the reason I go early,' Keita said quietly. 'Her legs pain her terribly.'

Lynelle noted Keita's flushed cheeks and how Ian's eyes were fixed solely on Keita's pretty face.

'I'm sorry to hear-' Ian's gaze swept to Lynelle.

She stiffened and looked directly into his surprised brown eyes, hoping to appear relaxed and unconcerned.

'What are you doing here?'

'I am escorting Keita home. Her mother is unwell and Keita has asked me to see her.' She swallowed. 'I am a healer.'

'But–'

'Please, Ian,' Keita said, and she laid her hand on his upper arm. 'Mother needs help and I fear if she's not treated soon, she will die. We promise to be back before anyone knows we have gone.'

Ian stared at Keita, and Lynelle was certain she saw his features softening. He threw a glance toward the castle and turned to face Lynelle again.

'I'll have your word that you *will* return and with haste.'

This was the second time someone had offered their trust in place of her giving her word.

Her word.

Something she'd thought useless until a few days ago. A heady feeling of importance filled her. 'I promise to return as quickly as possible.'

Ian stared at her and she prayed he realised she spoke the truth. With a curt nod he turned and strode to the boat and untied the rope from its mooring.

Lynelle and Keita shared a triumphant glance before they climbed into the boat and were rowed to the far side of Castle Loch.

They reached the pier on the other side and clambered out. With parting words of thanks to Ian, Lynelle and Keita began the half-mile trek to Closeburn village.

Keeping a brisk pace, Lynelle asked about the death of William and Edan's sister. In a solemn tone, Keita described the harrowing days leading up to Rhona's passing. Everyone had mourned her loss, for she was so young and vibrant and kind to all.

Then only two days later, more shocking news had swept through the castle and village on disbelieving tongues. Ilisa Kirkpatrick, the highly respected and much loved lady of Closeburn, had succumbed to the same dreaded ague.

A heaviness settled in Lynelle's chest as Keita recounted the terrible events of the year past. Merciful heavens. Poor young Edan had lost his sister and then his mother. He must have been devastated. How had their deaths affected William?

She pushed such questions and others concerning Jinny's banishment aside for another time as they arrived at Keita's cottage, nestled on the outskirts of the village.

The disarray inside the cottage did not detract from the cosy atmosphere that enveloped Lynelle as Keita ushered her to her mother's side. After being introduced to Elspeth, and Keita's brother Carney, Lynelle was soon bathing the festering sores and applying a salve to heal them.

She then left an assortment of herbs with instructions on how to continue treating the ulcers. With a chorus of thanks and a kiss on her cheek from Carney that made her blush, Lynelle headed back to the castle alone. She could find her own way back, knowing Keita was needed by her mother.

Wood smoke, carried from the cottages on a gentle breeze, scented the air as she followed the well-worn path through the clearing. Her gaze drifted to the small rolling hills to the south and the trees, filled with twittering birds, bordering the open spaces to the north.

Surrounded by the beautiful landscape, a quiet sense of peace flowed through her. Not another soul was in sight, but Lynelle didn't feel lonely. Though the sun hadn't shown its face, a brightness warmed her, shining from within. It was the same special feeling that seeped through her each time she helped the sick or the injured.

Tipping her face to the pewter-coloured sky, her serenity faded as a pair of eyes, matching the hue of the heavens, took shape in her mind.

Saint Jude, save me. William was so beautiful to look upon. He unsettled her, excited her. Made her want to do things that had never entered her head before.

She longed to touch him, trace his lips with her fingers and test the strength of his arms and chest with the palms of her hands.

She wanted him to touch her.

But more than anything, she wanted to ease his suffering.

Keita's story gave her a better understanding of why William lacked faith in healers. She still didn't know precisely what had happened to cause Jinny's banishment, but she sensed there was more to the tale. Edan's earlier mention of swans and curses only added to the mystery.

She rounded a slight bend in the dirt path and wondered how to begin soothing William's pain. He suffered an ache of the heart rather than a physical hurt. No herbs or potions would aid him. But could she truly help him?

The path straightened and Lynelle peered across the meadow. The fortress stood proud and formidable in the centre of the island, looking as magnificent as she'd imagined, but the swarm of people dotting the grassy embankment near the outer curtain wall doused the warmth inside her.

Her steps faltered and her heart tripped in her chest. A cold wave of alarm rushed from the top of her head to the soles of her feet.

One figure stood at the very edge of the water, alone. She did not need to be gifted with the sight to know who it was. Even at this distance, she felt the rippling waves of anger wafting from his powerful form.

Saints above. She'd wanted him to touch her and she'd wanted to ease his suffering.

Who would ease hers once he was done with her?

***

Jaw clenched, William stared at the lone figure approaching the opposite bank, surprised she returned alone. Surprised she came back at all. 'Now, Ian,' he said to the red-faced boatman. Ian started rowing across the loch to meet the woman and deliver her to William.

Mary's distress at finding the healer and Keita gone had resulted in a full-scale search of the keep. He'd ordered the distraught older woman to remain with Edan while he joined the hunt. After finding neither woman inside the castle, the inhabitants had moved outside to search the inner bailey. Still nothing. Then Ian had told him all.

Men, women, children, even the hounds now milled about on the grass between Castle Loch and Closeburn's defensive wall. They were waiting to see what he would do to the woman responsible for turning his home upside down. They whispered among themselves, keeping their distance from him, but their gazes burned a hole in his back.

He hadn't yet chosen what form of punishment to use. Several choices came to mind. Throwing her in the dungeon and starving her was one. Tying her to the whipping post and stripping the flesh off her back was another. But when images of using his bare hands to punish her turned to thoughts of using his mouth and then his body, he'd decided to wait until his mind cleared and his blood stopped racing. He only knew he couldn't lay hands on her yet. Not until his fury ebbed.

She was almost at the pier on the other side. If he'd known she would cause this much strife, he'd have thought twice about bringing her here. He peered up at the sombre grey sky, trying to ease the tension in his neck. At least it wasn't raining.

Multiple gasps sounded from the throng behind him and a cry rent the air. 'Naeeee!'

Straightening, he looked ahead and watched the Englishwoman toss aside the sack she carried, heft her skirts in one hand and begin running toward the west side of the castle.

What in God's name was she doing? Trying to escape? Now?

His feet began to move before he willed them, following her along the inner bank. His gaze fixed on her. But she stared in the direction she ran in, never once glancing at him or anything else. Her free arm pumped beside her, a sense of urgency showing in her frantic movements.

Suddenly, she plunged into the gloomy waters of Castle Loch. Shock jolted through William, swiftly followed by awareness as he finally saw what he and all the others had not. He raced forward and jumped, the chilly depths closing over his head, stealing his breath. William searched the dark, murky water by feel, fighting the pull of the loch on his fully clad form, struggling to reach the surface at the same time.

Something brushed against his elbow. He turned and latched onto fabric, dragging the tiny weight to his chest. His head finally broke free of the cold water and he drew a much-needed breath. He swam to the bank and passed the small bundle into the arms of a sobbing woman.

'Davy, oh my poor, wee, Davy.'

The little boy coughed and started crying.

'Where is she?' William gasped, pushing wet strands of hair from his face. He spun around and stared at the rippling water. Nothing else moved.

'The woman never came up,' someone shouted.

William gulped a lungful of air and dived deep, stretching his arms before him, raking the gloomy water, clawing with his hands. Something soft tickled his fingers and he grasped at it, kicking forward until his other hand clutched something solid. He pressed the form to his chest and with an almighty thrust of his legs, surged to the surface.

He gasped for air, swam to the bank and hefted his burden into Donald's waiting arms. William climbed onto shore and bent double with his hands braced on his knees, filled his chest with heaving breaths. He looked to where his kinsman had set the healer down and was thumping his fist on her back.

Dread sparked and swelled inside William as Donald's efforts went on without result. On unsteady legs he approached them, ready to shake life into the troublesome woman. She would not die on his lands. He would not allow it.

A choking sound filled the waiting silence. Water spewed from her mouth and a violent fit of coughing shook her body.

Donald supported her weight and when she quieted, William sank to one knee. Leaning forward, he brushed strands of sodden hair from her face. He traced the line of her jaw with his hand, cupped her chin and gently tilted her head up.

Her skin looked ashen, cold to his touch. Her lips were almost as blue as the watery eyes she lifted to his. William stared into them, astounded by the throbbing relief pulsing in his veins. A shiver rippled through her, the tiny tremor dancing up his fingers.

'Come.' His voice sounded rough. He cleared his throat. 'We need to get you dry.' William stood and scooped her into his arms.

'I'll carry her, Will,' Donald said as he fell into step beside him.

'Nae sense you getting wet when I'm already soaked through,' William said, loathe to give over the dripping woman nestled against him. 'How's wee Davy doing?'

'Davy's fine. He's had a fright and I don't think he'll be back testing the water any time soon,' Donald assured him.

'Good. Kindly inform Mary of what has transpired and ask her to fetch me a dry set of clothes.'

The inquisitive mob parted as he strode into the walled courtyard and entered the castle. He peered down at the woman in his arms, noting that her thick moist lashes were lowered and clumped together. The memory of her lifeless form pressed to his body flashed in his mind. 'You little fool.'

Her gaze snapped up and collided with his as he climbed to the second landing.

'Put me down,' she said weakly.

William ignored her and kept on climbing.

'Put...' She hit him in the chest. 'Me...' Another blow. 'Down.' And another.

He looked into her eyes, surprised by her strength, her daring. Anger blurred by pooling tears glared up at him, while his own anger grew, replacing his relief. She twisted in his grasp. He tightened his hold. 'Why did you do it?'

'You're the fool if I need to explain,' she said, pushing against him once more.

He adjusted his hold on her and opened the door to her chamber. 'Can you swim?' he ground out, slamming the door closed with his heel.

'Of course not.' She continued struggling in his arms. 'Let me go.'

He dumped her on her feet and her gasp echoed about the room. She staggered and swayed and he lunged forward, capturing her waist and drawing her against him.

Her breath rasped hot and fast. His wet garments were no barrier as each puff of warm air caressed his skin. Her fingers clawed his shirt and his stomach tensed beneath her touch. Waiting to feel more. Wanting to feel more. A hint of lavender teased his nose.

Her palms flattened, searing his flesh, pushing him away. Moving his grip to her upper arms, William allowed her a small distance, but refused to release her. He wasn't ready. Not yet. 'Why did you steal away?' He spoke to the crown of her head.

'Keita's mother is ill.'

Her voice sounded bland, uncaring. 'Why did you not ask to tend Elspeth?'

'I ... I didn't think you would allow it.'

'You believe me such an ogre to deny her aid?'

Silence.

Clenching his teeth, he battled to control his welling ire. His fingers flexed on her arms. 'Do you?'

'I-'

'Look at me,' he demanded, annoyed that she stood docile when moments ago she'd fought him. 'Are you a coward as well as a fool?'

Her head snapped back, wrath-filled eyes stabbing him with fury. 'Do not call me that.'

'Which? Coward or fool?'

'Neither. You do not know me, yet from the first you named me something I am not.'

'I know more about you than you think.'

Her eyes flared wide for a moment and then she bowed her head again. God above. What secrets did she hide? What did she fear he knew?

'I know you are unwed and have suffered the loss of a loved one.' A tremor fluttered through her. 'I know you are ungainly at times, though I struggle to believe it.' He watched as she curled her unbound hand into a fist. 'You heal quickly, too, it seems.' His fingers flexed. 'You cannot swim yet you risk your life to save a bairn.' She stiffened beneath his hold. 'And I have just discovered that while you appear meek, you hide a temper behind your mildness.' The tautness under his fingers relaxed. Was she mastering her temper even now? 'You have been called pretty but once.' Her arms turned rigid. 'An offense to my mind,' he finished softly.

She strained to pull free.

Placing his hands on each side of her head, he tipped her face up and stared into beautiful blue eyes, quickly shuttered with the lowering of her thick red-gold lashes. His gaze drifted to the fullness of her pale pink mouth.

Why is it I long to taste your lips, feel them soften beneath mine?

'Why is it I seem to be wet more than dry since meeting you?' he asked instead.

Tears seeped from the outer corners of her closed lids. His gut clenched. He wanted to lick the tear-trail from her skin, erase them from sight. He gently wiped each trickle with the pad of his thumbs.

A knock sounded. Mary's worried voice rang through the wood. 'William? Are you all right, lad?'

Nae.

He stepped back, his hands sliding to her shoulders. The pounding on the door grew frantic and her eyes fluttered open. The longing, shining in the blue depths, mirrored his. He wanted to ignore Mary's pounding plea and satisfy his own.

Fighting the need to slake his hunger, he made certain she could stand without collapsing and forced his hands to release her. He strode to the door and wrenched it open. 'I'm fine, Mary.' He fought to keep the growl from his tone. 'The healer needs your assistance.'

'Oh the poor lass.' Mary pushed past him and into the room, clucking about how cold the brave soul must be.

William stepped to the grate and knelt to light the fire. Striking flint to tinder, thoughts of how to manage his hammering need crammed inside his head. Eight days remained of her stay at Closeburn. Plenty of time to find out everything he wished to know about her and perhaps ease the unwanted desire simmering in his blood.

The kindling sparked and greedy flames soon spread and licked high in the hearth. He warmed his hands over their heat for a moment, then stood and strode to the door.

A last look at the sodden, bedraggled form showed her standing stiff with her chin angled stubbornly.

Damn her beauty and her courage. Devil take her for making him fear for her life. Curse her healing skills and her tears. She was much too dangerous for his peace of mind and far too alluring to ignore.

Chapter 14

The door closed and Lynelle sagged with weary relief. Angels of mercy, she thought he'd never leave. Now he'd gone, she longed to call him back. Craved his touch, so gentle, feather-like, barely there. Yet her arms could still feel the heat of his hands. The tender flesh beneath her eyes sang in memory of his whisper-soft caress.

Mary stripped the wet clothes from her and wrapped her in a rough drying cloth, so harsh against her sensitized skin. With the older woman's gentle prodding, she approached the stool set before the hearth and perched upon it. Legs weak, every inch of her skin prickled with goose flesh, she didn't resist Mary's attentions. She didn't even have the strength to shudder from the cold.

The echo of her heartbeat pounding sluggishly in her ears failed to drown out the deep timbre of William's voice, or his words. His naming her a fool, again, had unleashed her anger, given her strength. His rumbling words of admiration had pierced the well of sadness hidden in the recesses of her soul. She'd fought, begged and struggled, but she'd been powerless to stop the trickle of tears seeping free – a silent watery tribute to how much his praise touched her.

Heat stretched out from the fire to coat her face and the front of her body with soothing warmth. She stared into the hungry flames, wondering at the strangeness of the day. Had she really run and leapt into the loch to rescue the little boy? It seemed too unimaginable to be real.

Had William then plunged in and pulled the child from the water, and then returned to save her? It seemed too impossible, but it was true.

Dear God, she owed him her life. A shiver skittered over her skin. How would she ever repay him? What payment would he expect?

In a daze, she lifted her arms while Mary slipped a nightgown over her head. With effort she stood and the older woman slid the drying cloth free, the well-worn fabric fluttering down her length, tickling the tops of her feet.

Guided back onto the stool and encouraged to turn her back to the flames, Lynelle sighed as Mary passed a comb through her hair, humming softly while she worked. Her heavy lids dipped closed. Strands crackled and wisped about her cheeks like caresses, reminding her of the stroke of William's fingers. A wondrous touch that burned yet held her in place, willing to suffer the heat, craving more.

On legs that seemed to belong to someone else, she made it to the bed and slipped beneath the covers. Caring hands tucked the bedding about her and a kiss of motherly kindness brushed her forehead.

Drifting off to sleep, her mind manifested a vision of lips, thinned by anger, fuller when at ease, and surrounded by the faint shadow of a beard. How she longed to feel those lips pressed to her mouth, her cheek, her...

***

A noise tugged at the fringes of her sleep. In her dream there were no voices, no sound. Only feeling. The disturbance came again, a quiet voice accompanied by a pat on her shoulder. The mouth, the warm breath in her slumbering illusion faded, cooled, vanished.

Reluctantly opening her eyes, she searched the shadows. A flare of light drew her upright in the bed and she stared into Mary's face, mottled and distorted by the candle flame she held beneath her generous chin.

'Ah. Finally awake, lass.' Setting the lit taper onto the table, Mary dipped the wick of another into its flame and placed it onto the mantle. 'Did you rest well?'

Colour stained Lynelle's cheeks. Her wicked thoughts still hovered at the edges of her wakefulness. Thank the saints the room swam in relative darkness. 'Yes, thank you. I am much restored.'

Mary added wood to the fire and approached the bed. 'Time to rise and eat, lass.'

Ducking her head to hide the hot blush consuming her face, she swung her legs free of the covers and murmured, 'I am a little hungry.' Finding her feet, she walked the small distance to the table and sat. Her mouth watered as she spied the steaming fish on the trencher.

'Well, 'tis to be expected. You barely nibbled your noon meal.' She hadn't the stomach to eat then. 'Too busy planning your grand escape, nae doubt.'

Jerking her gaze from the salmon to the older woman, she found Mary studying her from beside the hearth. A hint of a smile curved Mary's lips. 'You don't believe I erred, then?'

'Oh, I wouldn't say that.'

Laying her palms on the scarred tabletop, Lynelle braced herself for the scolding to come.

'I do wonder why you didn't ask William to visit Elspeth and why Keita hadn't spoken about her mother's ills sooner.'

Jumping at the chance to steer the conversation away from herself, Lynelle said, 'Perhaps Keita was aware of William's mistrust of healers and didn't wish to trouble him further.'

'Hmm! Perhaps.' Mary lifted Lynelle's cloak from the peg on the wall, shook it out and turned it about before draping it back on the hook. 'Now only your actions elude me.' The older woman's direct look caused Lynelle to inspect her trencher.

'Do you think he will confine me to this room?' she asked, pushing the greens about the platter with the tip of her spoon.

She loathed the idea of being secured away after her small bout of stolen freedom. It saddened her to know the privilege of exploring the healing chamber would be lost too. But it might be for the best. A little over a sennight remained of her allotted time and she believed she could endure William's nearness in short doses when she was summoned to care for Edan. Any further incidents that would lead to being held in his arms were too unsettling to think on.

'I cannot say what William will do.' Lifting a blanket from a pile of linens, the older woman ambled over and draped the soft folds about Lynelle's shoulders. 'I only know I am disappointed.'

Closing her eyes and bowing her head, Lynelle fought to overcome the dreadful hurt caused by Mary's last words.

'I miss little of the goings on at Closeburn.' She sounded disgruntled. 'And to be one of only two souls to have missed the day's excitement just ties my hose in knots.'

Lynelle gaped at Mary and noted the twinkle in the older woman's eye. 'Forgive me for neglecting to inform you first, Mary.' Smiling, she added, 'I will do my best to give you warning the next time I throw myself into the loch.'

Lips twitching, Mary said, 'See that you do, lass.' Pausing at the door, she turned. 'Eat now and then I will take you to Edan.' She opened the door. 'The lad is anxious to see another hero in the flesh and I am certain your ears will bleed from the incessant praise pouring from his mouth.' With the click of the latch she was gone.

Lynelle paid little attention to the older woman's final words. Her mind had fixed on visiting Edan, which entailed seeing William. She hardly needed to lay eyes on him to conjure his image. Not when she could still feel the imprint of his powerful frame against her softness.

Filling her spoon, she chewed the cold fare, barely tasting the food. She was torn by the impossible need to avoid William and desperately wanting to have her sinful dreams become reality.

***

'...and it was kind of Donald to tell me everything,' Edan continued. 'But I'd much rather have witnessed the excitement myself.'

Edan's constant chatter provided Lynelle with a much-needed distraction. William had been leaning against the wall by the window, his relaxed appearance belying the intensity of his regard. She'd bobbed her head in greeting before dragging her gaze away, but she could do little to stem the memories of his hands upon her. Or the feverish dreams inspired by his touch.

Absently nodding each time Edan paused to draw breath, she prepared the potion and fought the urge to look at William from beneath her lowered lashes. Her mind and body were so keenly aware of him, she knew the moment he moved. The air in the chamber seemed to thicken as he shifted to the opposite side of the bed.

Sipping the brew, she passed it across to his silent figure, struggling to hold the vessel steady. His fingers brushed hers as he took the cup, sending a frisson of sizzling heat up her arm. Her traitorous gaze snapped up and collided with his, then flared wide at the smouldering eyes fixed on her. He tilted the cup and drank.

'It's like someone licking a spoon dripping with honey and telling you how sweet it is.' Edan sighed.

William slowly lowered the cup.

'But it's not the same as tasting it yourself,' Edan finished.

No. Just as dreaming of kisses was a far cry from actually being kissed. Her breath locked in her throat. Fire burned in her cheeks and a shiver flashed through her as her gaze strayed to where she begged it not to.

The tip of William's tongue played over his moist upper lip, making her want things she knew nothing about. Wrenching her gaze away, she made the mistake of looking up into William's eyes. Knowing eyes.

Turning, she clumsily set out fresh bandages and ointment, trying to slow the pounding of her heart and ignore the tightening of her breasts.

She accepted the empty cup from Edan and placed it on the small wooden table before retrieving the pot of salve. 'I, for one, am pleased you were not present.' She dipped her fingertip in the ointment and swiped a smear on William's proffered wrist, masking her shiver by quickly scooping more onto her burning finger.

She looked into Edan's face, his expression showing confusion. Licking her dry lips, she hastened to explain. 'Plunging into cold water will do your leg little good.' Painting the pink, puckered flesh of his wound, she continued, 'It is healing well and I've no doubt that had you been anywhere near the loch when Davy tumbled in, you would have given no thought to your own wounded state and risked all to save the boy.'

His face brightened. 'Do you really think so?'

'Most definitely.'

He looked thoughtful. 'Aye. You're probably right.'

With a nod and a secret inner smile, she bandaged his leg, checked his other injuries, packed her herbs and prepared to leave.

'What does being a hero feel like?' Edan asked.

Her hands stilled. 'I do not know,' she said quietly. Securing the top of her sack, she looked at Edan. 'Heroes hardly need rescuing, do they?'

'I suppose not,' he said.

'You should ask your brother. Today he played the hero more than once.' Snatching up her belongings, she headed to the door, Edan's frustrated voice following her.

'I already asked Will, but he denies being a hero, too.'

'Wait.'

The command halted her steps and she stared at the closed door, wishing she could melt into the thick timber. The air about her came to life as William neared. She inhaled sandalwood and him, felt his heat when he halted beside her.

'I will escort you to your chamber.'

'Please do not ... trouble yourself'. She hated the tremor in her voice. 'I can find my way.' There, much better.

'I'm certain you can.' He opened the door. 'But I will rest easier knowing you arrived *directly.*'

She'd kept the soft woollen blanket Mary had wrapped about her shoulders in place for modesty's sake. She discovered it proved a useless barrier against William's nearness as he followed her into the corridor.

'I trust you have recovered from your noon ... ordeal?' he said.

A delicious shiver rushed down her nape and rippled across her shoulders. 'Yes.' She swallowed. 'And you?'

'Aye.'

She didn't dare look behind to see how close he stood. But it felt as if not a whisper of air could pass between them. Why did he not open her door?

'Davy's parents send you their good wishes.' She blinked at the wooden panel in surprise. 'I too am grateful for all you have done this day.' His voice deepened to a quiet rumble. 'For Davy and for Edan.'

Stunned, she watched the door swing inward, revealing her cosy chamber. Resisting the ridiculous urge to sink back against him, she forced her feet to move forward into the room.

'Despite all that has happened,' he said, 'You are not excused for stealing away from my keep.'

She turned around, just as the door closed softly in her face.

Chapter 15

After a night filled with dreams of torture, imprisonment and masculine heat, Lynelle returned to her chamber after giving Edan his morning tonic. The fog of weariness cloaking her every movement, her every thought, had helped lessen her reaction to seeing William. Thankfully, he hadn't spoken a single word. No doubt he was too busy contemplating ways to punish her for escaping from his castle.

Now, slumped across the table in her room, her palms supporting her head, she stared into the last glowing embers in the grate, relieved by her confinement.

Well, it was better than being manacled to a slimy wall in the bowels of the keep, or tied to a post in the courtyard. Worse still, she could be tethered to William, forced to breathe the same air, smell his manly scent, view his dark visage and, in their bound state, accidentally brush her body against his.

Saints above. Her dreams tormented her, even when awake. Or had she fallen asleep where she sat?

A heavy fist rapped on the door. Jumping to her feet, she clutched her hands to her middle as the thick oak panel opened. She felt her stomach drop to her toes as William's steely gaze perused the chamber.

She'd seen him dressed in plaid and shirt and leather vest, but the thick, menacing sword now dangling at his hip had been absent since they'd arrived at Closeburn. He looked every inch the warrior.

'Don your cloak.'

Her eyes snapped up from the gleaming blade to his flint-coloured stare. Surely if he meant to sever her head he wouldn't care if she were cold or not.

On stiff legs, she crossed to the hook and reached for the garment. She would need it, if she were to be thrown into the castle's dungeon. Her fingers fumbled with the ties at her throat.

'Fetch your sack of healing herbs.'

Locking gazes with him, she wondered if he was giving her the means to tend her ills while wasting away in the damp confines of his keep.

God above. In her dazed and weary state, her imagination was rampant. She could ask his intentions, but her stubborn streak, the trait she so often kept buried, had her sinking her teeth into her tongue and holding her silence.

Retrieving her worn herb sack, resolve stiffened her shoulders. She would show no signs of fear.

'Come.'

Lynelle refused to cower, answering his summons with a toss of her braid and an up-thrust of her chin, before marching into the dim corridor.

Holding her sack tightly against her belly, she descended the stairs. Thank God she'd eaten every morsel on her tray this morning. It could be a long while before she received further sustenance.

The sound of voices grew louder as she neared the level to the great hall. Keeping her eyes averted, she avoided searching the faces of those she knew were appraising her. They were Scots, William's people, and she didn't want to witness their expressions of smugness.

She focused on the rough stone wall making up part of the entrance alcove, as a sudden hush greeted their descent into the hall. Drawing a huge breath, she compelled her feet to make the turn to the left toward the dungeons, as the air in her lungs shuddered out.

A large warm hand grasped her shoulder, halting her as her foot hovered in the empty space above the first step down. Strong fingers urged her away from the shadowed stairwell, coaxing her around until her eyes rested on the centre of William's wide chest.

It seemed she wasn't to escape the clan's sneering gazes. He must want the meting out of her punishment to be made public, her humiliation complete.

She lifted her chin, focusing on the muscled cords in his neck. He didn't know she'd endured scorn her entire life. Though the people might be different, condemnation was always the same.

'Where do you think you're going?' William asked quietly.

His hand left her shoulder and she drew a slow breath. So he wanted her to admit her fate to all.

'To the dungeon,' she said loud and clear.

'Ah. You do think me an ogre.' He spoke softly and his devil lips that had haunted her sleep for the past two nights thinned.

Lynelle held her tongue.

'Well, before I consign you to whatever brutal punishment you believe I have in store, there is someone who wishes to meet you.'

He stepped to the side, revealing a horde of people crowded in a half circle. She skimmed their silent faces and found two she recognized, Mary and Malcolm. The older couple smiled at her, as did the rest of the throng. Where were the narrowed eyes and condemning expressions she expected?

A man and woman stepped free from the others and stopped a slight distance from where she remained, frozen. With a small movement of her hand, the woman drew Lynelle's attention to a little boy of two, perhaps three years of age, who tottered toward her on tiny leather-clad feet.

Beneath her furrowed brow, she watched his approach, desperately trying to make sense of what was happening. The boy stopped before her and looked up, his brown lashes surrounded deeper brown eyes that matched the mop of dark hair on his head. Drawing his hand from behind his back, he thrust something toward her.

Lynelle peeled her gaze from his earnest young face and looked at his offering. Tears suddenly welled, blurring the untidy cluster of wilting flowers he strangled in his fist. He tilted his head to one side and said, 'I, Davy.'

Awareness took hold. This was the little boy who'd fallen into the loch. Furiously blinking the moisture from her eyes, she drank in Davy's features in wonder. He seemed to be studying her just as closely, when suddenly his fine brows lowered over his dark eyes. She eased back a fraction and glimpsed the flowers still clutched in his tiny hand.

Adjusting her hold on the herb sack, she reached forward and accepted the offering from his stubby fingers. 'Thank you, Davy,' she said softly and was doubly rewarded by the return of his impish smile.

Davy's parents edged closer. 'Bless you for saving our boy,' Davy's father said quietly.

Lynelle swallowed, trying to find words to explain their praise was misplaced.

Strong fingers gently curled about her upper arms, coating each limb with prickling heat. Only one person's touch had such an effect on her. William stood almost flush against her back, far too close.

'I believe the healer appreciates Davy's gift and your blessings.' Warm breath tickled her ear and washed over her cheek. Lynelle could only nod in agreement.

'Come.' His hold steered her to the keep's entrance, where he plucked the flowers from her hand. 'Mary, kindly see to these.'

Lynelle let him lead her outside into the courtyard, relieved by the touch of his guiding hand. Her encounter with Davy had drained the strength she'd mustered to face her punishment and she couldn't seem to form a rational thought.

'It seems my clansmen have grown lax.' A huge sigh escaped William as he paused and searched the inner courtyard. 'Can you see any sign of the gallows I ordered to be erected?'

'What?' Her gaze flew to his. Barely noticing the sun's warmth on her face, she scoured the bailey for a hitching post.

'Never fear,' he said, taking her elbow and ushering her forward. 'I'll have the curs whipped later for their tardiness.'

As they passed through the curtain wall's massive gates, Lynelle struggled to keep up with his purposeful stride.

'All is not lost. There are many fine oak trees near the village. Finding a sturdy limb should prove an easy task.' He stopped, glanced at her from head to toe, before tugging her along once more. 'A twig would hardly bend beneath your scant weight.'

She tore her arm from his grasp and stumbled to a halt. 'You mean to hang me?' She stared wide-eyed, as he turned to face her. It was one thing for her to entertain thoughts of her punishment. It was quite another to hear William speak of them aloud. Her knees threatened to buckle and she had to fight to remain upright.

'I know,' he said, his voice resigned, though his expression appeared disappointed. 'There's little enjoyment to be had from a simple hanging.' He slowly shook his head. 'It's over far too quickly.'

She gaped at him, the blood draining from her head to pool in the soles of her feet.

'Have you any suggestions?' he asked.

Her jaw dropped impossibly wider.

'Aye, how could I forget?' His features hardened to match his tone. 'You believed I intended to toss you into Closeburn's dungeon, most likely to wither and die.'

Lynelle tried to swallow, but her mouth had gone dry. She clutched her sack so tightly her fingers ached. William stepped toward her, so close she had to tilt her head back to view his angry face. She wanted to look away, but the fury swirling in his turbulent gaze held hers.

'I prefer not to be deemed a monster until my actions prove me such.' Each word he forced out strained through his gritted teeth.

The truth of what he said set her cheeks aflame.

Shame for having judged another, as she'd been judged all her life, swamped her. Her heart constricted and heat prickled behind her eyes. Desperately needing to offer the solace she'd never been granted, she reached up and skimmed his cheek with the tips of her fingers. 'Forgive me,' she whispered.

He jerked away. His sooty brows lifted, showing his surprise, but he was no more surprised than she. Her hand fell stiffly to her side, fingers curling inward, the feel of his roughened jaw safely trapped within her palm.

Splinters of silver flashed in his slate coloured eyes, enchanting her. Something unknown passed between them. Something...

The sound of someone clearing their throat broke the spell. 'Are you ready, laird?' An older man stood at a slight distance, his eyes downcast.

'Aye, Geordie. 'Tis past time we left.' His voice sounded rough, gravelly. 'Come.' Turning, he gestured to the pier, where Geordie held the rowboat steady.

Ignoring his command, Lynelle stood firm and lifted her chin. 'Lest my imagination take flight again, I'd prefer to know your plans for me.'

He slowly faced her, setting his fists on his lean hips. After giving her a meaningful look, he nodded and said, 'You have unfinished business in the village. I am here to see you complete what you began.'

Her brow knotted, and her puzzlement must have shown.

'Elspeth is expecting you.'

'She is?'

'Aye, if we hurry, perhaps we will make her cottage by nightfall.'

He was punishing her by giving her permission to continue tending Elspeth. She stared at him and realised he hid a softer side beneath his fierce visage – and perhaps a sense of mirth. Hope welled in her chest.

'We'd best make haste then.'

Consumed by a weightless sensation, she seemed to float to the dock, and with William's aid she climbed into the small boat. Unfurling her fisted hand, she peered at her fingertips. They looked unchanged, but they still tingled.

A gentle nudge signalled they'd reached the loch's outer pier and she quickly tucked her fingers back into the centre of her hand. Silly, but she was certain she'd captured something special and she didn't want to lose it.

Aided by the boatman, she clambered to shore. Half way to the village she suddenly stopped. 'Wait. Where is Ian?'

William halted and faced her. 'Ian is none of your concern.' He turned and resumed walking. Lynelle trotted after him.

'Please do not punish Ian. I alone am to blame for leaving the keep.'

Skidding to a stop, she shrank away from William's wintry grey gaze.

'I am laird here and will deal with those who compromise my clan's safety as I see fit.'

He set a brisk pace and as she struggled to keep up, guilt churned in her belly. If Ian suffered punishment because of her, she'd never forgive herself. The blade of William's sword glinted with each long stride he took, escalating her heartbeat and her fears for the young boatman. Where had his softer side gone?

Likely buried back in the pit of his soul.

Lynelle desperately tried to erase the grim images swirling through her mind. William's hand clutched her shoulder, startling her to a halt. She stared at the plume of smoke rising from the cottage she'd visited the day before.

A calloused hand cupped her chin and tilted her face up, sending sparks of warmth down her neck and along her jaw. Flint-coloured eyes studied her and then darkened to resemble storm clouds. 'Ah, I see your imagination has flown again.'

'Lynelle. Lynelle,' a little voice squealed in excitement.

Shaking free of his hold, she spun around at the sound of her name. Carney charged toward her with all the speed a three-year-old boy's legs could muster. She braced herself a moment before he barrelled into her thighs.

'You come back. You come back,' he said clutching her legs and gifting her with an enormous smile.

Her chest constricted and warmth fused her cheeks at the little boy's unfettered delight. 'Yes, Carney. I've come to see your mother.'

His bright eyes found William, and Lynelle was quickly forgotten.

'You come back, too.'

Carney knew William? Lynelle stared at William, wondering when he'd visited the village.

Surprising her further, William snatched Carney up from the ground and perched him on one of his broad shoulders, drawing a giggle from Carney.

First the softening and now this gentle play. If she hadn't witnessed both acts herself, she'd never have believed him capable of either. It took her a moment to gather her wits and start after them.

Keita dashed out to meet her, as William disappeared around to the rear of the cottage with Carney, whose childish laughter filled the air.

'I thought you worked at the keep till noon,' Lynelle said.

'The laird has given me leave of my chores until mother's legs are better.' Keita's smile showed her relief.

Lynelle added kindness to William's growing list of hidden traits.

'How is your mother?'

'Oh, much better, thanks to you.' Keita grasped her hand and pulled her to the door. 'Come in and see for yourself.'

Keita had been busy. The disarray she'd seen the day before had vanished. A large iron-pot bubbled quietly over the fire and the smell of vegetable broth scented the dim interior.

Elspeth lay propped up on one of the heather-ticked mattresses positioned against the side wall; the other lay bare, save for the woollen blanket neatly folded at its foot. Kneeling beside her, Lynelle could see the purple shadows beneath the older woman's eyes had faded. They exchanged greetings and smiles.

As she peeled away the bandages from Elspeth's legs, joy flowed through her. The angry redness surrounding each sore had eased and the yellow pus weeping from the ulcers had lessened. Using the same methods as the day before, she quickly tended to Elspeth's wounds.

'Keep resting Elspeth, and you'll be on your feet and dancing before you know it.'

Elspeth's soft laughter made her smile as Keita walked her to the door.

Stepping outside, Lynelle leaned close. 'Keita, I believe your mother is going to be fine, but I'm worried for Ian.'

'Why?' Keita said, with a puzzled expression.

Grasping the young woman's sleeve, she said, 'It wasn't Ian who rowed us across the loch today, but another man. I fear the laird may be punishing Ian for aiding me.'

To Lynelle's surprise, Keita smiled and blushed. 'The laird has been very kind and I hope Ian doesn't feel he is being punished.'

The sound of rumbling voices grew louder as William, Ian and Carney strolled into view. The two men appeared to be deep in conversation, while Carney seemed intrigued by the flashing sword hanging from William's hip.

'Ian arrived at first light this morn,' Keita whispered. 'He has already repaired the chicken enclosure, and chopped wood for cooking and heating.'

The young maid's excitement was evident in her tone, and Ian didn't look as if he'd been beaten or whipped, as Lynelle had imagined.

Her gaze crept to William and her heart tripped within her chest. She didn't know what to think of the insufferably handsome man. Why did he act the tyrant with her, yet allowed her to see snippets of his caring side while dealing with others?

She murmured her farewells and she and William soon retraced their steps to Castle Loch. Lynelle failed to notice the luscious scenery or feel a sense of peace, as she had on yesterday's journey.

On waking this morn, she'd been prepared to face any form of punishment metered out for escaping the castle. Instead, she'd received flowers and had been asked to tend Elspeth. Moreover, Keita's duties had been suspended until her mother recovered and Ian's had altered so he could assist Keita's family.

Saint Jude, save me. She'd never been so addled in her life.

Without turning her head, she stole a peek at the man beside her. There was an air of confidence and purpose about his lean, muscular frame. Head held high, an aura of pride and satisfaction surrounded him as he surveyed his lands.

Simply watching William walk sent tiny tendrils of excitement skittering through her. How fierce would the heat become if she were the object of his undivided attention? Casting her eyes forward, she locked out such thoughts.

Despite her desperate struggle to avoid William at all costs, her gaze constantly slid back to devour his dark, tempting countenance. Her traitorous mind began conjuring ways to spend more time with him.

Dear Lord. If she thought she'd slept poorly last night, she knew there'd be no respite from her tormenting dreams tonight.

Chapter 16

The moment Lynelle returned to the castle, Mary swept her down through the stone passageway to the healing room. A shadow of disappointment seeped into her chest at being separated from William so soon after she'd decided to stop avoiding him. Having witnessed his softer side, she wanted to glean any other attributes he kept hidden beneath his harsh, brooding exterior.

Together, she and Mary began sorting through the room's abandoned wealth. They dusted and removed wooden stoppers from each small jar and clay pot and sniffed the mysterious contents. A chorus of sneezing erupted as their labours stirred to life seasons of neglect and potent aromas from long-stored plants.

Lynelle discovered several rolled leather satchels and set them aside for closer inspection later. It felt good having something to occupy her hands, but the physical exertions, Mary's chatter and the wonders she found couldn't stop her from thinking about William and wishing the day would end so she could lay eyes on him again.

Opening a large earthen pot, she lifted it to her nose and quickly drew back from the bitter, aromatic scent of tansy leaves. She set the jar to one side, planning to mix the leaves with freshly scattered rushes to dispel fleas and lice.

A sharp knock rattled the doorframe and a heavily bearded bear of a man filled the doorway. The thunderous scowl creasing his forehead sent a shudder of fear down the length of her spine.

'Ah, Dougal,' Mary said, reminding Lynelle she wasn't alone. 'Is your tooth causing you grief again?'

'Aye, Mary.' His soft reply, murmured from one side of his mouth, was at odds with his savage appearance. Lynelle's brows shot straight up. 'I can't sleep and it pains me to eat. I'll soon be wasting away to naught if something isn't done.'

'Come, Dougal,' Mary said, waving him into the chamber. 'Come and sit.' Mary helped him ease his bulk onto the stool she'd vacated. 'Can you aid the lad, Lynelle? The poor mite's been suffering with the aching tooth since last winter's onset.'

'Yes, yes ... of course,' Lynelle said, trying to overcome her surprise at Mary's fragile description of the hulking Scotsman who sat slumped forward with his elbows on his thighs and his head in his hands.

Racking her memory, she searched her mind for herbs to remedy his ailment. 'I will prepare him a brew to lessen the pain, but I will need wine to make a mixture to cleanse his mouth.'

'You're an angel, lass,' Mary said. 'I'll fetch the wine, while you prepare the brew.' Mary walked to the door and turned. 'Dougal, this is Lynelle. The lass has agreed to help you, so mind your manners while I'm gone.'

'Aye, Mary,' Dougal said, barely lifting his head.

Lynelle quickly blended a tonic to ease any swelling inside Dougal's mouth, knowing the feverfew would also calm the giant. 'Drink every drop. It will help with your pain.'

His large, meaty hand swamped the vessel she offered and he downed the lot without hesitation. 'I thank you.'

She nodded, returning to the newly cleaned workbench to begin grinding the wood betony leaves, tossing in a pinch of salt and a sprinkling of dried mint. Knowing her preparations would give Dougal relief was heartwarming.

'The next tonic is not to be swallowed, but to be held and swirled around inside your mouth and then spat out.'

Dougal grunted in understanding.

'Once done, I will need to look to see how diseased the offending tooth has become.' His next grunt sounded higher pitched than the first.

Turning to face him, she found his brown, pain-glazed eyes watching her.

'I can see how badly the tooth troubles you,' she said softly. 'But if left untreated, it will fester and may spread to other, healthy teeth.'

He gave her a brisk nod.

'Here's the wine, lass,' Mary said, re-entering the room.

Pouring a good measure into the cup containing the crushed herbs, Lynelle stirred it through. Locating a deep, wooden bowl and a clean strip of linen, she draped the cloth across Dougal's knees and handed him the cup and bowl. 'Remember, take a goodly swig, swirl it round for a moment or two and spit it into the bowl. Be sure to do it several times, until the tonic in the cup is finished.' He eyed each wooden vessel and then did as she bid.

She retrieved one of the burning candles mounted in an iron holder and placed it on the bench near Dougal. Taking the empty cup and bowl of used mouth cleanser from his bear-like hands, she set them atop the work table as he wiped his mouth on the linen cloth. Even through the dark grizzly hair sprouting from his cheeks and jaw, she could see the swelling on the left side of his face.

'I need to take a look now, Dougal.'

Heaving what sounded like a resigned sigh, he swallowed and opened his mouth.

Lynelle grasped the candle, stepped closer and with gentle fingers she tilted his head to allow her a better view. A rank odour rushed out to greet her as Dougal expelled a breath. Not even the mint or pungent scent of the feverfew could mask the smell of diseased flesh. Blinking the tears from her stinging eyes, she moved the candle higher until she found what she was looking for.

The problem tooth was positioned half way along the left side of his lower jaw. A gaping hole in the tooth's centre stared back at her and the gum cradling the rotten tooth flamed a fiery red.

She straightened, put down the lit candle and moved to where she'd set aside the leather satchels she'd found earlier.

'Did you find the troublesome tooth?' Mary asked.

'Yes,' she said absently, unrolling the soft, worn leather. 'And I believe I can fix it.' Staring at the strange metal implements tucked safely in the satchel's folds, she bypassed the long, thin knife and blanched at the thick, jagged-edged blade in the next pocket.

'How?' Dougal's mumbled question snapped her attention to the third metal instrument. Drawing it from its niche, she studied the two grasping jaws that opened and closed as she worked the two short handles, the feel of the cold steel seeping into her fingers. She replaced the tool and looked over at Dougal.

'Firstly, I will make more of the cleansing wash. You must rinse your mouth again thoroughly this eve and then again in the morn. It would be best to ease the swelling before we proceed further.'

'And then?'

'Then I suggest you consume a generous amount of ale.'

'What?' Dougal groaned and cupped his jaw with his massive hand. Mary patted his huge shoulder, but Lynelle could see the same question painted on her kind face.

Shifting closer, she peered into Dougal's distressed eyes. 'The tooth has to be removed, Dougal, or your pain will only worsen.'

She heard him swallow. 'Why not just do it now, eh?'

'As I said, 'tis best to allow time to reduce the swelling and ... I also need to garner someone's help.'

Dougal heaved a resigned sigh and said, 'The morrow it is, then.'

'Give me a moment to prepare your mouth tonic.'

She quickly blended the crushed herb, mint and salt in with the remaining wine. She gave Dougal the jug, repeating her instructions, all the while avoiding Mary's inquisitive eyes and willing the giddiness in her belly to disappear. She knew its cause, but had no wish to discuss it with the steward's wife.

It was one thing to spend time with William to find out more about him, but having to ask for his help meant giving him an opening to ask something about her. Was she willing to reveal her well-kept secrets to aid Dougal? She had the skills to rid him of his pain and couldn't allow him to continue suffering.

The last time she'd asked William for help it had been a ruse. This time, she truly did need his aid. She needed his strength. In the process, if it assisted in restoring his faith in the healing arts, so much the better.

Selfishly, and to her own consternation, she was pleased that having him assist her also gave her the chance to spend more time in his company.

Perhaps her plunge into Castle Loch the previous day had affected her ability to hold sensible thoughts. Or maybe, she'd just experienced her first.

***

Invisible sprites danced a jig in Lynelle's stomach as she returned to her chamber and wrestled with the enormity of asking William for help. Would he refuse? Perhaps concentrating on mundane tasks would distract her and calm her.

Pouring water from the ewer into the basin, she quickly splashed the dust from her face and was securing the ends of her re-braided hair when Mary delivered her trencher.

The meal of stuffed pheasant, turnip and greens looked delicious, but worry for how William would react curbed her hunger. She picked at her food and then checked her herbs, adding some of the boiled and dried bandages to her sack.

She stared at the door and pressed a splayed hand to her middle in an effort to settle the mingled anticipation and trepidation welling inside her. The waiting seemed worse than the imagined outcome.

Thankfully, Mary soon came and ushered her into Edan's chamber. On entering, she looked to the wall near the window and then glanced at the hearth, the places William usually occupied when she arrived. The places she'd always avoided looking before.

Her breath stalled in her throat. Both places stood empty. The trapped air in her lungs rushed out as she focused on the muscular, plaid-draped figure bent over the bed.

Dark eyes turned from his task of unravelling the bandages from Edan's chest and latched onto her. Her breath hitched again and her heartbeat thundered at a rapid pace.

'Thank you, Mary.' His gaze never strayed from her. 'We will manage from here.'

The soft click announced Mary's departure and distracted Lynelle enough to stop her ridiculous gawking. She moved to the unoccupied side of the bed.

'Good eve ... gentlemen,' she said, not certain how the laird's name would sound coming from her lips.

'Hello, Lynelle,' Edan responded cheerfully.

'Good eve,' William said.

She wondered if he too found it awkward to speak her name aloud.

'How are you feeling, Edan?' She unpacked all she needed from her sack.

'Mostly fine,' he replied. 'But my leg itches something fierce.'

'A sign your wound is healing well,' she assured him with a smile.

'It is?'

'For certain,' she said, grinding the herbs for his potion, while furtively watching William's long, capable fingers unwind the dressing from his brother's thigh. 'It proves your skin is stretching as the wound grows smaller.'

'Praise Saint Patrick,' he spouted on a sigh.

Lynelle's lips twitched at his exaggerated relief and she flicked a glance at William. Her tiny smile froze when she found him staring at her mouth. Her smile slipped. His gaze lifted to hers. For several missed breaths she peered back. But when a fine sheen of sweat erupted over every inch of her skin and her lungs screamed for air, she ducked her head and finished making the tonic.

Dear God above. The man was a danger to her health.

And a trigger to her senses.

She sipped the brew and offered it to William, forcing herself to look at him. If she expected his help with Dougal and wanted to know him better, she needed to be able to make eye contact without turning away every time their eyes met.

He watched her as he drank.

Breathe. Hold still. Breathe. Hold still.

William looked down at Edan and passed him the cup. The shift of his focus eased some of the tension throughout Lynelle's body, but her stomach remained taut as she bathed Edan's exposed thigh wound, pleased to see it was indeed healing. Retrieving the pot of salve, she painted the back of her hand with the ointment and drew a deep breath before turning to William.

As she coated his inner wrist with the decoction, she returned his stare and prayed he didn't notice, couldn't feel her trembling.

'Enough. See to Edan.' William almost growled.

Lynelle smeared Edan's injury, using the last of Iona's salve. 'I will cover your wound tonight, but as of tomorrow you will no longer need the ointment applied and therefore it won't be necessary to bandage your leg.'

'You truly mean it?'

'Yes, and perhaps in a day or two, after I remove the stitches, I may allow you to stand – with assistance, of course.'

'Did you hear that, Will?' Excitement rang in his tone. 'I'll be up and about before you know it.'

'Aye, lad. Aside from you, nae one is more pleased than I.'

'Your arm and ribs will take longer to fully mend.' She loathed causing the small frown of disappointment creasing Edan's brow, but he had to understand it wasn't only his leg that needed to heal.

'How long then?' he asked, sounding frustrated.

'As long as it takes, lad.'

William's intervention surprised her, and pleased her. His gaze lifted from his brother and settled on her. She gave a small nod to indicate her gratitude. He returned the gesture, stunning her further. A spark of hope flickered to life. He just might help her.

Once again, they worked together, binding Edan's ills and hurts. But each time William's fingers accidentally brushed hers, she didn't withdraw and avert her gaze. Instead she paused, savouring the tingling heat, allowed it to almost run its course before casting her eyes upon him to discern if he noticed or if he too was affected.

Every fleeting lull prolonged the bandaging process and by the time they were done, she had to hide her laboured breathing and desperately wished to fall in the loch to cool her heated body.

William showed not a single outward sign that he was suffering anything remotely similar to her burning breathlessness. Not until he straightened and bestowed his full attention on her. His fierce regard, so intense, turned his eyes a shade barely shy of black.

Under the guise of packing up her herbs, she groped for something to support her, as her knees threatened to buckle. But even as she fumbled and struggled to remain on her feet, a whisper thread of excitement entwined around her heart.

She wasn't alone. William felt it too.

Snuffling, open-mouthed snores floated up from the bed, signalling that Edan had already slipped into slumber. She gathered the remnants of her physical strength and her rattled wits and headed for the chamber's exit, knowing well the laird would follow.

She turned and faced him. 'I have a request.'

He stopped an arm's length from where she stood – a short arm, by the warmth she could feel radiating from his lean form.

'I am listening.' His eyes smouldered deepest charcoal.

'One of your men, Dougal, has a putrid tooth that must be removed.'

'And?'

It had been easier to look at him with a bed holding his brother's sleeping form between them. She licked her suddenly dry lips. 'I have given him a herbal rinse to cleanse his mouth tonight and once more in the morn. I then instructed him to consume a good measure of ale afterward to cloud the pain when the tooth is taken.'

'I am sure wee Dougal did not argue against that particular command.'

'Well, no. He didn't.'

'Please go on.'

'Yes, well. I am confident as to which tooth is causing him such distress–'

'Nae doubt the lad will be eternally grateful.'

'If you will stop interrupting me, I can make my request and find my bed.' Ignoring the tightening around his mouth, she continued. 'I have the necessary tool to extract the tooth, but I lack the physical strength needed to pull it out.'

Staring down at her, his lips compressed and a muscle flexed along his shadowed jaw.

For a heartbeat, she wanted to stomp her foot. 'Well?'

'Have I permission to speak?'

'Of course. Will you help me or not?'

'You want *me* to pull Dougal's putrid tooth?' His dark brows thundered down in a scowl.

'He is your clansman.'

'God's teeth,' he said, tipping his head back.

'No. Dougal is the one with the problem tooth.' Her lips twitched.

His head snapped forward and his stony gaze bore into hers. The hint of humour caused by her last remark withered and died in her chest.

'He is in pain,' she said softly. 'He needs your help.'

'Fine,' he said, spearing his fingers through his hair. 'I'll do it, after we return from the village.'

'The village?'

'Aye. I've decided to escort you to Elspeth each day until she has recovered.'

'Oh. I ... thank you.'

'Don't thank me. That's your punishment for stealing out of my keep.'

Angels of mercy. Did he think she'd view having him conduct her to tend Elspeth each day a penalty?

'One more thing before you find your bed.'

She stiffened. 'I know the routine. You have agreed to my request and will now ask a *simple* question.' Although she'd expected it, she couldn't hide the trace of bitterness and underlying fear of what he might want most to know. She squared her shoulders and looked directly into his beautiful, slate-coloured eyes.

'Why do you smile so seldom?'

Lynelle couldn't have been more stunned if the world turned upside down and dropped her on her head. She searched William's face, sure he must be jesting. She delved deep into his troubled, serious gaze.

'Is it an offence to not smile in Scotland?' She wished she could bite off her tongue the moment the caustic remark fell from her dry lips.

'Nae. But you should find a reason to smile more often. It becomes you.'

He reached past her then and opened the door. She hesitated before spinning on her heel and marching from the chamber. Pushing her door wide, she sailed into her room, turned to close the door and came face to face with William.

'Till the morn, healer.'

'Good night, Sir.'

He stepped out into the corridor, pulling the panel with him as he withdrew. Lynelle was certain she heard a mumbled 'Sweet dreams' before the latch clicked into place.

Wandering to the table, she set down her sack.

Why do you smile so seldom?

She smiled often. Didn't she?

Lifting a hand to her mouth, she traced her lips with her fingers. Thin. Tight. She closed her eyes and William's image filled the dark void behind her lids. Her frown loosened, eased. The taut flesh beneath her fingertips relaxed. Her lips softened.

A gentle shiver rippled through her heart.

She'd never had reason to smile, but now...

Chapter 17

'Is something wrong, Will?'

Edan's question broke into William's harsh thoughts. He forced his feet to halt their incessant pacing and looked at his brother.

God's blood. Everything is wrong.

He'd barely caught a wink of sleep last night and every time he'd found the elusive state, he'd soon woken in a lather of sweat, rock hard and wanting.

'Nae, Edan. Naught is wrong.'

Spearing his fingers through his hair, he silently cursed the healer and her pouting lips. Full, soft lips that in his slumber smiled constantly for him.

'Aye, Will. Whatever you say.'

William walked to Edan and sat on the side of the bed. 'I didn't sleep well, lad.'

'You don't need to stay with me every moment of the day, Will. I'm not a bairn.'

Peering into his brother's grey eyes, William noticed the clouded frustration caused by his infirmity, along with a hint of sadness. 'I spend my time here because I want to,' he said. 'All know as well as I that you're far from being a babe.'

'At least have a pallet brought in then, instead of sleeping in a chair.'

'The chair suits me. I think idleness is to blame for my poor sleep. But as I told you, I have a few things needing done this day and Mary will be back soon to keep you company while I'm gone.'

A light tapping at the door signalled Mary's arrival. William stood. 'Enter.'

Mary sailed into the room, with Lynelle close at her heels. As she'd done the previous night, the healer glanced to the window and then the hearth. Was she searching for him? Turning, her gaze found him and she noticeably stiffened.

'Good morn, gentlemen,' she said, approaching the bed.

'Good morn, Lynelle.' Edan's face visibly brightened.

'How are you feeling, Edan?'

'Much better now, thank you.' The lad was definitely easily influenced by a pretty face.

Her mouth tilted up at the corners as she looked down at his brother and William caught a glimpse of white teeth between her soft lips. Those damn lips had tortured him the whole night through. His hands curled into fists.

She shifted, using the table to mix Edan's brew. The fragile smile still hovered about her mouth – a smile for his brother, never for him.

He turned away at the black thought and found Mary staring at him with an all-knowing look on her kind, annoying face.

The healer sipped and passed the potion across to him. He drank and waited a moment before allowing Edan to drain the vessel.

'I'll be back as soon as I can,' he said, gently squeezing Edan's shoulder. His brother nodded, but William didn't miss the disappointment in his eyes.

'I'll see you this evening, Edan,' the healer said and headed for the door.

William followed and Mary sidled over to him and whispered in his ear. 'You shouldn't frown so. You'll frighten the lassies and the children.'

He glared at her and closed the door firmly behind him.

'Is there anything you need to fetch to tend Elspeth?' he asked Lynelle as they stood alone in the dim corridor.

'I have everything here,' she said, indicating her sack.

'Good. Let's away then.'

They descended the stairs and upon reaching the great hall, William paused to assess the two men seated on a bench at the far side of the room.

'If there is something you wish to do, I will wait here for you.'

'Nae. All seems as it should be.' He caught her questioning look as he gestured for her to precede him out into the courtyard. 'I have given Donald the pleasure of watching over Dougal while he numbs his pain.' Still she appeared confused. 'Consumes a generous measure of ale.'

'Oh.' Her frown disappeared. 'Has he begun already?'

'He started at dawn.' Her large, blue eyes rounded before she peered skyward. 'Aye. Two full hours have passed and nae doubt half a cask of Closeburn's fine heather ale, too.' They strode through the massive timber gates standing ajar and trod the slight slope down to the pier.

'Lord above. He'll be insensible for days.'

'Not likely. With Dougal's size, it takes the man a full day and copious amounts of the heady brew to even dampen his wits.' William aided her into the boat Geordie held steady, and then found his seat once she'd settled on the plank opposite.

'It's just as well he's made an early start, then.'

'Aye.' He scanned his lands, anything to divert his attention from the woman throwing numerous fleeting glances his way.

Something in her manner had changed.

Her gaze continued to settle on him frequently, when prior to last night she'd done her best to avoid looking at him.

Last eve, when her fingers brushed his, she hadn't jerked away, hadn't gasped or lowered her lashes as they dressed Edan's injuries. But he'd witnessed her trembling and he'd recognized the awakening desire shimmering in the depths of her troubled sapphire eyes.

His groin stirred at the memory, and a rush of heat pulsed through his veins, just as it had last eve.

The boat docked and William shot to his feet. They climbed ashore, and with a nod to Geordie they headed for the village.

'Is it difficult being laird?'

The soft, breathless sound of her voice made him turn and he noticed her efforts to keep even with his brisk stride. He slowed his pace.

'It must be like having a mountain sitting on your chest. So much responsibility for so many.'

'I wasn't born to be laird,' he said. 'Nor raised.'

A look of astonishment appeared on her flushed face. 'If not you, then who?'

'My brother.' His heated blood ran cold, chilling him and banishing his swelling arousal.

'Edan?'

'Nae. Roger.'

'You have another brother?'

'Had.' His chest tightened as he uttered the single word. Thankfully, she held silent for several moments, giving him time to release the painful breath trapped in his throat.

'When did Roger pass?'

Pass? She made it sound like some peaceful, gentle thing.

'He *died* last autumn.' On a day drenched in sunshine. 'Their boat overturned in the loch.'

'Their?'

'His wife was with him. She was carrying their first child. It would have been born this spring.'

Her gasp echoed in his ears, reminding him of Roger's battle to breathe when he'd dragged him from the water.

'Three lost all at once.'

'Nae. Only two. Margaret was already gone when I pulled her from the loch. Roger survived for two days more.'

'Dear God. To hold such hope...'

'Not hope,' he cut in. 'Roger gave up the moment he learned the fate of his wife and unborn babe.' Fury spiked in his heart and he clenched his fists till his knuckles ached.

"Tis not your fault,' she said quietly.

'Nae. 'Tis Roger's.'

'You are vexed at him for dying?' She sounded incredulous.

'He didn't have to die. He gave up, sought death rather than to live without his wife.'

'He must have held a great love for her,' she said softly.

'Aye, but he had us. He could have lived for Edan's sake. For mine.'

Horrified by what he'd revealed, William stopped and turned in her path. His face close to hers, he said, 'You go too far. None of this is your concern.'

'You said I judged you an ogre without knowing you,' she said, staring up at him. 'A misdeed that shames me deeply. But now when I attempt to know you, to understand you, you tell me I go too far.'

He scowled. 'Perhaps it would be best if you see me as the monster you first believed me to be.'

'I didn't truly think you were a monster,' she cried.

'Of course not,' he scoffed. 'Yet you were prepared to march straight to the dungeon where you believed I was escorting you.'

'I was prepared to suffer whatever punishment you named, because I'd erred. Not because I thought you a monster.'

William stared down into blue eyes brimming with truth and dismay. Her defence of him added to the burden of trying to draw air into his constricted lungs. A malady she seemed to be suffering too, by the swift rise and fall of her cloaked chest.

'What if I confessed to being the fiend you so prettily defend?' His voice rang low, his heartbeat quickened as he awaited her reply.

Her tongue darted out to moisten lush pink lips as her gaze searched his face.

'I would still wish to know you and make my own judgment,' she finally said.

Little fool. His heart hammered. He fought the urge to crush her against him and plunder her mouth with his, to prove a beast did indeed lurk inside him. He allowed a hint of ravenous lust to show in his eyes. She swallowed, but stood her ground.

'I have seen monsters portrayed as men,' she said with quiet confidence. 'I do not think you are one of them.'

William clenched his jaw, rattled by the calm words and the decisive look in her unblinking eyes. God's blood. The troublesome wench had turned his attempt to unsettle her back upon him.

She is a healer and an English one, he reminded himself sternly. 'Come,' he ground out. 'Elspeth will wonder what keeps us.'

They covered what little distance remained to Elspeth's cottage, and he scooped Carney up and onto his shoulders as the lad dashed out to greet them. The unnerving woman entered the cottage while he carried his wriggling burden around the back in search of Ian.

William's tension soon eased as he watched his young clansman strain with the honest labour of working the patch of land marked for planting. The boatman turned farmer set aside his shovel at Carney's call and approached, wiping the sweat from his brow.

'Morn, laird,' he said with a smile.

'Ian.' William gave him a nod. 'Your new duties seem to please you.'

'It's harder than pulling oars, but aye, it suits me.'

William didn't doubt having Keita nearby fuelled Ian's grin.

'Is Lynelle tending Elspeth?'

William nodded, his mouth tightening at the sound of the woman's name on another man's lips.

'I'll fetch you a log to rest your legs while you wait, then.' Ian started for the pile of chopped wood neatly stacked under the lean-to.

'Don't bother, Ian. I'll not be here long.'

'Ah.'

'What?' William asked, lifting Carney from his shoulders and setting the fidgety lad on his feet.

'Well. Keita mentioned some of the womenfolk from the village have come to call. She says they heard about Lynelle tending her mother and are keen for her to ... well, to see to their ills, too.'

William stared hard at Ian for another long moment before his gaze shifted to the thatched cottage close by. A feeling of betrayal swelled inside him. But hot on its heels came the knowledge that his clansmen needed aid, the kind of aid he couldn't provide. Some of them, like Elspeth and Dougal, were suffering, had been left unattended for too long.

Because of him.

His gut churned. Closing his eyes he inhaled deeply. When he opened them, he looked into Ian's worried face and said, 'Come. We'll finish turning the soil together.' He ignored Ian's surprised expression and headed for the uneven turf.

Perhaps a bout of physical labour would settle his stomach. If only it was so easy to dismiss the guilt pricking his soul.

***

William noticed the flush in the healer's cheeks as they left the village and followed the familiar path back to Closeburn Castle. He perused the clear sky, noting the sun wasn't far off reaching its peak, and savoured the slight tightening in the muscles of his arms. It seemed an age since he'd exerted himself physically, an eternity since he'd practiced with his sword.

He peered down at the smooth hilt his fingers played over. An excuse to avoid staring at the wisps of red-gold hair defying the healer's tight-woven braid and curling about her face and ears. Curls he longed to wind about his itching fingers. Ears he'd readily trace with his tongue.

God's eyes. He'd arrange a bout of swordplay with Donald the moment he set foot inside the keep. Right after he rid Dougal of his blasted diseased tooth.

The iron yett yawned open, granting them entrance and his steward met them with a haunted look on his face. 'Ah, Will. 'Tis glad I am you've finally returned.'

'What ails you, Malcolm?' Then William heard it. A pitiful wailing echoed from inside the great hall. Malcolm's neck seemed to disappear as his shoulders lifted in attempt to cover his ears.

'He's been at it for the past hour,' the older man said. 'The servants refuse to set out the tables and the kitchen maids say they cannot dress the trestles if they're still upended against the walls.'

'Who is it? They must be in dreadful pain.'

William glanced down at the woman straining her neck to peer around him. 'It's wee Dougal,' he said, cringing, as another string of wailing rang from the chamber within. 'He's murdering an old Scots ballad.'

'Oh.'

'I suggest we end his misery and thereby end our own.'

'Oh, of course,' she said. 'But I need to fetch the pincers from the healing room.'

Turning back to Malcolm, William said, 'Kindly escort the healer below. I'll see to Dougal.'

Donald stood from the bench seat he shared with Dougal, a pained expression on his face. 'Saints be praised you're here.'

'Perhaps you should have shared a cup or three with the wee lad,' William said.

'Aye,' Donald said, rubbing the back of his neck. "Tis a shame the idea didn't tweak earlier.'

'Hooo,' Dougal breathed, peering up at William through a slack-jawed smile. 'Hellooo, laird. Have a pint wi' me, heeey?'

'Christ.' William turned his head. The fumes wafting up from the man burned his eyes and were enough to send a full-grown ox to the floor. 'Thanks, Dougal, but I'll pass for now.'

'Suit yourssself...' Squint-eyed, he peered past William. 'Hellooo, Lynelle, have a pint wi' me.'

William turned to see her smile at the beaming, drunken souse, before looking at him. 'Malcolm has gone to fetch a few stout men to hold Dougal steady.' She set a flaming candle down on the trestle at the far end and turned to Dougal.

'I need you to lie on the table, so we can remove your troublesome tooth.'

Dougal didn't move, didn't even blink.

Malcolm shuffled in with two men from the kitchen. Amid a chorus of grunts and groans, Malcolm, the two burly men and William heaved Dougal's bulk onto the table. The hopeless drunk's smile never wavered.

'Thank you all,' the healer said. 'If you can grasp a limb each to ensure Dougal doesn't move, we can have this unsavoury business done with.'

William accepted the odd-looking instrument she offered, his hand tightening around the cold metal. God above. He prayed she knew what she was doing.

'Dougal, you need to open your mouth and remain completely still,' she said gently to the grinning drunkard staring up at her.

She waved William closer and held the lit taper above Dougal's gaping jaw. 'I will point out the tooth you need to pull,' she said softly. Her sweet breath fanned his face. 'Do you see it?' He forced his gaze from the smooth turn of her cheek and peered into Dougal's mouth. 'On the left, the one with the hole in the centre.'

'Aye. I see it.'

'Good. Please be sure you have a firm hold with the pincers before you pull.'

He slowly lifted his gaze until it rested on her face once more. 'I'll do my best.' He heard her swallow, but she kept her eyes downcast.

William looked down again to his task and a smattering of unease trickled through him. Firming his grip on the tool, he found a comfortable hold with his fingers and forced the metal jaws open.

'Be still,' she urged Dougal, cupping his grizzly cheek with her free hand.

William shifted his stance, groping for a firm hold on the tooth.

'Tilt your head forward a mite,' she said to the prostrate man, allowing William better access.

The implement's jaws slid and then found purchase on either side of the decayed tooth. Holding his breath, William squeezed the pincer's handles tight and pulled with all his might. After an initial resistance, the tooth came free with only a slight grunt from Dougal. William stared at the ruined tooth clutched in the tool's steel jaws, long roots tinged grey with disease and red with blood.

'Pretty blue eyes,' Dougal mumbled. 'As big asss the ssky,' he slurred.

William's gaze slid to Dougal and found his bewitched clansman still staring up at the healer, as she tried to clean away the bloodied spittle. He fought the sudden urge to pull more of Dougal's teeth from his thick head, be they rotten or nae.

Coaxed by the healer and with help from the others, they turned Dougal onto his side, where the slack-jawed oaf promptly fell asleep.

'Thank you.'

The genteel voice and the hint of lavender drew his attention back to the woman at his side. Pools of blue, shimmering with gratitude in the glow of the candle she held aloft, stared up at him. A faint smile sparkled in her eyes, for him.

God above, he could sink into the soft depths without reason, without struggle.

A hefty blow to his back saved him from such inane thoughts. 'Saints be praised,' Donald said.

Thrusting the tooth-grasping tool into her hand, William turned to his two burly helpers. 'Leave Dougal to sleep it off. Set out the tables and have the serving wenches bring out the noon meal.'

'Aye, laird.' The menservants left for the kitchens.

'Malcolm,' he continued. 'Kindly escort the healer to her chamber and relieve Mary of Edan's company. I'll not be long.'

Malcolm nodded.

Facing Donald, he said, 'Care for a round of swordplay before we eat?'

'Aye,' Donald said with enthusiasm. 'The morn's idleness has stiffened my joints and I welcome the chance to best you with my blade.'

'You can but try.'

Without a backward glance, William strode for the keep's entrance, desperate to feel the wind on his face and the action of battle.

Dougal wasn't the only one suffering from a form of intoxication.

Chapter 18

'Get an eyeful, lass?'

Startled by the sound of Mary's voice, Lynelle almost toppled from where she stood high on the window-ledge in her room.

The clang of steel striking steel had drawn her to the window, and after shucking her boots she'd clambered atop the stool to view the commotion in the bailey. Still lacking height, she'd levered herself up onto the slim stone ledge, clutched the rough edges of the narrow opening with shaking fingers and peered out.

'Merely curious as to what caused all the noise,' she said calmly, despite the mortification burning her cheeks. What would Mary think, finding her in such an ungracious position?

Her efforts had been worth every graze scoring her hands, her foot and one side of her flushed face.

Praying conversation would distract the older woman and erase the image of William's naked, sun-slicked torso from her mind, she carefully climbed down and asked, 'How is Edan?'

'The lad's fine, though getting more fidgety by the hour.' Mary slid the tray she carried onto the table. 'And Dougal still snores the sleep of a drunkard.'

'Good. Though I worry his head might ache more fiercely than his tooth ever did.'

Mary chuckled. 'Don't concern yourself. It won't be the first time wee Dougal's suffered from a sodden head. Come and eat.'

Lynelle placed the stool beside the table and sat. Looking down, she tried to focus on the trencher piled high with smoked ham, cheese and thick chunks of brown bread, but the deep-throated grunts accompanying each ringing clash from outside teased her ears and freshened the vision she struggled to clear from her head.

'How was your visit with Elspeth?'

'Oh, it went well,' she said, grateful for the diversion. 'Her leg ulcers are healing quickly.'

'You've done a fine job with both Edan and Keita's mother, lass.'

Lynelle glanced up at Mary, renewed warmth filling her cheeks at such praise. 'Two village women also asked for my assistance.'

'Truly?'

'Yes,' she said, nodding with pleased excitement. 'One is round with child and the other suffers a persistent cough.'

"Tis not surprising they sought you out,' Mary said, heading to the door. 'As you know, it's been some time since we had a healer at Closeburn.' She turned at the entrance. 'Nae doubt they heard good tales about your tending of Edan and Elspeth. I'd wager others will come to you while you're here.'

While she was here. Lynelle needed to remember her time at Closeburn wasn't permanent.

'The laird told me of Roger's death.' She spoke to ease the disappointment that suddenly flared to life with her last thought.

'Ah.' Two grey brows lifted high on Mary's forehead. 'Now that does surprise me.'

Dismayed by her loose tongue and Mary's obvious interest, Lynelle busied her hands laying cheese and ham upon the loaf, determined not to ask why or say more on the subject. 'I need to make more salve for Elspeth and brew a tonic for coughs.'

'I'll come for you once you've eaten.'

'Thank you.' Satisfied she'd diverted Mary's curiosity away from William and herself, Lynelle caught a glimpse of the older woman's wide smile before the door closed, and she heaved a sigh. Perhaps not.

She cocked her head to one side and listened.

Nothing.

Only the sound of her breathing filled the quiet. At least she *was* breathing. When she'd first seen William's sweat-dampened body, her breath had gotten lost somewhere deep in her belly. Each of his graceful movements had sent muscles rippling and bulging beneath his smooth, tanned skin.

She took a generous bite of her layered victuals, chewed slowly and gazed up at the high window.

Why couldn't her chamber be located directly below, on the ground floor?

***

A familiar pattern shaped the following days, causing them to pass swiftly. Aware of her daily visits, the villagers formed a line outside Elspeth's cottage every morning where Lynelle met and appraised each of their ailments. Keita suggested she make use of the empty cottage at the far end of the village, which left Elspeth to recover without swarms of people invading her home.

Each afternoon, the castle's inhabitants sought her out to cure their ills while she prepared tinctures and ointments in the healing room. Her evenings were spent tending Edan and sharing his growing excitement as he improved.

The nights, however, seemed to lengthen and drift by far too slowly. Despite the sinful dreams she suffered, dreams invaded by William's powerful form, nothing came close to matching the dizzying heat that swamped her each morning as she endured her so-called punishment.

Forced to trek to the village with William, she couldn't help perusing the lean length of him, filing away images and snippets of information and bringing them to life as she slept. She also looked forward to their discussions as they walked, but made sure they spoke of safe topics, such as the needs of the clansmen she tended, giving him no opportunity to question her about the life she'd lived before coming to Closeburn.

Had she really lived somewhere else?

Her fading memories of Fenwick dimmed further with every passing day. As her confidence in her healing abilities swelled, awareness of a different kind clouded her thoughts.

The end of her allotted time at Closeburn was quickly approaching. She should be relieved. But a bleak sadness filled her chest and an unwavering ache settled in her heart.

She did her best to conceal her inner turmoil. The last thing she needed was for William to become privy to her thoughts. Would he care? Or would he find a way to use her weakness against her?

On the eve of her departure, she entered Edan's chamber. Before she'd set her herb sack down, her gaze locked with William's and a jolt of longing speared her heart. How would she survive each day without seeing his handsome face?

Was it anger flashing in his dark eyes?

Dear God. She didn't want his anger, she wanted...

A crack of thunder shook the walls, heralding the arrival of nature's onslaught that had hovered and threatened all day.

'I ... I need to fetch feverfew from the healing room.' She swallowed and pressed her sack hard against her middle. 'I will be back soon.'

Turning, she left the chamber and hurried down the stairs, removing one of the flaming torches from the wall as she went.

Entering the healing room, she dropped her sack on the stool and slid the torch into the wall sconce. With her hands now free, she hugged herself tightly, fighting to regain some of her scattered senses.

Holy Mother Mary. She'd fulfilled her promise and should be pleased her time here was almost over. Then why in heaven's name did she feel as if she were being torn apart? Even the thought of returning to Fenwick and finally gauging her father's reaction, failed to lift her spirits.

Unsettled by her bewilderment, she set about preparing Edan's tincture.

The fine hair at Lynelle's nape lifted as the air within the small chamber changed. She knew without looking who had come. So powerful was his presence, it was as if he'd brought with him the spring storm that raged outside.

William Kirkpatrick, laird of Closeburn.

For almost two weeks she'd made use of this tiny room inside his castle, nurturing her healing skills amid vial-cluttered shelves and clumps of herbs dangling from the rafters. He'd never ventured here before. Why had he followed her now?

'Is it ready?'

His deep, rumbling voice rolled through her like a clap of thunder. She fought to steady her hand as she lowered a full vessel to the scarred workbench. Checking to make sure none of the liquid had spilt, she took a moment to calm the tide of jumbled emotions washing over her.

'Yes,' she said, hearing the tremor in her voice. He stood behind her, far too close.

'Come. Edan awaits.'

Inhaling slowly, she retrieved the goblet containing the potion and turned. She should be relieved knowing Edan wouldn't need her tonics or her aid after drinking this mixture. Good food, gentle exercise and time were all he'd need to fully recover.

But her satisfaction was swamped by a fluttering nervousness. William's broad shoulders seemed to fill the room. With potion in hand, she refrained from looking into his face. Instead her gaze touched his linen shirt, unlaced and exposing the bronzed skin and the smattering of dark curls at his throat. Her breathing quickened. She tightened her hold on the pewter goblet, fighting the sudden urge to test the hardness of his wide chest.

'You first, healer.'

Why did he never use her name? Irritation surfaced and her eyes snapped up, colliding with his stony gaze.

'Now?' How she wished he'd take a step back.

'Aye, now.'

Veiling her expression, she lifted the cup and drank. He still didn't trust her or her tonics. The initial bitterness of the healing herbs disappeared beneath the sweet taste of honey. She swallowed and licked a stray droplet from her bottom lip.

A large hand cupped her elbow, warm fingers circling her bare flesh. Fire shot down her arm. The goblet slipped through her nerveless fingers. Liquid splashed the hem of her gown, seeping into the rushes scattered upon the floor.

Horrified, Lynelle stared at the moisture glistening on his leather boots. Her breath caught in her throat.

Her eyes lifted, skimming over the plaid draping his lean hips, past the corded muscles in his neck to the dark whiskers defying this morning's efforts with his sharp blade. His jaw clenched and relaxed repeatedly. Her heartbeat thumped in time with the flexing movement.

'My touch repulses you?' His voice was hoarse, almost ... uncertain.

'No.' Her response slipped out before her mind fully registered the question. She searched his eyes, seeing nothing in the cool, grey depths to confirm what she'd thought she'd heard. Did he truly believe she found his touch repulsive?

'How does it make you feel?'

Warm. Wanting. Alive.

'Frightened.' Not of him, but of how he made her feel.

His eyes narrowed as he studied her closely. She tried to hide her emotions, but knew she'd failed when his features cleared and the hint of a smile tugged at his lips.

'It won't take long to make another potion for Edan,' she said, turning away from his enchanting mouth, desperately needing a chance to collect her wits.

'In a moment.' He grasped her arm again lightly, making her gasp. 'I still need to taste the spilled potion.'

Lynelle turned and frowned up at him, struggling to understand his words.

"Tis impossible. The rushes have absorbed the mixture.'

'Nothing is ever impossible,' he said, locking his other hand about her free arm and stepping closer.

Heat stretched across the minute space between them. A melting sensation spiralled through her. The smell of leather and man filled her giddy senses with excitement. And danger.

She swallowed, and remnants of her potion slid down her throat.

The potion William was determined to sample.

Saint Jude, save her. She wanted this.

'Don't do this,' she pleaded, afraid not for herself but her sanity.

'I must.' His head lowered.

''Tis madness,' she whispered.

'I know,' he said softly.

Her lips remained closed beneath his gentle assault. Strong hands caressed her arms and shoulders, his palms cupping her head as his expert fingers kneaded her neck, making her tremble. His tongue skimmed and pressed against her sealed lips and she shivered with delight.

The insistent pressure lifted from her mouth as a finger pushed against her chin.

'Open for me, Lynelle.'

She obeyed, enslaved by the low rasping sound of her name. His lips settled over hers once more and her eyes drifted closed. Tingling warmth spread from her mouth to her scalp and down until her entire body quivered with wanting. His probing tongue slid inside her hungry mouth and she forgot who she was.

Clutching the fabric of his shirt, she stretched onto her toes, seeking more. Her tongue tangled with his. Heat engulfed her, inflaming her senses until all she knew was his taste, his touch, him.

Powerful arms enfolded her and she sank into his embrace. Her nipples hardened, crushed against the solid wall of his chest. Her insides turned into liquid fire and she floated on a sea of sensations, so foreign, yet invigorating.

With a suddenness she was unprepared for, his tongue and lips withdrew, leaving her chilled. As she slowly drifted back to earth, the pounding of her heart and her panted breaths filled her ears. Lifting her lashes, she focused on her hands still curled within the folds of his shirt. His heart thudded beneath her fingers and his breathing rasped, swift and shallow.

'That was foolish.' His voice was unsteady.

She peered into his handsome face. His dark brows drew together, giving him a troubled expression. A glow from the flickering torch shone in his eyes and resembled a streak of lightning slashing across a bruised and clouded sky.

'And completely unnecessary,' she said breathlessly, releasing her hold. 'You must know the potion wasn't tainted.'

Her legs were weak and her body strangely unbalanced, but somehow she managed to stand on her own. She watched as he raked his fingers through his dark mane. He looked wild, untamed and far too appealing.

Yes, the kiss had been foolish, but she didn't regret it. Never had she experienced anything so glorious, so hot. His kiss had ignited a flame deep inside her, a burning craving for more. She pressed her fingertips against her lips, marvelling at how sensitive they were.

'I don't believe it was completely unnecessary.'

'Why?' Her hand dropped to her side. 'What have you gained by confirming I hadn't poisoned Edan's tonic?'

'Gained? Nothing about the potion, but I have learned something that has tormented me for far too long.'

'What?' She hated the way her voice shook, but she couldn't help it. He loomed over her, unconcealed desire glinting in his gaze.

'I discovered your lips are as soft as they look, and your buried passion is fuelled by more than anger.' His voice lowered to a hoarse whisper. 'I want to taste you again.'

***

Lust surged through William's veins. His groin leapt and swelled under his plaid as he devoured her swollen lips with his gaze, plump lips that tasted of innocent yearning and honeyed herbs. Her eager response proved he wasn't suffering this maddening desire alone.

'William.'

The sound of his name washed over him on the single breathless word. His heart raced. The hand she gently pressed against his chest seared the flesh beneath his shirt. He closed his eyes, savouring her willing touch and drew a deep, shuddering breath, fighting for control. When he kissed her again, he wanted to relish each skim of her lips, every tentative slide of her tongue.

'I have fulfilled my promise.'

His eyes flew open and fixed on her round, blue-eyed stare. 'What promise?'

Her palm fell from his chest and coldness rushed in to replace the warmth.

'Edan is almost fully recovered.'

Her pink tongue flickered out and moistened her lips, distracting him.

'My allotted time here ends at dawn.'

Dawn. Nae. Too soon.

Anger and unfulfilled desire swept through him. Had she returned his kiss so eagerly knowing she'd soon be gone from here, out of his reach? His hands turned to fists. He could kiss her again, now, certain she'd respond as keenly as she had moments ago. His rampant desire demanded action. His cursed honour screamed in protest.

William stepped back, giving her space, an opening for her to escape. His lust howled in silent denial.

She didn't move.

'Donald will take you home at dawn.' He turned, heading for the healing room door. He should never have entered this cursed chamber.

'Wait. Please.'

He stopped at the room's threshold, his heart beating a dull thud.

'I can't leave at dawn.'

Hell's fire! William strove for patience, for calm. He stared into the dim passageway, suddenly desperate to be gone from this place, far from her alluring presence.

'What time of day better suits your departure?' He forced the mannered question through gritted teeth.

'The time of day is not important. I cannot leave here and return to Fenwick with certain matters unfinished.'

His heartbeat quickened. Slowly turning his head, he studied the woman splashed with dancing torchlight. 'Certain matters?'

'I promised to aid Leslie during birth.'

Disappointment twisted his insides. Was her promise to Leslie the only reason for prolonging her stay? 'When will the bairn arrive?'

'A sennight, perhaps two.'

Relief ploughed through him. He had seven days, two weeks at best, to explore the maddening lust she inspired.

'Done.' William strode from the room.

Chapter 19

Lynelle stared at the empty doorway until William's footfall faded. The hissing of the torch and her thudding heart were the only sounds filling the chamber.

Saints and Glory. William had kissed her and she'd responded with unfettered abandon. She could still feel the gentle pressure of his hands on her neck, her shoulders. Still taste his masculine heat on her lips, her tongue.

Sliding her arms about her middle, she hugged herself, afraid the warm tingling feeling would disappear if she let go. A shiver of relief blossomed from inside out. She wouldn't be leaving tomorrow.

While Leslie's condition provided a reason to remain, William's kiss inspired a desperate need, an uncontrollable longing to stay and to have him kiss her again.

Emboldened by certainty and a sense of purpose, Lynelle brewed Edan's potion and left the healing room. Potion and herb sack in hand, she returned the torch to its holder on the landing and climbed the remaining stairs with excited determination.

She paused to catch her breath outside Edan's chamber and a niggling doubt pricked holes in her newly found resolve. How would William treat her now? What must he think of her? Her heartbeat quickened. Did she look different?

Smoothing a wayward strand off her brow, she tried to quell the fluttering in her stomach. She inhaled deeply and knocked on the door.

'Enter.'

The deep-voiced command reached through the wooden panel and her breath hitched. Tucking her sack under one arm, she unlatched the door and stepped inside.

William stood two paces in front of her, his powerful form blocking the view of the night outside the window. Her heart pulsed at a feverish rate and fire burned in her cheeks.

'What took you so long, healer?'

Healer? Why didn't he use her name? He knew full well the reason for her delay. Had he forgotten their kiss so soon? She searched his eyes and noted the steely glint lurking in the grey depths. Heat pooled in her belly.

He hasn't forgotten.

'Edan wanted to surprise you,' William said.

Edan? Dear Lord. She'd forgotten why she was here, hadn't even noticed Edan standing beside William.

'You're standing,' she finally said.

'Aye. I walked the full length of the room.' A beaming smile lit his young face. 'Will had Keith fashion a crutch to aid me. See.'

Lynelle studied the thick, wooden staff propped under his arm. She'd removed the stitches from his thigh two nights before, but hadn't expected him to be walking so soon.

'Oh Edan, what a splendid surprise.' Resisting the urge to look at William, she lowered her healing sack to the floor. 'Perhaps tomorrow, if the weather is fine, your brother could help you outside for some sunshine.'

'Really?'

'Yes.' She smiled at Edan's whoop of delight. 'But you must take it slowly and be careful not overdo it.'

'I won't. I promise,' Edan said. 'Is that the potion you brewed for me?'

'Yes.'

'May I have it now?'

'Of course.' Stepping closer, she noticed the fine sheen of sweat dampening Edan's brow. Despite the crutch and William's support, standing proved a strain for him.

Lynelle quickly lifted the cup and sipped, before passing the potion to William to sample. She caught his warning glance and swallowed the suggestion that

Edan should return to his bed. Her gaze fixed on his throat as he drank and a rush of longing to press her lips against his neck stole her next breath. She wanted his mouth to cover hers, to feel his hands wander the length of her body.

Her heart leapt at the prospect, but she could discern nothing of William's feelings from his guarded expression. Was she alone in yearning for more?

'Ah. I thank you, Lynelle.' She started at Edan's words and accepted the empty cup he held out to her. 'Now, allow me to see you safely to your room.'

'Oh, 'tis unnecessary, Edan.' She heard the desperation in her voice. Time alone with William as he walked her to her room suddenly seemed precious.

'After your tireless care of me, it would be my honour to escort you.'

She stared into grey eyes so similar to William's in hue, but so different in how they viewed her. Instead of fire and ice, gratitude shone clear and bright. The strain of being on his feet after two weeks confined to his bed showed too, yet he suffered without complaint, for her. Shame for thinking to refuse his offer squeezed her selfish heart.

'It would be my pleasure to have you accompany me to my door.'

He stretched to his full height, which left the top of his head even with William's shoulder, and gave her a brisk nod. The tightness about her heart eased.

'I fear I cannot take your arm...'

'Hush, Edan,' she chided gently, noting the pained grimace he fought to hide. 'I am weary and would appreciate your escort now.'

She retrieved her sack and glanced at William, who remained steadfast beside his brother. She opened the door wide, wondering at his silence.

With a small smile for Edan, she slowly left the chamber. Each dull thud of his staff on the wooden floor preceded a sharp, indrawn breath. She winced at every harsh inhalation but refused to turn about and let him witness her concern, afraid of wounding his pride.

Reaching her door, she threw it wide and the light from the lit candles within her room spilled out into corridor. She cleared the worry from her brow and, forcing a smile, she looked behind her.

Edan panted slightly and his face was flushed.

'Thank you for your escort,' she said, inclining her head.

'It is ... my pleasure.'

'I bid you good night,' she said and entered her room.

'Till the morn.'

William's deep, rumbling voice shattered her feigned calm. A threat or a promise? She gripped the door latch with white fingers. As the brothers awkwardly retraced their steps to Edan's chamber, William looked over his shoulder and his gaze collided with hers.

Lynelle closed the heavy door, spun around and sagged against the solid timber. Her sack slid from her fingers and she pressed her palms onto the cool wood.

Her pulse thudded wildly in her neck and her knees threatened to give way. How long must she wait to feel his hot, hungry mouth upon her starving lips?

***

William prowled the windowed wall of Edan's chamber, keeping double-time to his brother's slumbering snores. He threw the door another menacing glance, daring it to open of its own accord, affording him an excuse to march into the passageway and pound on her door.

Did she sleep while his lust for her robbed him of rest, stole his very mind? One more taste of her sweet lips would confirm whether this maddening desire was for her alone, or if he'd simply gone too long without slaking his base needs.

Liar.

Throwing himself into the large, sturdy chair he'd pretended to sleep in for the last two weeks, he wiped roughened hands over his face. Kissing her had ignited a fire in his blood, sparked a burning need to sample more than her lips.

He didn't believe he was alone in his torment. She'd kissed him back with equal ardour and he hadn't mistaken her struggle to keep her attention fixed on his brother afterward.

Edan mumbled and shifted in his sleep. William leaned forward to study him in the dim light. Praise God his wounds were healing and his spirits were high. William's chest tightened at the memory of Edan's chivalrous display. He'd felt Edan's trembling weakness and wanted to order the lad to bed, but he didn't have the heart to trample on his brother's burgeoning pride and sense of honour.

Slumping back in the chair, he closed tired eyes. Edan had called him a hero days before. What name would Edan brand him when he discovered William planned to seduce the woman responsible for saving his life?

***

Lynelle clutched her herb sack in one hand and brushed stray wisps of hair from her cheeks with the other. It seemed she'd been standing by her door for untold hours, waiting for William to come for her.

Last night sleep had eluded her, providing her with boundless time to think. William held sway over the one thing she desired most.

To live. To feel alive.

His kiss had awakened a need so great, so real, she didn't believe she'd survive without more. It showed her the difference between enduring life and living.

She wanted more.

A knock sounded. She stiffened. Pressing a hand to her middle, seeking to calm the fluttering in her belly, she smoothed the fabric of her gown for the hundredth time.

Anticipation shivered through her.

She freed her hand from beneath her cloak, stepped forward and unlatched the door. William filled the opening, his fresh, masculine scent filling her next breath.

She sank her teeth into her tongue and met his dark gaze. Heat flooded her cheeks and she grasped the edges of her cloak to stop the need to fan herself.

I want to taste you again.

The words he'd spoken last evening shone clearly in his eyes.

Her breath caught. Lowering her lashes, she stared at his mouth, his lips, up-tilted slightly at the corners. She struggled to appear composed.

'How is Edan?' she said, studying the square line of his jaw, wondering if the faint shadow would rasp against her skin.

'Edan is well.' He shifted. 'Come. Others await your skills in the village.'

Inhaling deeply, she moved past him into the corridor and forced her legs to keep moving as a hand cupped her elbow. Her cloak proved no barrier to the warmth racing up and down her arm.

As they descended into the great hall, he released his hold and her blood seemed to slow within her veins. Servants stopped clearing the tables from the morning meal to throw glances their way. She returned their smiles, buoyed by their friendliness.

They stepped out into the sunlight, and William's hand settled on the small of her back. His fingers softly stroked her sensitive flesh like a bard strumming his lute. His touch sent tendrils of heat sparking along the length of her spine as he guided her through the gates and down to the pier.

He ceased playing her as she climbed into the boat and her senses started to reassemble, only to scatter the moment he sat beside her on the bench seat, his hip and thigh pressing against hers.

Why did his caresses linger today, when he'd previously avoided touching her? Did he simply taunt her, or was he too hoping for more?

She turned and peered into the water as the vessel glided across the loch, the surface rippling in their wake. God help her. If she planned to savour his taste when he kissed her again, she needed to find a way to remain coherent. In her present state, she feared her body would soon resemble a steaming puddle in the bottom of the boat.

A bird cried overhead and she stared at the osprey's white underbelly. What would it be like to know such freedom? Freedom to be herself, freedom to feel. She continued to watch the bird until it flew from sight.

Climbing ashore, she accepted the hand William offered. As her fingers wrapped around his, sparks rushed up her arm, but she drew strength from the sensation and welcomed the quickening of her blood.

She turned to the boatman. 'Thank you, Geordie.' Her voice rang clear and loud, despite her inner turmoil.

Geordie responded with a nod and his weathered cheeks coloured slightly.

A gentle tug on her hand had her turning about and together she and William struck out towards the village.

He released her hand, but his fingers slid along the tender skin of her wrist, where they stopped to encircle her lower arm. He remained silent and she wondered if he were speaking to her with his touch rather than words. Her mouth grew dry and she could feel herself sinking into oblivion again.

'Tell me about the swans.' Her question broke the serenity and his leisurely stride. His fingers firmed a fraction before slowly lowering her arm to her side and letting go.

'Do you believe in myth and magic, curses and legends?' he asked softly.

Lynelle's stomach clenched. People said she was cursed, and blamed her for everything that went wrong. Even her own father shunned her.

'I believe people seek answers from wherever they can when deeply troubled or hurt,' she said.

'It is easier to accuse something that has been whispered about for a hundred years,' William said. 'A story that holds nae truth, but saves those responsible because of who they are.'

'A story told for so long must hold some truth,' she said. 'How did it begin?'

William sighed and she feared he'd refuse to tell her the tale.

"Tis said many years ago, two swans used to visit Closeburn Castle. At least twice their appearance heralded the miraculous recovery for ill members of our family.'

Lynelle's heart warmed at the notion.

'The swans came to be regarded as tokens of good luck,' William continued. 'That was until one of my ancestors, it is said, cruelly shot one through the breast with a crossbow bolt.'

Lynelle gasped and looked at William. He strode on as if unaffected.

'Thereafter, the apparition of a swan with a bleeding breast foretold a death or misfortune for the Kirkpatrick clan.'

Angels above.

'Has anyone ever seen the bleeding swan?'

'A few believe they have.'

'Have you?' Lynelle couldn't take her eyes off William as she awaited his response. But from the rigid set of his jaw, she already knew his answer.

'Nae.'

'But why would they lie about seeing—'

He stopped and turned to her. 'People see what they want to see when grieving. It is easier to blame an ancestor long gone, instead of accusing those who still live and are really at fault.'

His strained expression and pain-filled eyes told her more than anything he could say. He'd banished Jinny but bore the guilt for his family's demise himself.

Reaching out, she grasped his fist and gently squeezed. 'You are not to blame for their deaths, William.'

He shook free of her hold and his eyes narrowed. 'You are now a seer as well as a healer?'

'No.'

'Then you speak out of turn.'

His harsh tone silenced her for a moment, but the despair in his eyes loosened her tongue.

'In your grief, you sent Jinny away. You needed someone to blame and should not feel guilty.'

His expression turned to stone. His eyes glittered darkly. An aura of barely leashed anger surrounded him as he stood in silent fury before her.

'You know nothing of my grief. Or guilt.'

Tears welled in her eyes and she blinked them away.

'I may know nothing of yours, but I carry my own.' The words spilled free, without thought, and she suddenly knew she wasn't to blame for surviving her birth when her mother and twin brother had died. How could a newborn babe be responsible for another's death?

But why had she lived when they hadn't?

'You said you weren't born or raised to be laird, but what if you were meant to be leader of your clan?'

'I would rather have my family back.'

'Of course, but do you not think things happen for a reason?'

'Nae. Things happen because we grow lax and allow them to.'

'But–?'

'Enough.' He speared his fingers through his hair. 'Come. The day passes and we've done naught but talk nonsense.'

Lynelle stared at William's rigid back as she followed him the rest of the way to the village. For her, it hadn't been nonsense, but a revelation.

In her father's grief, he'd needed to focus his pain and suffering on someone. That someone had been her. The people of Fenwick had followed his example and though she'd borne their condemnation, she at least now understood why.

If William had suffered because he was meant to be laird, why had she survived? Could it be her whole cursed existence led her to this place, to William? If so, what was her true purpose here?

Was it to become the healer she claimed to be by aiding the sick? Was she meant to restore William's faith in healers? Or was she here to experience life as she'd never known it before?

Chapter 20

God above. Was the healer trying to absolve him of his guilt while he'd been attempting to seduce her?

Her view of why his family had died, while he yet lived, cast a little light on his shadowed soul. Then again, perhaps it had only been a reflection of her goodness.

Was she right? Had he always been meant to be laird?

The thought persisted as he helped Ian form dirt mounds and lay seed for Keita's family. Once done, they visited the other cottages and aided the men with their spring planting. It was a task he'd often performed before Roger's death, after which other matters had consumed his time and stolen his peace of mind.

Now, as he stood alongside his clansmen and appraised their handiwork, a sense of pride washed over him. He hadn't realized how much he'd missed the manual labour and the satisfaction it granted.

He had a good comradeship with the clan folk and was respected by Closeburn's men-at-arms. He also felt responsible for every soul living within the castle and village confines.

But he'd never believed he was born to be laird. Feeling responsible and actually being accountable were two different things entirely. The first was a choice. The second was an expected duty.

Feminine voices drifted on the breeze, dragging him back from his reverie. Sunlight glinted red in Lynelle's golden hair as she approached with Keita. His body tensed. Christ! When had he started thinking of her as Lynelle?

When you kissed her.

'Are you returning to the castle now, laird?'

William turned at the sound of Ian's voice.

'Aye.'

'Can I walk with you? I need to see my father.'

'I welcome your company, Ian.' He told himself his agreement had nothing to do with the sudden need to avoid Lynelle's probing questions.

They bid the villagers farewell and started back along the path. Despite Ian's presence, the woman walking beside him proved a constant distraction.

There was something different about her. An air of confidence and certainty shimmered around her, as if she'd discovered a well-kept secret. He could think of many ways to encourage Lynelle to share her knowledge with him, but doing so would mean being alone with her.

The short journey across Castle Loch seemed to take forever. Though he stared at the rippling water, he remained acutely aware of every word Lynelle spoke, every gesture she made. Relief ploughed through him as the boat bumped into the pier.

William kept a slight distance between them as he escorted Lynelle into the keep. No words passed between them, but her gaze locked with his for a whisper of time before she descended to the healing room below, and he took the wide stairs up to Edan's chamber two at a time.

***

'I win!'

William groaned inwardly. Not again. How could Edan win the second game of draughts with such ease? Seated in the bailey, enjoying the mild sunshine, William was having trouble concentrating.

Edan's triumphant grin widened as a group of giggling young serving maids approached. They spouted on about Edan's daring and bravery, causing his underdeveloped chest to swell.

Standing, William offered his seat to the bright-eyed maids, allowing Edan some privacy to soak up their praise.

William strode around to the back of keep, drawn by the sound of steel clashing with steel. Donald had kept up the men's training since William had become laird, though it was a duty he'd previously enjoyed. Removing his shirt and picking up a heavy sword, he sparred with several of the men, relishing the physical exertions placed on his body.

After splashing his face and upper body with cool water, he left Donald to guide the aspiring swordsmen. Today, he lacked the clear-headed concentration required to hone their skills.

Donning his shirt, he sought out Malcolm, Closeburn's steward. Food stores of fresh meat were low and William decided to organize a hunt in a week or two to replenish the larder. As they spoke, his gaze constantly drifted upward to the keep's highest level and the window that no eyes had peered out of for half a year.

The sun hung low in the west by the time William sought out Edan. He patiently waited for Edan's flock of admirers to disperse, then carried his grumbling brother back to his chamber.

William teased Edan about the young lasses vying for his attention as they shared the evening meal. Edan repaid him by beating him at draughts for a third time.

'What's troubling you, Will? You've hardly eaten and I've never bested you at draughts three times.'

Pushing out of the chair he'd placed beside the bed, William paced the length of the chamber. He halted at the far side of the room and looked at his brother's concerned face.

'Tell me, Edan. If there was nae such thing as the curse of the bleeding swan, who would you blame for the deaths of our loved ones?'

All colour drained from Edan's cheeks.

A flash of pain seared William's chest as his brother lowered his gaze to the coverlet. He desperately wished he'd held his tongue.

'Forget I spoke, lad. It was a foolish question.'

'Nae! It wasn't.' Strong emotion shone in his brother's eyes. 'Do you think me too young to have shared similar thoughts?'

Aye, he had. William approached the bed and resumed his seat. 'Then tell me.'

Edan looked at him. 'The hurt was so great I believed I would die along with them.' He swallowed. 'But I didn't, and then I grew angry with each of them for leaving me.'

William understood such anger. He'd suffered the same burning fury.

'Then I was glad I wasn't struck down with the ague, and relieved I hadn't gone out in the boat with Roger that day. I hadn't died, but my selfishness caused the most pain of all.'

'It isn't selfish to want to live, Edan.'

'Then why do I feel guilty for being alive?' Anguish almost robbed him of his voice.

William's heart constricted. Reaching forward, he gripped Edan's hand and squeezed. 'I haven't the answer as to why, lad, but I assure you, you don't suffer alone.' William tightened his hold on his brother's hand.

'The swan curse was an easy choice and saved me having to find fault with anyone,' Edan said. 'But after being wounded, I've had plenty of time while lying here to think about who is to blame.'

William stiffened, fearing Edan's next words.

Grey eyes lifted to meet his.

'Nae one is to blame, Will. Not Jinny, not me and certainly not you.'

A whisper of light broke through the darkness around William's heart. He stared at his brother, surprised by Edan's maturity.

'I should have asked your opinion sooner,' William said as he stood, releasing Edan.

'Aye. You should have.'

William heard the serious note in Edan's tone. 'I'll not forget to ask your thoughts next time.'

'I'll ensure you don't.'

William's smile mirrored Edan's. 'There is something I need to do,' he said as he walked to the door. Turning back, he said, 'I'll fetch Mary to keep you company. With your luck today, you may even best her at the board.'

'Not likely.' Edan's groan was cut short as William closed the door.

He spared a glance at the stout oak door across the way. He'd been granted absolution from the living twice this day, and the woman sleeping within the sealed chamber had been the first. Her faith in him had formed a crack in the blackness surrounding his heart. Edan's belief in him had widened the breach and doubled his hope.

But before he opened his heart to bask in full light, he had one last ghost to lay to rest. He needed absolution from the dead.

***

Lynelle pressed her ear to the wood and held her breath as she listened for further signs of life outside her room. The murmuring of voices had stopped and there were no more sounds of footsteps or latches clicking into place.

If Edan was ill or someone needed her skills, she was certain they would send for her. No one came.

Sighing, she turned and gazed about the chamber she'd spent the last few hours prowling around in. Everywhere she looked, William's face seemed to take shape. She saw him in the pale stones forming the walls, in the low flames flickering in the hearth.

She made her way to the window, peered into the night and found a sense of space in the darkness. But the illusion soon faded and left her feeling confined, once again. Restlessness was new to her. She'd always bided her time, holding no expectations for anything.

But today things had changed.

Until she returned to Fenwick, it was pointless dwelling on what her father's reaction would be. Helping Leslie deliver a healthy babe was something she prayed would transpire, but she had no command over when it would happen. Though on seeing Leslie today, looking more swollen than the previous day, Lynelle was sure the babe would come in a day or two.

Would William send her on her way the moment the infant drew its first breath?

Saint Jude. She was running out of time.

While the timing of certain matters was beyond her control, there was one outcome she could hasten, if she only had the courage.

Wrapping her arms about her middle, she closed her eyes and drew forth the memories and sensations evoked by William's burning kiss. A shiver rippled through her, leaving a trail of gooseflesh dotting her skin and a deep yearning in her heart.

Resolve filled her. She had to know William's thoughts, was desperate to know his feelings. She wanted...

She marched across the room, pulled the heavy door open and made her way to Edan's chamber before her courage failed her. Fear of being rejected made her hesitate, her hand poised to knock. She could withstand rejection, but could she return to her room without knowing what William's choice would be?

Her soft knock went unanswered. As she shifted from foot to foot, contemplating going back to her chamber or knocking again, the door suddenly opened, revealing Mary's kind face.

'What is it, lass?'

'Nothing. I ... how is Edan?' she said, hoping the poor light in the corridor hid the flush warming her cheeks.

'Edan is sleeping as all healthy young lads should. Especially since I allowed him to best me at draughts.'

Lynelle returned Mary's smile with a nervous one of her own. 'I am pleased to hear he is well.'

The door cracked open a fraction wider and Lynelle couldn't stop from straining to see past Mary's generous form and into the chamber.

Edan was alone.

Her attention fell on Mary, who appeared to be inspecting her thoroughly.

She peered down at her form and the fire in her cheeks spread down her neck and across her chest. After a busy day tending clansmen in the village and then in the healing room, she'd stripped off her clothes, washed, and welcomed the feel of the loose linen nightgown Keita had loaned her. Though it covered her decently from neck to toes, it was hardly attire fit to wear outside a bedchamber. Saints above, even her feet were bare.

'Forgive me. I didn't mean to disturb you. Goodnight...'

'Wait, lass.'

The urgency in Mary's tone stilled Lynelle's flight. She turned around to face her. 'Is something amiss?'

Mary slipped out into the dim passageway, leaving the door ajar. A deep frown scored her forehead, as she peered down the length of the corridor toward the stairs. Lynelle looked in the same direction, a coldness seeping into her belly.

'I worry for William,' Mary whispered.

'Why? Is he ill?' Lynelle couldn't hide the fear in her voice.

'Nae, but he looked troubled.'

'Where is he?' Lynelle's mind raced. 'Has he gone from the castle?'

'Nae.' Mary slowly shook her head. 'He didn't say where he was going, but I watched him climb the stairs.'

'Are there chambers above?'

'Only one,' Mary said solemnly.

'And?' Lynelle's heart pounded. 'Please, Mary,' she said clutching the woman's arm.

"Tis the laird's chamber.'

Lynelle stepped back, struck dumb for a moment by such an ordinary answer. 'Mary, William is laird. It seems natural for him to...'

'You don't understand, Lynelle. William hasn't set foot there for the past half year.'

'But why?'

'William blames himself for not saving each of his family. The foolish man doesn't think he deserves to be laird of Closeburn.'

Lynelle had sensed William's misguided guilt. She'd even shared her thoughts on the subject with him this morn. But she hadn't suspected the depths he'd gone to in denying his rightful place as laird. Why had he changed his mind about entering the chamber now?

'William is a worthy laird, but deeply troubled.' Mary's expression was grim.

Lynelle searched the end of the passage as if the flickering shadows concealed the answers.

'I would go to him myself,' Mary said. 'But I gave my word I'd stay with Edan.'

'I'll go.' Clutching her nightgown with clammy hands, Lynelle headed toward the stairs.

Chapter 21

William stared at the imposing door before him, the iron-studded timber softened by the glow from the taper he held. Dread prickled his skin. He wanted to run, to leave the hurtful memories and the possibility of reliving them.

Inhaling deeply, he reached for the latch and pushed the door inward. Cool air rushed out to meet him, threatening to douse the candle and plunge him into darkness. He shielded the flame with one hand and waited until it settled. Then squaring his shoulders, he stepped over the threshold and closed the door behind him.

A hint of disuse tinged the air. He willed his eyes to adjust to the room's dim interior and battled to slow his racing pulse. The candle's meagre light pushed back the shadows, offering a glimpse of the chamber's secrets.

The ornate fireplace on the far wall stood still and silent. No fire danced in its belly, no flickering flames illuminated the intricate patterns he remembered adorning its sides and the thick, stone mantle above. He refused to look higher. Not yet.

His gaze skittered over numerous trunks stacked in the corner to his left. The timber screens failed to hide the solid reminders of those who'd come and gone. Behind the door stood the robe Mary visited daily to fetch William's clothes, and the carved wooden chest filled with the rest of his belongings.

He turned to the massive bed located on the dais. The closed hangings hid the silky coverlet and matching pillows from sight, but couldn't shut out the recollections of Roger's last drawn breath, or those of his mother, Ilisa.

Stabbing pain sliced through his heart. He squeezed his eyes shut, as if shuttering the view could somehow block the ache. Forgotten images crowded his mind.

Memories of Roger and William scrambling onto the high bed, their mother's laughter filling the air as the brothers raced each other on hands and knees to reach her loving arms. The scent of roses as he sank into her hold, blinking across at Roger's smiling face as they shared their mother's loving embrace. The sound of their father's booming voice, causing both their eyes to widen. A swift tightening of the arms around them before powerful hands snatched them up, throwing a son over each shoulder, a tickle and their childish laughter that continued long after they'd been shooed from the room.

Lord God how he missed them.

But knowing he could recall such memories, something he hadn't acknowledged until now, eased the anguish twisting his heart.

He opened his eyes and rolled his shoulders twice before forcing his feet to cross the large square rug muffling his footsteps. Crouching low, he set alight the neat pile of logs he suspected had been awaiting his return. Strangely, his heart no longer raced.

The woody scent from the crackling fire swirled around him as he straightened and touched flame to the fat candles at each end of the stone mantle. Setting his taper down, he wiped damp palms over the plaid draping his hips and slowly looked up.

The framed portrait of his parents loomed above him. Roger Kirkpatrick's deep brown eyes shone with pride and strength. William studied the square jaw and dark hair, physical traits he'd inherited. At twelve, the news of his father's death in battle had stunned him, but his distress had paled in comparison to his mother's quiet devastation.

Shifting his gaze to the face of the young woman beside his father, William's chest constricted. Long brown hair, a shade lighter than his, fell about her slender shoulders. Her ever-present smile forever caught on canvas, dazzled brilliantly. It always had, even after his father's death. But William had often noticed the slight trembling of her lips when she thought no one was looking. Her courage, right up until her death a year ago, humbled him even now.

Clutching the cold stone mantle, he searched his father's gaze. Did he only imagine a sense of approval in the unblinking eyes?

Had he been torturing himself with self-blame and guilt for things he had no control over?

A log snapped in the grate, the sound breaking the hush of the chamber. As he stared into the growing flames, a sense of serenity seeped through him.

He clenched his fists against the contentment he was certain he shouldn't be feeling and studied the trunks along the wall, waiting for the familiar ache to return.

Sadness loomed, but it was without blame, born only of grief for losing someone precious. Spinning about, he strode to the window and pulled back the shutter. A chill breeze swept in, cooling his face and neck. He inhaled the cold night air, but still the calming warmth invading his chest remained.

He gripped the sill and stared into star-studded darkness. The village slumbered beneath the moon's light and as his eyes adjusted, he caught stray wisps of smoke rising from each cottage. Faces of the villagers and castle folk flashed through his head. His people. His knuckles strained as a surge of protectiveness swamped him.

Suddenly, Lynelle's face appeared in his mind. His heartbeat quickened at the thought of being her protector. He groaned as his body tensed with the desire to do more than defend her.

He'd planned to seduce her slowly, had enjoyed every shiver his caresses had evoked, every quiver she'd tried to hide. He was sure she'd been unaware of the tiny breathless gasps his touch had inspired and his body had roared to life at her guileless reaction.

But he wasn't prepared for her innocent seduction of him. Her methods had surprised him most.

Using words of kindness, she'd encouraged him to forgive himself. Her optimism had ignited a spark of hope in his cold heart. He'd known her for such a short time, but she seemed to understand him, perhaps better than he did himself.

He was here in this chamber tonight because of her.

He was in danger of falling under her spell.

Praise Saint Patrick she was secured in her room below, out of his reach. He didn't have her gift for words, but he could show her how grateful he was with every inch of his body.

A knock startled him. Nae one aside from Mary knew he was here and he'd left her to watch over Edan.

Edan.

He raced to the door and wrenched it inward. 'What...?' Any further words died on his tongue.

The fire blazing within the room brushed over the figure standing in the doorway. His gaze drifted down the linen-clad form to the bare toes hardly visible in the shadows, before skimming back up to the high neck of the nightgown. His hand clenched on the door, remembering what lay beneath her modest attire.

'Edan...?' The rasping voice didn't sound like his own.

'Is well. He sleeps and Mary still watches over him.'

The tension riding his shoulders eased as fear for his brother ebbed.

'Are you all right?' Concern coated her soft-spoken enquiry and the tip of her tongue licked her upper lip.

His body tightened at the memory of how sweet her mouth tasted.

'Aye. There's naught wrong with me.' He should bid her good night and close the door. 'Why are you here, Lynelle?'

'Mary worried for you but didn't like to leave Edan and–'

'So you came in her stead,' he interrupted.

'Yes.'

'Once again putting yourself in danger–'

'Danger? I simply climbed the stairwell–'

'In complete darkness.' His voice deepened with his rising frustration. 'Even I had the sense to carry a candle,' he said, gesturing inside the room.

Her gaze followed the direction of his hand and her effort to see inside the chamber gave him a glimpse of her slender throat as she craned her neck.

His nostrils flared as her slight movement released the faint smell of lavender. Scaling the stairs in the dark wasn't the only danger she faced as she stood before him, painted in shadows and firelight.

How would she react if he were to plunge his fingers through her soft golden hair, tilt her head and praise her foresight with his lips, his tongue?

'Are you certain you're well?' she said. His gaze lifted from her mouth to find her studying him, her brow furrowed. 'You seem ... distressed.'

Distressed?

If wanting to drag her into the chamber and turn his thoughts into reality caused him to appear distressed, he couldn't argue with her assessment.

'It might help to speak to someone of your troubles,' she continued.

Dear God. If he weren't struggling so hard to keep his body in check, he'd laugh. Did she have no clue that she was the cause of his distress?

'My *troubles* are my own. But I thank you for your concern.' He sounded calm, polite.

'But–'

'I suggest you return to your bed,' he interrupted. His will to leave her untouched was rapidly failing. The stricken look in her wide eyes didn't aid in his battle.

'Good night, Lynelle.' He made to close the door.

'Wait!' She stepped forward, barring it with her hand.

Her actions brought her closer. The smell of lavender grew stronger. His control slipped another notch and he had to concentrate hard to keep his breathing even.

'What now? I am weary and wish–'

'A kiss,' she said softly.

Christ Almighty. His body turned rigid, every muscle locked in place.

'Just one kiss and I will leave you in peace.'

Peace? He hadn't known a moment of peace since she'd traded herself for Fenwick's heir. Blood pounded through his body. Heat – bred by the need to hold her, taste her, lose himself within her goodness – seared his heart.

His restraint hung by a gossamer thread. Directness hadn't driven her from his door, but perhaps a threat would.

Deepening his tone, he said, 'Heed me, Lynelle. If I grant you your wish, I will not stop at a single kiss.' He leaned toward her a fraction and her palm slid from the door to her side. She didn't back away.

Stubborn woman.

Locking his arms across his chest, he formed what he hoped was a dangerous expression on his face. He skimmed her form with his gaze, expecting her to flee while he looked his fill. She stood her ground. The only difference in her appearance was the increased tempo of her chest as it rose and fell beneath the clinging fabric of her nightgown.

Christ! How much more could he take?

Then she moved. But instead of turning for the stairs, she brushed passed him into the room. Her eyes never once left his. Firelight shone in her gaze, but a flicker of something else brightened the glow.

With a single step, he closed the distance between them. Cupping her head, he tilted her face up and captured her tormenting mouth with his.

Her soft lips parted and lust roared through his veins. He feasted on her eagerness and innocence, ravenous, as if starved of warmth and light.

Stop!

Wrenching his mouth from hers, he stared down into glazed pools of blue. Ragged, panted breaths filled his ears. His. Hers. He wanted her with a desperation he didn't understand. An aching need so powerful, he believed he'd shatter if he moved.

A soft touch seared his chest. Clenching his eyes shut, he waited for his body to splinter into a thousand shards of fired steel.

Calling on God and the saints to give her the sense to escape while she could, William forced his fingers to loosen their hold in her hair.

His desire for her was too great, too consuming. This woman stirred feelings of more than lust, made him crave more than her body alone. Somehow she'd slipped inside the barriers of his bruised heart. After wallowing in self-imposed darkness, Lynelle had gifted him with light to free his soul.

She'd fulfilled her promise, earned her freedom. He couldn't ask more of her. He had no choice but to deny his need, leaving her as virtuous as the day they'd met.

He opened his eyes and inhaled deeply. Her clear gaze met his unflinchingly before roaming his features. He let her look her fill, willing his hands not to reach for her.

Long lashes dipped over her enchanting eyes as she blinked.

He forced the words asking her to stay with him to lie unspoken on his tongue.

She turned to the open door.

William ground his teeth, his hands curling into tight fists as painful disappointment ripped through his chest.

Let her go.

One delicate hand lifted, pushing the door closed, sealing her inside the room. Sealing her fate and his.

Chapter 22

Lynelle had barely turned around before powerful hands grasped each side of her head and demanding lips crashed over hers. Opening her mouth, she begged his tongue inside, her body quivering with fervent need.

He tasted of fire and a desperate longing matching her own. Her fingers burrowed into his linen shirt, dragging his heated body nearer.

Dear God, it wasn't enough. She wanted him pressed tightly against her, desperate to feel every masculine inch of him.

His mouth left hers. She gasped 'no' and then shivered as his lips burned a path along her cheek.

'Too late, Lynelle.' His hot breath scorched her ear. 'You should have escaped while you could. I'll not let you go now.'

Praise God.

A shudder ripped through her, stealing her breath, her voice.

Sliding her hands over his shoulders, she clutched his head and pulled him closer. Her actions would have to speak for her.

His palm cupped her breast and her back arched as she thrust her chest forward. Her fingers tangled in his soft dark hair as his lips and hands brought her body to life. Heat prickled her skin and she was sure she'd burst into flames. Questing lips again sought hers and she relished the air he breathed back into her struggling lungs.

Strong arms swept her off her feet. Clinging to his neck, she revelled in his taste as he carried her further into the room. Their lips parted and her eyes flew open as she settled onto something soft and silky.

Panting heavily, she stared into William's serious visage. His smouldering eyes blazed in his flushed face and his harsh breathing awakened something primitive within her.

Fingers skimmed her calves, pushing her nightgown higher. She wriggled, trying to aid him as his other hand plucked loose the laces at her neck. William whipped away the confining cloth.

There was no time for modesty as with frantic hands she helped him shed his shirt and plaid. Finally as naked as she, he collapsed on the bed, kissing her with increasing urgency. She drank him in, absorbing his wildness, becoming his equal.

The coarse hairs on his limbs and chest grazed her sensitive skin. Lips seared her throat, her breasts, and she cried out her joy, her need, welcoming his weight as he settled atop her. She opened her arms and her heart as he probed her woman's core. Pressure nudged at the juncture between her thighs. Wet heat filled the centre of her being. She clawed at his arms, blindly seeking more.

Palms cradled each side of her head as his mouth took hers in a flaming kiss. She stiffened as a flash of pain tore through her lower body. Soothing, whisper-soft kisses fluttered over her eyes, her cheeks and the corners of her mouth.

His hips shifted, gently rocking against her and the discomfort faded as a new sensation built inside her. Rising beneath him, she met each flex of his hips as the unfamiliar feeling swelled and spread within. Their movements became frenzied. She strained against him, with him, desperately trying to reach the illusive prize she sensed hovering a wisp away.

Blazing heat and light rushed through her, as if she'd touched the sun. She gasped and shuddered and clung to William as a mighty roar echoed in her ears. Tiny shivers rippled inside her and trembled across her flesh. Her heart thudded wildly in her chest and she gasped for air.

Her pulse slowed, her body hummed.

Bone weary, she couldn't move.

She'd never felt so alive.

William shifted, sliding off her. She wanted to protest, but couldn't speak and her limbs ignored her command to draw him back.

A moment later his warmth returned and she curled against his side, as gentle caresses skimmed her face and trailed through her hair.

'Forgive me.'

His low-voiced words confused her. Lifting heavy lids, she gazed into William's eyes, now darkened with concern.

Her heart twisted in her chest. There was nothing to forgive. She'd wanted this as much as he had. Had vowed to again have his strong arms around her, his lips upon hers.

Lacking strength and words to reassure him, she gave the only absolution she could.

She smiled.

***

William stared down at the woman cushioned against his side. Her eyes slid closed, but her smile lingered on her reddened lips. A smile for him. He resisted the urge to lean down and kiss the curved bow of her mouth.

She looked small and fragile. Her smooth, pale skin so different compared to his rough, tanned flesh.

Beautiful.

He'd asked for forgiveness, but not for joining with her. He'd never experienced such pleasure, such magic. But when he'd broken through the barrier proclaiming her innocence, he'd caused her pain.

The moment she closed the door, making love to her was inevitable. His struggle for control had been overwhelmed by passion and a desperate urgency to have her, to know her intimately.

Her trust humbled him. He'd relished every nail she'd scored down his back. She'd clung to him, her sweat-slicked body wrapping about his as if he were vital to her existence. Her gasps and cries of pleasure echoed in his ears. Her violent trembling when she'd reached her peak fired his blood.

His body hummed with life at the memory. Stroking damp tendrils of hair from her forehead, he forced his breathing to slow, willed his body to relax. Easing his head onto the bolster, he continued caressing her, savouring the feel of her in his arms.

***

Inhaling feminine heat and lavender, William emerged from a deep, peaceful sleep. The lithe form curled in his embrace stirred as he slipped from the large bed. He perused her pale, slender body with hungry eyes.

Mine.

The thought loomed, and he quickly draped the silk coverlet over her enticing restlessness.

Padding to the open window, he stared out as night's chill breath wafted through the portal, cooling his rising flesh. The half-moon hadn't completed its duty, but hung mid-way on its descending journey, proving he hadn't slept for long.

Unwelcome thoughts crowded his head. How many times would the moon rise and fall before Lynelle left?

His chest tightened.

He wanted her to stay.

He rubbed roughened hands over his face and walked to the hearth. Stoking the embers, he added more wood, silently berating himself for a fool.

He should have ignored her kindness, turned his back on her encouragement and mastered his lust, his desire.

Too late.

Her unwavering spirit had seeped into the closed confines of his heart and sprinkled seeds of hope. Her caring, gentle ways nurtured aspirations of trust and ... love? Emotions he'd believed lost to him.

He stood, shaken by the knowledge that he could still feel so deeply. Though he stood within the safe confines of his castle, the strange feeling of being out of place surged through him.

He retrieved his clothes from the floor and dressed. Scooping up Lynelle's nightgown, he laid it at the end of the huge bed. His gaze trailed over the rumpled covers to the face peeking out from within the folds.

Again, his chest constricted at the sight of her. She'd burrowed beneath the protective walls he'd erected around his heart, when he'd been certain he was safe from the mightiest foe.

But not safe from one small, foolishly brave English healer who had a life far from Closeburn.

Marching to the door, he escaped the room, crowded as it was with too many startling revelations, and descended the stairs to the next level. Slipping into his brother's chamber, he found both Edan and Mary sleeping soundly.

He returned to the dim corridor and crept down the stairwell to the great hall. Keeping close to the wall to avoid his clansmen's pallets, he entered the deserted kitchens and lit a fire in one of the giant cooking hearths.

While he waited for the water in the deep iron pot to boil, he prepared a meal of bread, smoked ham and cheese, and sat at the long, scarred table to eat. The mundane activities and the quiet of the room washed over him, soothing him. But he couldn't escape his thoughts.

He was tired of brooding. Lynelle was still here. It was up to him to convince her to remain at Closeburn after the birth of Leslie's babe. He alone had the power to persuade Lynelle to return to his bed for however long she decided to stay.

But first he needed to know if she despised him. She'd ignored his warning and he'd carried out his threat, giving her much more than a kiss.

The sound of bubbling water drew him. Downing the last of his ale, he placed the wooden cup on the table and rose. He poured the hot water into a pail and prepared a tray of food. Controlled determination filled his every movement as he carried both the water and tray above stairs.

His steps faltered as he entered his chamber. Lynelle sat in the centre of the huge bed. She looked soft and tussled, the silken covers wrapped loosely about her lush form. His body hardened.

Forcing his legs to move, he closed the door with his foot and set the pail on the floor and the tray upon the square table beside the bed. Drawing a long, slow breath, he fought his rampant desire.

He turned and studied her.

Colour stained her cheeks, and patches of red marred her slender throat and the smooth ridge of her shoulders. All proof of his fierce hunger and whiskered jaw. His gut clenched.

'Did I hurt you?' His voice rang low.

Her brow furrowed. 'No.'

His muscles relaxed and he exhaled the breath he'd been holding.

Her eyes suddenly widened. 'Why? Did I hurt you?'

Lord God, she was serious. Her guileless concern caused his heart to stall in his chest. His heartbeat resumed and he wondered how she'd react to seeing the scratches he could feel beneath his shirt.

'Nae.'

Her forehead cleared and she seemed to sink deeper into the bed.

'Any regrets?' He had to know.

'For not hurting you?'

He stared down at her. Was she teasing him? A small smile tilted the corners of her still swollen lips.

'No, Will. I have no regrets,' she said softly.

'Good.' His mouth relaxed. His pulse thudded wildly through his veins. 'It is early yet. Eat if you're hungry and bathe if you wish. I must see to Edan, but I will meet you in the great hall to escort you to the village.'

She nodded.

William escaped the chamber before he gave in to the need to make her his prisoner, a captive of his fierce passion and desire.

But he knew she wasn't the only one in danger of being enslaved.

Chapter 23

Saint Jude, save her. She was in love with William Kirkpatrick.

Toppling onto her back, she clutched the coverlet tightly over her naked chest and squeezed her eyes shut. God and heaven's angels. She was in love.

She was in trouble.

How could she have been so unaware of her feelings? Had she truly not known she was falling in love when her skin tingled at the sound of his voice? When her heart had fluttered on seeing him? When she'd craved his touch and yearned to caress him?

Only moments ago, she'd had to dig her fingers into the bedding surrounding her to stop from dragging William back onto the bed.

Wicked. Sinful.

Alive. In love.

Wrenching free of the covers, she pushed herself upright. Her sigh echoed about the room.

Lord above. What was she to do now?

Climbing from the high bed, her toes curled as her feet touched the cool timbered floor. She winced at the stiffness in her limbs and the unfamiliar soreness between her legs.

She peered at the tray of food and though it looked tempting, she decided to make use of the hot water first. Naked, feeling unusually daring, she tiptoed to the trunk behind the door and lifted the heavy lid. William's scent drifted from the contents. Drawing a deep breath, she smiled. Within the trunk, she spied a pair of calf boots, several clay pots and the linen cloths she'd been searching for. After taking two cloths, she removed a stopper from one of the pots and took a few precious soap flakes before securing the jar and closing the chest.

Sprinkling the sandalwood scented slivers into the steaming water, she used the smaller cloth to freshen her skin. Each place she bathed triggered memories of William's passionate attentions. Her cheeks, her neck, her sensitive breasts, all came to life as she skimmed the fabric over her body. She shivered and gentled her touch as she bathed the red-hued stickiness from her thighs and the tender place above.

The deep timbre of his voice when he'd questioned her, coupled with the strained expression on his face, showed his obvious concern for her. The food and heated water spoke of his thoughtfulness. But was he prepared to offer anything else? What more could she want?

Much more.

After drying, she donned her nightgown and carried the tray to the hearth. Sitting on the soft fur rug, she nibbled at the fare, silently telling herself she must be content.

Her mind understood, though her heart rebelled – a state she'd suffered since the day she was born. Yet she'd survived.

Returning the tray to the table, she straightened the coverlet and peered out the open window. Dawn was near. The heavy weight of longing pressed down upon her shoulders. She and William had no future together. She loved him, but couldn't tell him.

Should he discover she was the outcast daughter of an English lord, he'd want to know all her secrets. She couldn't bear to have him look at her with disgust, to shun her if the reasons for her disgrace were revealed. She'd earned his trust and couldn't bear to lose it. Her heart would surely stop beating if he ever had cause to loathe her.

Straightening, she had no choice but to bury her dreams of shared love and focus on the harsh reality of her life. But she was determined to enjoy each moment and savour every experience with William while she was here.

She slipped down to her chamber undetected, dressed and fixed her hair in the usual style of a single thick braid. Then she sorted through the contents of her herb sack, as if this morning was the same as any other.

When she judged it time to meet William, she descended the stairs to the hall. Her belly fluttered with nerves and her palms grew hot and moist at the thought of seeing him again.

After making love, they'd spoken in fire-lit darkness. He'd stood before her, barefoot and handsomely dishevelled, while she'd been wrapped in the coverlet with the evidence of their intimacy still coating her inner thighs. Now, daylight pierced the shadows and there would be no more talk or teasing as lovers. Her heart whimpered in protest. She quieted it with steely resolve.

William stood at the bottom of the stairwell, neatly attired in fresh garments, his hair as tidy as his untamed soul allowed. His scorching gaze skimmed her from head to toe. Her body heated beneath his intense regard and heat filled her cheeks. On legs suddenly gone weak, she descended the last few stairs feeling that she might melt into a puddle at his booted feet.

'Come.'

The warmth in his tone trickled through her like un-watered wine.

He turned for the keep's entrance and she followed close behind. As they stepped outside into the blessed fresh air, he slowed his step.

'You're blushing,' he said softly.

Her face flared hotter, and she ducked her head to hide the pleasured smile hovering on her lips.

William greeted Geordie as they climbed into the boat and Lynelle lifted her chin a notch to give the older man a glimpse of her smile.

Turning, she stared at the water, sure it seemed clearer today. The breeze was fresher, the early-morning sun warmer.

They alighted on the far shore and began the trek to the village.

'My mother, Ilisa, walked this path daily.'

Lynelle glanced up at the man beside her, surprised by the topic he'd chosen.

'Oh?'

'She deemed it her duty to pay a visit to the people who chose to live on Closeburn land, but away from the castle.'

'Your mother must have been a caring, thoughtful woman.'

'Aye. She was.'

And beautiful. The stunning woman in the portrait possessed an unsurpassed elegance.

'What of your mother?' William said. A chill skittered down her spine. 'Or is your father the beauty who gave you your enchanting looks?'

A roaring sound rushed through Lynelle's head. She stumbled on the smooth path. William caught her upper arms, steadying her. His troubled gaze searched her face. She looked away.

'Lynelle, what is it?'

'I...' Her heart pounded. Lord God, what could she say? 'I never knew my mother. She died moments after I was born.' It was safer to speak of her long-dead mother than of the father who refused to know her.

'Forgive me, Lynelle. I didn't know.'

A sharp pang of loss spiked in her chest. She swallowed. 'There is naught to forgive, William.'

She'd never grieved for her mother. No one had ever given her the chance. Until now. Until William.

Pain sliced through her at his kindness, and her deception. Moving closer, she reached up and captured his face in her hands. Pulling his head down, she kissed him with all the love and passion consuming her soul. Her tongue surged inside his mouth and she pressed for more, trying to erase everything but the taste of him. Begging him for forgiveness.

William took control, gentling the kiss. She followed his lead, basking in the soft skimming of his lips before he lifted his head. A shuddering breath escaped her. Looking up, she stared into his smouldering eyes.

Over the thudding of her heart, she heard the ragged sound of his breathing.

He stepped back, releasing his hold and glanced toward the village. 'A pity you're expected.' Blazing eyes returned to her. 'Else I would have you here, now.'

A shiver ripped along every nerve ending. Please. Now.

'Tonight,' he said. ''Will you come to my chamber tonight?'

'Yes.'

His chest swelled as he inhaled deeply. 'Come then, before I again forget myself and why we're here.'

Lynelle trailed slightly at his side, relief pulsing through her veins. She'd averted further conversation about her mother and, more importantly, her father.

She despised herself and the secrets she must keep. But if she wanted William to continue gazing at her with hot, fervent need, she would continue to use any means to distract him.

Touching her fingertips to her lips, she cherished the tenderness his kiss left behind. Anticipation for the coming night warmed her blood, her entire being.

But first, she had a full day of caring for those in need.

Tonight, she'd see to William's and her own.

Chapter 24

William stared out into the star-studded sky, as the furious pounding of his blood finally slowed. The day had seemed endless, but Lynelle would come to him soon.

Thank God.

Mary's joy at knowing he'd spent the past night in this chamber, his rightful place, had been obvious. She'd volunteered to stay with Edan again, but only after she'd hinted at her suspicions that he might not have spent the previous night alone.

When he'd asked if she were concerned for Lynelle's wellbeing, she'd stunned him by saying it was *him* she worried most for. He'd left her then, unprepared to deal with the apprehension clouding her wise eyes.

His time with Lynelle was short, and hinged on the expectant birth of a bairn. Days? Hours? Perhaps knowing had sparked and heightened his suppressed passion the night before.

Tonight, he planned to take command.

A slight sound drew his attention to the door he'd left ajar. The opening widened, revealing a figure brushed with firelight. His heart seemed to sigh at the sight of her. His pulse quickened, his body hardened, but determination held him rigid.

He vowed to keep control, to take it slow. He would savour every touch, every taste, every quiver, as he explored every inch of her. Tonight he planned to linger, as if he were a condemned man and she his final sustenance.

The door clicked shut and she crossed the rug toward him. On bare feet, he met her advance in front of the hearth. His composure slipped a notch as his gaze stared into her desire-filled eyes and then dipped to her moist, parted lips.

She reached for him and he captured her seeking hands. 'Nae, Lynelle,' he said softly. 'Tonight is mine.'

He released one hand, and it fell to her side. Her puzzled expression disappeared as he unfurled the slender fingers still in his grasp, and pressed his lips to her palm. His tongue skimmed the cupped centre and he relished her tremor. The shimmering gleam of desire in her eyes held a glint of understanding. He grappled with the excitement roaring through his being at her hint of surrender.

Her plaited hair unravelled with the gentle urging of his fingers, the red-gold mass tickling the backs of his hands like strands of cool silk. He stepped closer, cradling her head and tilting her face to one side. Pressing his lips to her ear, he traced the pale shell-like skin with his tongue, his reward a gasping shudder that threatened to break his hard-fought control.

Lavender filled every unsteady breath as he laved the delicate, pounding flesh of her neck, his deft fingers already loosening the ties of her nightgown. He spread the fabric wide, as his lips continued their eager quest to the curve between throat and the sweep of her shoulder.

With care, he pulled the material lower, till it pooled at her waist and trapped her wrists, laying her upper body bare to his eager mouth. Her rasping breaths matched each heave of his chest as he battled for air and composure.

His lips descended and hovered above the pebbled peaks of her breasts. Her back arched, thrusting the soft mounds within a whisper of his starving lips. Cupping the underside of one firm globe, he splayed a hand at her back. Parting his lips, he drew her pale softness into his mouth and fed his rampant desire.

Her legs buckled and a moan of tortured delight filled the chamber. William caught her crumbling form, swept her into his arms and carried her to the bed. He stripped the gown from her writhing figure, tore his shirt from his body and pushed the plaid from his hips. He joined her on the coverlet, every ounce of control banished by the taste of her, the sound of her pleading moans, his desperate need to end her torment and his.

He sank into her wet heat and a shudder ripped through him. Her body strained to meet his as he surged inside of her. Grasping fingers clawed his back, his shoulders, clung to his head and hair. Her body tightened, clenching him fiercely, her cry of fulfilment spurring his own release. He filled her honeyed depths, his rapturous groan mingling with her shuddering sighs.

Collapsing, almost drained of all strength, he managed to roll to his side, drawing her against him. His thudding pulse eased and his struggle to breathe lessened as his body relaxed, sinking deeper into the bedding. Lynelle pulled closer and the muscles of his arms quivered, locking about her.

God above, he was helpless to contain his desire. A muffled cry and a feather-like touch proved enough to send all thoughts of control from his head. His lips started to lift at the notion of his weakness, but the smile never fully formed. Forcing his heavy lids to open, he shifted his head to stare at the woman resting in his arms.

Never had his flesh hungered so fiercely. Never had he suffered starvation after he'd feasted. He was ravenous for more.

But it wasn't only her body he craved.

He wanted all of her, heart, mind and soul.

Her smile had the power to wipe all thought from his mind. The way she viewed things and shared her ideas had him questioning his perceptions about others, about himself. Despite his mistrust and hostility, she'd shown unwavering kindness towards

Edan, the castle folk and the villagers. Everyone she met she touched with her gentleness, her compassion. Including him.

His clansmen flocked to her now, seeking her aid for all manner of ills. She'd earned his people's trust.

She'd won his battered heart.

Closing his eyes, he allowed the revelation the freedom he'd not permitted before. No stabbing pain pierced his chest. Instead, soothing warmth filtered through him as if he'd emerged from the darkest pit into the sun's beaming light.

Who'd have guessed he'd fall in love with the healer he'd done his best to despise.

Peering at the portrait hanging above the mantle, he finally understood the sparkle in his mother's eyes as she gazed towards his father. Would a similar glint show in his eyes now whenever he looked at Lynelle?

More importantly, did she look at him in such a way?

He searched her face, but her thick lashes remained closed, shielding her secrets.

Despite their physical closeness, a wall remained between them. This morning when he'd mentioned her mother, he hadn't been fooled by her diversionary kiss. He'd tasted her desperation, her fear. She was hiding something, but what?

Brushing damp strands of red-gold from her cheek, he wondered how he'd fallen in love with a woman he knew so little about. Aside from being English and skilled in the arts of healing, she resided at Fenwick, rescued kidnapped heirs and floundering toddlers and had lost her mother moments after she'd been born. But there must be more to her life.

Did she have brothers or sisters, and what of her father? If she did, surely they'd be desperate to have her back.

A chill swept through him. The birth of Leslie's babe was imminent, and then Lynelle would be gone. How did she feel about leaving? Would she happily return to Fenwick, or did she hope each day and night stretched longer, as he did.

He glanced at the door, pondering the strength of the lock, but dismissed any thoughts of forced confinement. Her passion matched his. Perhaps she'd willingly stay if he promised to love her with his body every night, and day, if necessary.

Tracing the path of her cheek, he skimmed his fingers down her slender throat, over the slope of her pale shoulder and along the length of her arm. Pausing, he rested his palm on the curve of her hip. Why in God's name was he worrying about her leaving while she still lay warm and soft in his arms?

He craved to know her feelings, but didn't dare reveal his own. Not until he discovered the secret she'd concealed with a kiss.

His hand slid to the juncture of her thighs. Her sigh swiftly altered to a whimpered plea. Desire speared through him and he doubled his intimate efforts. Seeing her falling apart in his arms restored his pride a fraction.

He wanted more, but this was enough ... for now.

***

Lynelle discreetly followed Geordie from the keep into the bailey and beyond the castle grounds through the yawning gate. While the boatman continued down the slope to the pier, seemingly unaware of her presence, she stopped at the top of the rise knowing full well the guards patrolling the battlements watched her. But they didn't question her.

The early-morning breeze teased her hair as the meagre warmth from the awakening sun kissed her cheeks. Exhaustion dragged at her limbs and her lashes seemed weighted, too heavy to hold open.

Yet never had she felt such vitality.

She'd left the cause of her lethargic vibrancy slumbering peacefully in the huge bed above stairs. She needed fresh air to gather her scattered wits, unable to think clearly while cocooned in William's enchanting embrace.

A shiver rippled through her as she remembered the past night. Thrice she'd reached heaven, enslaved by William's masterful touch. She'd dozed between bouts of lovemaking, roused from sleep each time by his questing hands and searching lips. She'd responded readily, eagerly. Her body gave her no choice. Her heart overflowed with wonder, with love.

How was she to go on?

Her gaze brushed the rolling hills to her right. She'd ridden over the gentle mounds, drenched by teeming rain on the day she'd arrived here. Her past lay in that direction. She shuddered at the thought of returning. Beneath her cloak, she hugged herself. Dear God, she didn't want to go back.

But if she didn't she'd never gain her father's approval.

Delving deep, she searched her heart and soul. Could she ever find peace without having her father acknowledge her?

Yes!

The swiftness of her answer rocked her.

She'd gladly sacrifice hearing her father call her his daughter for William's love.

She never thought her life-long dream could be replaced by another. But she'd never imagined falling in love either.

Inhaling deeply, she drank in the lush scenery beyond Castle Loch. The flat meadow, which she crossed daily to walk the path to the village, seemed so familiar now. A band of stout oaks, their solid branches reaching out to touch the tree alongside, formed a formidable barrier to the north, shielding the inhabitants of Closeburn, keeping the rest of the world at bay. The verdant beauty of the landscape stole her breath. But it was much more than the picturesque surroundings calling to her.

She'd found purpose here. Using her burgeoning skills as a healer to help those in need had given fullness to her wasted existence, enriching her life and sparking her first taste of happiness.

Would the clan folk welcome her if she stayed? Did William want her to? If so, in what guise was she to live here? Healer? Lover? Both? Would it be enough?

'Tell me your thoughts.'

Lynelle started. Her heart pitter-pattered in her chest as William's low, deep voice washed over her. Turning her head, she looked up into his glittering grey eyes and forgot to breathe.

I've fallen in love.

Her fingers dug into her sides as she tore her hungry gaze away and stared at the view. She loved William with all her body and soul, but aside from his desire to wring mewling cries from her lips as he joined his body with hers, she had no clue about his feelings for her. He held power over her and she feared revealing her heart's secret. She'd withstood rejection all her years, but could she survive his?

'It is beautiful here.'

'Aye.'

Peeping to the side, she found him studying his lands, fierce pride painting his features. Her heart seemed to melt at the mere sight of him and a delicious shiver coursed through her.

'Are you cold?' His question proved his attention wasn't fixed solely on the scenery.

'No. Only eager to be on our way.'

'Let us go, then.'

Lynelle didn't miss the faint curve of his clever lips, or the knowing look in his eyes. She willed her legs not to give way as they descended to the loch. Lord above. He hadn't even touched her since he'd joined her on the grassy rise, yet her heart raced with remembered delight. Worse still, the handsome beast seemed to know she struggled for composure.

'I'm surprised you can walk at all after last night's vigorous activities,' he said softly.

Lynelle's steps faltered on the dock's wooden planks. Strong fingers curled about her elbow, steadying her and at the same time unsettling her as he handed her into the rowboat. Averting her flushed face from

Geordie, she sagged onto the timber board and fought to slow her feverish pulse.

She enjoyed his teasing; this William was such a contrast to the brooding laird she'd dealt with when they'd first met. Had she played any part in his transformation? She liked to think she had.

They bumped into the outer pier and, after assisting her from the rocking boat, William released her hand. She missed the thrill of his touch, but understood the need for discretion. Rejoicing in his caresses in the confines of his chamber was altogether different to being in full view of curious eyes.

If she stayed at Closeburn, would they forever have to keep their passion hidden?

When they reached the bend in the path, powerful arms swept her off her feet, robbing her of breath and thought. His mouth crashed into hers and she parted her lips for his onslaught, demanding his surrender with every tangling sweep of her tongue.

Her nipples hardened and she pressed them against the solid wall of his chest. She speared desperate fingers into the dark, silky strands at his nape and gloried in the urgent, blazing sensations swarming through her.

The soles of her boots touched ground as William ended their mind-numbing kiss. Her hands slid from his hair, down his body to where his heart thudded into the softness of her palms. Their panted breaths mingled in the small space between them and Lynelle had to blink several times before her eyes could focus on the man before her.

'You're like a fire in my blood,' he rasped. Lynelle's heartbeat skittered and thumped at his admission. 'Come. If we do not go now, you are in danger of being ravished right here on the path.'

She concentrated on taking one shaking step at a time. Patting her hair into place with trembling hands, she hoped she didn't look as if she'd just been kissed senseless.

At the first glimpse of a wattle and daub structure, William said, 'When I finish mending Arthur and Blair's roof, I will come for you.'

It took a moment for Lynelle to grasp what he spoke of. Keita's words suddenly sprang to mind. The young couple had gone east to attend Arthur's sister's wedding in Saughtree before Lynelle had arrived at Closeburn.

She nodded and couldn't help a final peek at William's form as he made his way to the absent couple's cottage at the far end of the village.

With a fortifying breath and a fierce act of will, she thrust the image of William's prowling grace and potent kisses from her head. She couldn't give her full attention to healing with thoughts of William stealing her wits.

Chapter 25

William leaned against the rough wall of Leslie's cottage, trying to appear relaxed, bored even. Having repaired Arthur's roof in short time, he'd gone back to the castle, set his plans for noon into motion and then retraced his steps back to the village.

On his return, one of the village women had informed him that Lynelle was visiting Leslie. He'd since walked a decent rut in the earth running alongside the expectant woman's home.

He glanced up at the sun as it began its downward slide, and did his best to curb his impatience. A door creaked. He straightened and took a step forward. His chest filled with warmth at the sight of her and his blood pulsed, awakening, engorging the length of him beneath his plaid.

She turned back and stared at the cottage's entrance. Her troubled expression doused his ardour and his feet carried him to her side without thought.

'What is it?'

She looked at him and back to the door before heading out of the village. 'Leslie's back aches.'

William walked beside her, at a loss. 'This concerns you?'

'Well ... yes.'

Cupping her elbow, William stopped her as they started along the path. 'Why? Is the babe coming?' If it was time, why was she leaving with him?

'Not right now, but soon, I think.' Her brow creased with worry.

Was her frown for the babe or because once it was born, she would leave?

His chest tightened. 'Come,' he said, still holding her arm and urging her forward. 'I am in need of your skills.'

'Are you hurt?' she asked, almost running to keep up with his brisk pace.

The note of concern in her voice eased the constricting band around his heart. Her gaze raked over him from head to toe, firing his blood.

'It isn't your healing skills I refer to.'

Her puzzled expression was short lived, before her lips parted and her eyes widened. Colour flushed her cheeks a delightful pink.

How many blushes could he evoke with wicked words and probing caresses before the sun set? Would they be enough to convince her to stay?

At the curve in the trail, he steered her into the trees. Black stood where William had left him, tossing his head as they approached.

'What–?'

'Ride with me,' he said, cutting her off.

She stared at him. The look in her eyes softened and a smile touched her lips. 'Yes.'

William's heart thumped wildly. He mounted and offered his hand. Lynelle took it and placed her foot on his boot. With an effortless tug, he pulled her up, across his thighs.

She didn't question where he was taking her, simply snuggled against him. Her trust shattered the last barrier surrounding his heart. He loved her. She deserved to know. He would tell her, but not yet.

Picking his way carefully, he guided Black through a tunnel formed by the gnarled branches of ancient oaks. The forest appeared impenetrable, but not for a lad who'd explored every inch of his family's land.

The air was thick and cold beneath the leafy canopy. Dead undergrowth littered the ground. Black's hooves stirred it to life, and the smell of the damp and the old wafted about them. Ducking low, William shielded Lynelle from stray wooden limbs, and inhaled her lavender scent.

Pinpricks of light signalled the thinning of the trees. Sunlight washed over them and William gave his mount leave to gallop for a short distance. Lynelle clung to him, hiding her face, while he relished the feeling of freedom caused by the short burst of speed.

Drawing rein in a glen dappled with willow and alder, William lowered his precious bundle to the ground and dismounted. Leaving Black to graze, he took Lynelle's hand and led her to a secluded glade. This was where the burn providing Closeburn village with water began.

At the water's edge, he turned to face the woman who had stolen his heart. Cradling her face in his hands, he prayed it was love for him shining in the sapphire depths.

He kissed her slowly, deeply, hoping she understood his feelings without him voicing them. He lifted his head and stared into eyes glazed with desire.

Releasing her, William removed his plaid and spread it on the grassy bank. He smiled inwardly as Lynelle swayed toward him before catching her balance. Shucking his boots, he stood in his shirt and swiftly divested her of her cloak, gown and shift. She shivered, though the day was warm, and then tried to hide her luscious form from his prying eyes with her arms.

His shirt joined her garments and before shyness could cool her blood, he drew her against him and tasted the honeyed sweetness of her mouth. Without breaking the kiss, he lowered her onto his plaid and lay down alongside her.

Reaching over her lithe form, he scooped cool liquid into his hand and sprinkled it over her bared paleness. Her gasps echoed in his ears. Tiny bumps erupted on her skin. Water droplets glistened on every part of her and he licked the moisture from her flesh, worshipping her. Lynelle's shuddering release quivered against his lips, his tongue.

Quenching his thirst only heightened his raging hunger. He crawled up over her, positioned himself where his mouth had been and stared down at her flushed features.

Her beauty awed him and her unwavering kindness humbled him.

She was his. He pushed into her wet heat. No one would dare to take her away from him.

Her hips rose to meet each gliding thrust. His arms shook as he drove into her, time and time again. Her cries of rapture filled the sunny glade, stealing his control like a thief. He roared as his life's essence spilled deep within her.

Tonight. Tonight he'd ask her to stay. Tonight he'd tell Lynelle he loved her.

***

Having donned his shirt and boots, William assisted Lynelle into her gown, unable to control the urge to kiss her neck and shoulder. He was helpless to stop his fingers from skimming her breasts and the curve of her hip as he did so. Lynelle's shy smiles and fluttering lashes made him want to tear the clothes right off her again.

But the day was waning. Using the anticipation of the coming night to quell his growing desire, he lay on the ground and rolled, wrapping his lower body into his plaid. Standing, he drew the end of the garment over his shoulder and tucked it at his waist.

Looking up, he found her expression had altered from playful modesty to one of rapt fascination. He did the only thing he could. He offered her a courtly bow. She rewarded his efforts with a glowing smile that made the radiance of the mid-afternoon sun seem bleak.

Beautiful.

He moved without thought. His hands cupping her face, his body as hot as newly forged steel. Wide, shining eyes peered up at him as his thumb slowly traced her lower lip. He pressed a kiss to the corner of her mouth. The warm breath from her parted lips brushed his cheek.

Forcing himself to step back, he stared into her misted gaze. 'We must go,' he said quietly. 'Now.'

Taking her hand, they walked to where Black stood nibbling tufts of greenery.

'Thank you for bringing me here,' she said, as he grasped the dangling reins and began leading them toward the trees. Her head was bowed and he wondered if she referred to the glade or to Closeburn itself.

Where the meadow collided with the forest, he lifted her and carried her through the shadowed wood. Holding her seemed right, natural. She relaxed in his arms and he rested his chin on the crown of her head, his mount trailing close behind.

Light penetrated the dimness as they neared the exit on the opposite side of the forest. William's chest tightened, as did his arms. The world would rush in the moment they left the trees. He didn't want their interlude to end, not yet.

Beneath the boughs of an ancient oak, he reluctantly released his hold and her slender form slid down his length. As he tucked stray wisps of red-gold behind her ears, slim fingers stilled his hands.

'I want to stay.' Her softly spoken words stunned him. 'I know we agreed on my leaving once Leslie's babe is born, but...'

Filtered light painted her face. Her eyes were large, her gaze direct.

'Why?' His heart knocked against his ribs.

'You have no healer. I like it here.'

'Are these your only reasons for wanting to stay? Honesty is important to me, Lynelle.' His heart pounded on the wall of his chest. Here was her chance to unburden the secret she'd concealed with a kiss.

'You,' she whispered. 'I want to be with you.'

His heart soared, but he needed more.

'Is it possible?' he asked.

She frowned. 'I don't understand.'

William lowered his hands and turned them so he was left holding hers. He loathed what he was about to do, but he had to know. He would have asked the same questions this night, if she hadn't broached the subject first.

'Is there nae one waiting for your return?'

'No.' She pulled her fingers from his grasp. Her lashes dipped, hiding her thoughts, once again.

His shoulders stiffened. Cupping her chin, he tilted her face up and searched her expression. Her gaze flickered and danced like a startled deer's. Why?

His body tensed. Forcing a light tone, he said, 'Will nae one sicken without your skills? Will nae avenging brother ride to your rescue?' She slowly shook her head. 'Nae irate father wanting to spill my blood?' he finished softly.

'If anyone cared, do you not think they would have come for me already?' A hint of bitterness scored her voice. Sadness clouded her eyes. 'Truly, there is no one.'

'Then it is my greatest wish for you to remain here.'

Lowering his head, he pressed a gentle kiss to her lips, hoping to erase her hurt and his guilt for causing it. He released her mouth while he still could. 'We'd best return, else Mary will have the entire clan searching for us.'

She gave him a true smile. He gathered Black's leather reins and they stepped out into the sunshine. Walking side by side, they headed back to the castle. The tension had eased from his body but his thoughts ran riot.

Where were they to go from here? He loved her, but did she feel the same for him? Wanting to be with him wasn't a declaration of love and if she did, she'd just missed the perfect opportunity to tell him, as well as the chance to share whatever troubled her. Such strong emotions were new to him and he suddenly shied away from revealing the secrets of his heart.

The castle came into view as they rounded a bend in the path. Raised voices filled the air. Narrowing his gaze, William studied the scene and the six mounted men clustered on the landside of Castle Loch. Numerous clansmen lined the banks on the opposite side, shouting at the intruders.

He turned to Lynelle and grasped her upper arms. 'Go back to the forest. Stay out of sight until I come for you.'

Placing a quick kiss on her mouth, he threw himself into the saddle and drew his sword from the scabbard secured to Black's flank.

'Who are they?'

'I don't know, but they're English.' He tore his gaze from the unwelcome strangers and looked down at Lynelle. 'Go into the trees, Lynelle. You'll be safe there.'

Black leapt forward at his silent command and thundered toward those who dared to invade his domain. Six against one were terrible odds, but as he drew closer he turned his mount slightly to the left, keeping the Englishmen between himself and the loch. If a fight ensued, he'd do his best to drive as many of the curs as he could into the water.

He drew his mount to a halt as Donald's voice rang clear and loud.

'Naught here belongs to you.'

'I will not go anywhere until you return what is rightfully mine.' Anger vibrated in the clipped English tone.

Fury ignited in William's blood. 'What precisely do you think we have that is yours?' He didn't shout, but the authority in his tone caused all six intruders to turn and face him.

The older man who'd delivered the threat nudged his horse to the forefront.

Leaning forward, crossing his wrists, William patiently withstood the man's lengthy perusal of himself and his drawn sword.

'Give me my son's horse and we will leave.'

His son's horse?

'Who are you?' William asked.

'I am John Fenwick, lord of Fenwick Keep.'

Running footsteps sounded. William spun about in his saddle and his heart plummeted to his toes. 'Stop, Lynelle.' With a jerk of his knees, Black shifted into her path. She dodged his mount, and without looking his way she pulled up near the English lord.

'Father!' she cried. 'You came.'

Father?

William stiffened. Her father was an English lord.

Truly, there is no one.

William stared at Lynelle. Pain twisted his heart.

'The horse was a gift to my son, my heir, for his last birthday.' The English voice penetrated the thick haze that was fogging William's mind. He saw Lynelle's smile slip, watched as her complexion paled.

'I've come for what's mine. Give me the horse and I will be on my way.'

William looked at John Fenwick and stared into cold, blue eyes. 'Donald,' William called.

'Aye.'

'Fetch the mount we borrowed from Lord Fenwick.'

The nobleman nodded and his mouth turned up at the ends in what William took to be a smile, though it looked more like a sneer.

Footfalls behind William drew his attention. He turned and watched as Keita's steps faltered. 'What is it, lass?'

'I've come for Lynelle,' she said as she eyed the strangers. 'Leslie's babe is coming.'

William peered at Lynelle. Her gaze was fixed on her father, her face crestfallen.

With a nod, William gestured for Keita to approach Lynelle, who jumped as the young woman touched her arm. 'Lynelle, Leslie needs your help.'

'Oh.' She looked up at him. Heart twisting further, William stared down at her. He had no clue as to his expression but Lynelle's face suddenly bleached of all remaining colour. 'Oh, of course.' She ducked her head and then left with Keita for the village.

Stunned, anger igniting beneath his skin, William sat his mount and watched her go. Why hadn't she told him who her father was? What other untruths had she shared? What other secrets did she hide?

The horse they'd used to drag Edan's litter was being brought across the loch on the flat-topped barge, along with Donald, Dougal and their horses.

'Are you Scots so barbaric or so desperate you would trust a cursed woman, a murderer, to birth your children?'

William slowly turned and witnessed the smirks on the faces of John Fenwick's men. They'd obviously heard their lord's comments and agreed. But Lord Fenwick's slight of William's people paled in comparison to how he spoke of Lynelle. The woman he loved. The woman who'd lied to him.

Muscles bunching and flexing as anger swelled into a controlled rage, William coaxed Black nearer to Lord Fenwick and leaned in close. 'Are you English so stiff or so unmanly you fail to acknowledge a daughter of your own blood?'

Lord Fenwick's lip curled. 'I have no daughter.'

William eased back in his saddle and studied the English lord. 'Aye, it seems I was mistaken.' He clutched the hilt of his sword. 'Lynelle has too much strength, too much courage to have sprung from your weak seed.'

Instead of drawing his sword, as William hoped, the nobleman blustered under his breath as his face mottled with rage.

'Here is your son's horse.' William turned to his men. 'Donald, Dougal, escort this English scum off my lands.'

Chapter 26

Lynelle struggled to put one foot in front of the other. Her heart sat like a rock in her chest. It hurt to breathe.

William's expression, a mixture of shock and accusation, haunted her. She flinched at the memory. What must he think of her now he knew who she was? What she was? Now he knew she'd lied?

Keita continued relaying Leslie's condition, but Lynelle only caught snippets through the buzzing sound and jumbled thoughts filling her head.

The gossamer thread of hope she'd foolishly clung to regarding her father had snapped and shrivelled to naught when he'd refused to even look at her. Strangely, she'd suffered not a twinge of pain as it broke and it had taken a moment for her to realise she was finally free.

But at what price?

A tortured cry split the air. Lynelle blinked and focused on the door Keita stepped forward to open. The young lass then chose to remain outside.

Heat from the fire splashed Lynelle's face as she entered Leslie's cottage. She swallowed past the lump of trepidation in her throat and looked around the stifling room.

Several iron pots of water bubbled in the centre of the flames. Linen strips, along with a sharp knife, herbs for cleansing and the lavender ointment she'd prepared days ago, all sat on a small rickety table nearby.

Elspeth nodded her welcome from beside the pallet where Leslie's bulging form reclined, and continued mopping the expectant mother's brow. Another wail of pain bounced off the roof and Leslie's wide eyes rounded further before clenching shut.

Lynelle shuddered. Why in God's name had she promised to aid Leslie in childbirth when she'd never even witnessed a babe entering the world?

Her stomach churned and beads of sweat popped out along her forehead. She couldn't do this. What if something went wrong? What if she made a mistake? What if one of them...?

'Bless you...' Leslie panted. 'For coming ... lass.' She offered a strained smile.

Pretending to feel confident for Leslie's sake, Lynelle smiled back. 'I gave you my word,' she said and made quick use of the cleansing herbs to wash her hands.

Knowing Elspeth had experienced two births of her own, and had assisted in others, boosted Lynelle's fragile confidence. The older woman murmured constant words of praise as she bathed Leslie's damp brow, and regularly peered beneath the sheet draping Leslie's bent knees to ascertain the babe's progress.

Lavender scented the hot, confined space as Lynelle rubbed salve onto Leslie's swollen belly and aching back. Her fingers grew numb as Leslie clutched her offered hand during numerous ongoing contractions.

Elspeth announced it was time, and things proceeded swiftly.

After a last grunting push, Lynelle held a wrinkled, mottled little girl in her hands and a tremulous cry filled the room.

Elspeth held the babe as Lynelle cut and secured the cord with a strip of boiled leather, and then took the precious bundle away to be washed while Lynelle took care of Leslie.

With the bedding changed, the room set to rights and Leslie crooning softly to the miracle in her arms, Elspeth sent Keita to fetch Hearn, the worried first-time father.

The big man's troubled face brightened as he crossed the threshold, his broad-grin easily seen through his thick, reddish beard.

Lynelle accepted the couple's words of gratitude and congratulated them again. She left them to their joy and along with Elspeth left the cottage and stepped out into the coming night.

Keita waited outside and told them Ian had dashed to the castle to pass on the good news.

'Come home with us, Lynelle,' Elspeth said.

'Aye,' Keita said. 'Supper awaits and there's plenty to go about.'

Lynelle's stomach shrivelled at the prospect of food, though she hadn't eaten all day. 'Thank you, but no. I have a few things I need to attend to in the healing cottage.'

'If you change your mind, come and join us,' Elspeth said with a smile.

Lynelle turned to go and paused. 'I appreciate your help today, Elspeth. I couldn't have gotten through it without you.'

'You would have managed, lass.'

A small smile tilted the corners of Lynelle's mouth. With a nod, she left mother and daughter and walked through the deepening shadows to the far end of the village.

The familiar scents of tansy and meadowsweet assailed her as she entered the cottage she'd been using during her visits to the village. Lighting a new candle, she held it aloft and gazed about the single room. The smell, the plants and pots all reminded her of the shack she'd lived in at Fenwick.

Sadness welled inside her. Not because she missed where she'd grown up, but because it seemed she'd ended up in the same situation in a different place.

Only she hadn't fallen in love at Fenwick.

Tears threatened. She willed them away. Despite being exhausted in mind and body, she washed from head to toe with cold water, hesitating as she discovered William's loving still marking her inner thighs.

The glade, the brook, his touch, his tenderness, the sunbeams tinting his dark hair as he made love to her, making her feel beautiful and special, rushed back.

You should have been honest. You should have told him everything.

Biting her lower lip, she tucked the precious memories away and bathed all trace of him from her skin. How she wished it were so easy to cleanse him from her heart.

Donning the same shift, she made up a pallet on the floor using an old woollen blanket and wondered if William was sleeping in the massive bed they'd shared only last night.

She sat on the makeshift bed, pretending the rough fabric was silk and didn't cause her skin to itch. Pulling her cloak to her waist, her shoulders sagged. What was she to do? Where could she go? Not back to Fenwick. Not now, not ever.

But could she remain at Closeburn, knowing she'd see William? Would he allow her to stay?

She doubted he would want anything to do with her now he knew who and what she was. An outcast. A murderer. *A liar.* It would be easy for him to forget her. He'd likely banish her as he had Jinny.

She collapsed back on the bedding, tugging her threadbare cloak to her chin. The tallow candle shrank beneath the flame's heat, flickered, hissed and finally guttered as one of the village roosters shouted dawn's arrival.

Spending the full night thinking hadn't given her the answer as to whether she should remain or move on. But she had made a decision regarding another important matter.

She was tired of wondering what tomorrow would bring. Until recently, she'd wasted her life waiting, believing she would eventually find favour with her father, but no more. Never again would she allow her life to be ruled by the whims of another. She'd never survive the waiting again.

Not even for William.

Tears lay wet on her cheeks when Lynelle finally drifted to sleep.

***

William stalked the length of the dark, narrow landing of the keep's upper level. He'd gained not an ounce of peace from his reckless afternoon ride. He'd avoided visiting Edan after leaving his wind-blown, sweat-matted mount to the stable hands and had growled at Mary when she'd asked if something was wrong. Even Ian's news of Leslie and Hearn's healthy babe had failed to shed any brightness on his black mood.

He couldn't sit or eat and hadn't bothered attempting to sleep. Deeming himself unfit company for the pigs lounging about in their muddied pens, he'd prowled the passageway outside the laird's chamber, his chamber, well into the godforsaken night.

Halting before the iron-studded door, he rested his forehead on the cool timber, reminding himself it was his right to enter the room. He'd spent the last two nights within, but he hadn't been alone and he feared a new string of memories would rise to haunt him if he dared to step inside. Not only private memories, but ones more pleasurable, more real, because they were shared.

His heart howled in silent grief and he hammered it mute with thoughts of Lynelle's mistrust. Why couldn't she have told him about her father? Who had she murdered? She'd said no one had died while in her care. Had she lied about that too? And he'd allowed her to tend to Edan.

A shudder racked him. Thank God Edan had survived.

Would she leave now she'd fulfilled her promise to Leslie? Where would she go? Back to Fenwick, and a father who didn't have the courage to spare his daughter a glance?

William clenched his jaw and his fingers curled into fists at the thought of John Fenwick. If her mother had died moments after her birth and her sire acted as if she didn't exist, how had she grown into such a caring, giving, beautiful woman?

Almighty Christ. He still loved her even though she hadn't trusted him enough to tell him about her life, about herself.

He'd opened his heart and soul, revealed parts of himself he'd never spoken of before. Perhaps he had because he loved her. Perhaps she hadn't because she didn't love him.

His chest constricted.

He was a fool, but even fools deserved answers.

Tomorrow he would use any means, any method of persuasion to discover her every secret, and he would hear them from her own sweet lips.

Chapter 27

A sharp knock woke Lynelle.

Keita popped her head inside. 'I've brought you something to break your fast.'

'Oh,' Lynelle said as she stretched her stiff limbs and rubbed sleep from her eyes. 'What time of day is it?'

'Mid-morn,' Keita said as she balanced the tray she carried and closed the door. 'When mother left at dawn, she said not to wake you too early, as you needed your rest.'

'Your mother is a clever woman,' she said, sitting up. 'Where did she go at dawn?'

'Arthur and Blair returned at first light.' Lynelle accepted the tray handed down to her. 'I've not seen her since.'

'I'll introduce myself to them after I visit the new babe.' She scooped some egg and a piece of oat bannock onto her spoon and ate, suddenly realizing how hungry she was. 'This is delicious.'

Keita smiled.

'Where is Carney?' Lynelle asked, sinking her teeth into the brown husk of bread.

'He's working, or playing rather, in the vegetable garden with Ian.'

'Ian has been a great help to your family, hasn't he?'

'Oh, aye. I'm so glad the laird sent him to us.' Keita blushed.

At the mention of William, Lynelle lost her appetite.

'This is lovely, Keita, but I'm afraid there is too much for me to finish.' She drank the cup of watered wine and rose to her knees.

'Never fear. The pigs will soon scoff anything you leave.' She took back the tray. 'I'll let you dress and see you later.'

Lynelle expressed her thanks again as Keita left her alone. She pulled the gown she'd removed last night over her head, folded the bedding, plaited her hair and opened the single shutter on the rear wall of the cottage.

As she stared at the sun-warmed grasses and assortment of trees to the west, she wondered how many times Closeburn's previous healer had admired this view from where she now stood.

Before she'd been banished.

Perhaps Lynelle could search Jinny out in Thornhill and live with her there. She smiled, for it was the first idea she'd had that held any promise. By day's end, she hoped to come up with many more. She had to.

Leaving her cloak, she stepped outside. Eager to meet the newly returned couple, she waited for any sign of movement from the neighbouring cottage. Nothing. She turned her gaze to the rest of the clearing and the dozen or so generously spaced thatched homes that made it a village.

She liked it here. The very air had a welcoming freshness and the people were helpful and friendly. But she had to leave. She had no choice. She couldn't risk staying, knowing she'd see William again.

Tomorrow.

If all were well with the new babe, she'd ask Ian to fetch her meagre belongings from the castle and be on her way at dawn.

As she walked to Leslie's home, a fluttering sadness filled her chest. She'd have to pass on farewell messages to Edan and Mary and all the others who had brightened her existence and given her confidence.

She tapped on the door and stepped inside at the call. Leslie and Hearn lay on their sides, stretched out on the pallet. Their tiny girl slumbered peacefully between them, oblivious to the awe-struck smiles raining down on her.

After being assured their babe was perfect, Lynelle left them to continue gazing adoringly at their bairn and headed back to her cottage.

She'd almost reached her door when Elspeth darted out of the nearby cottage and hurried toward her.

'Stop.'

Lynelle halted in her tracks at the abrupt command and frowned at the older woman's pale, drawn expression.

'What is it, Elspeth? Are you ill?' She wanted to go to her, but Elspeth held up her hand and seemed to be struggling to catch her breath.

''Tis Arthur,' Elspeth said, pressing her hand to her middle, wiping her palm down the front of her gown over and over.

'Is he sick?' Lynelle spoke calmly, though the food she'd eaten started to roil in her stomach. The woman who'd remained steadfastly composed throughout Leslie's birth nodded. 'Then I will see him and–'

'Nae.'

Lynelle flinched at the fierce denial.

'You don't understand,' Elspeth said. 'There is naught to be done.'

'At least let me–'

'Where are Keita and Carney?' Elspeth looked about the clearing, her eyes wild.

'In the vegetable garden with Ian.'

Elspeth stopped her agitated search and nodded continuously. 'Good. Good.'

'Please Elspeth, tell me what's wrong. You're frightening me.'

Elspeth stilled and gazed at her. 'Oh, lass. I'm frightened too.' Her voice wavered and fear shone in her troubled eyes.

Lynelle stepped forward. Elspeth retreated.

'Don't come near me, Lynelle.' Renewed strength hardened her tone.

'Why? If Arthur is ill, why can't I–?'

'Because I may be sick, too.'

Lynelle stiffened. Elspeth didn't look ill, despite her ashen pallor. Frightened, yes. Agitated, for certain. But what made her think she might be sick?

'I want to help, Elspeth, but I can't if you won't tell me what's wrong.'

Elspeth's expression softened and her usual composure suddenly returned. 'You're such a good, lass.' A strained smile touched her lips. 'But I fear your skills won't be enough this time.'

Puzzled, she said, 'At least let me try.'

'I believe Arthur has the Black Death.'

The world tilted. Lynelle sucked in a deep breath as her mind swam with recollections of what Ada had told her.

Ada had been a child when the pestilence swept into northern England. She'd survived, as had most of those tightly secured inside Fenwick's walls, but hundreds had died. Thousands.

Driving fisted hands into her stomach, she willed the gorge rising in her throat back down. What use was she to anyone if merely hearing the words made her panic? She needed to think. What should she do?

Leave. Now. What difference did a single day make?

She stared at Elspeth and tears of anger at her cowardly thought, prickled behind her eyes.

No! She would not run away in fear.

'I'm sorry I've upset you,' Elspeth said quietly.

Lynelle's eyes burned hotter. 'You ... surprised me.'

Elspeth nodded. 'I was shocked too, but I feel a tad easier now I've spoken of it to someone.'

'Are you certain?' Lynelle couldn't suppress the note of hope in her voice.

'Blair says Arthur started feeling unwell three days ago. She urged him to rest, but he refused. The fever came two days past and though she begged him to stop, he wouldn't. He kept telling her he wanted to be home.' Elspeth drew a ragged breath. 'They travelled through the night and he collapsed on the bed the moment he walked through the door.'

'In my haste to welcome them home,' she continued, a tinge of bitterness edging her tone, 'I comforted Blair and helped her restrain Arthur when he started thrashing about. We removed his shirt to bathe the heat from his body and ... and that's when I noticed the dark swelling under his arm.'

Lynelle stiffened, all hope of Elspeth being wrong banished by what she described.

'Does Blair know? Does she understand?'

'Nae,' Elspeth said. 'She is too distraught and weary.'

Lynelle's mind raced. 'We must inform the others. Certain measures need to be taken.'

They stood perhaps ten feet apart, but the distance suddenly seemed far greater. Sorrow crept back into the older woman's eyes.

'I know. I'll leave it to you.' Elspeth started to turn away and then swung back around. 'Tell Keita and Carney...' Her gaze dropped to the ground. 'Ask Ian to watch over them.'

Lynelle bit her lip as Elspeth headed back to Arthur and Blair's home. 'I'll see you in a little while,' she said, but Elspeth gave no sign she'd heard.

Dragging in a shaky breath, Lynelle gazed at the peaceful village. On such a beautiful day, the men would be working their small fields or tending animals or mending fences. The women would either be helping or cooking or washing clothes. The children...

She swallowed. She had no clue as to how the contagion spread. Was it already too late for the people in the village? Squeezing her eyes shut, she hoped not. But if it was she'd do all in her power to make sure it went no further.

The castle folk must be kept away. Including William. Her heart ached just thinking of him. He would come, she knew. He might despise her for not telling him exactly who she was, but his pride would demand the reasons why. She had to find a way to stop him, to keep him safe. It wouldn't be easy. She needed help.

Forcing her feet to move, she went in search of Ian and prayed to God for strength and to the Saints that He was listening.

***

William leapt from the boat and glared up at the sun. The ball of fire seemed to glare back as it slowly descended in the sky. His initial fury on waking at noon had eased, thanks to Mary's heated outburst.

'Tired of your temper.' That was the start of her set-down.

'We searched the laird's chamber, the stables and asked Geordie if he'd taken you across the loch.' How was anyone to know he'd slipped into Lynelle's chamber before dawn and slept within the bedding still thick with her scent? He'd almost believed she was lying beside him.

'Edan thinks you're angry with him.' The final part of Mary's tirade, and the most condemning.

He'd visited his brother, a necessary delay, and assured Edan his foul disposition had naught to do with him.

It was her fault.

She'd broken through his defences, made him love her and then tossed his shattered heart back at him with her lies.

He followed the curve of the track, doubling his pace to match his escalating pulse. Soon. He would lay eyes on her soon.

***

'Lynelle,' Keita said as she entered the cottage. 'The laird is coming.'

No! Not yet. She'd left Ian to watch for anyone approaching the village and knew she only had a few moments to reach the village outskirts before William did.

With a last glance at the tiny face of the babe in her arms, she passed her into Leslie's hands. 'Keita, will you help Hearn move the last of their necessities?'

'Aye.'

Hastening out the door, she almost collided with one of the women carrying a bundle of essentials. After she had broken the dreadful news to Ian, he'd called the villagers together and she'd told them the situation. They needed to know everything, deserved to know. She'd been almost brutal in her honesty, both regarding the plague's ferocity and her lack of knowledge about how to deal with it.

Wide eyes, gaping mouths and ashen faces had stared at her and she'd felt vile and evil for being the one to evoke their fear. Ian had stood tall and pale beside her until Keita had asked after her mother, and Lynelle had revealed the horrible truth. Dashing forward, Ian had caught Keita before she fell, and drew Carney's small body into the embrace.

After the initial shock, together they decided it was wise to move everyone into the first four cottages nearest the entrance to the village. It would be cramped and uncomfortable, but if shifting far away from those already afflicted without leaving the village saved lives, she didn't expect any complaints from any of those concerned.

Their laird's reaction would be another matter entirely.

She walked past Keita's cottage, the closest to the entrance of the small community, and continued a few paces along the path. The temptation to keep going niggled, but she thrust the awful whisper aside and stopped.

'Please God, give me courage,' she said softly.

A flicker of movement signalled William's arrival. He strode purposely toward her. Each long, powerful stride was an action of natural grace. Her heart shivered at the sight of him, then stilled as he lifted his dark head, revealing the look on his face.

'What in God's name...?'

The deep tone of his voice rippled through her. Gritting her teeth, she squared her shoulders and steeled herself against his effect on her.

'Stop. Please,' she said as he reached the wooden barricade the men had erected across the path, about a dozen feet away from the village's entrance.

'You think to keep me out of *my* village?'

'Never. But I hope once you hear what I have to say, you will choose not to come any further.' Life was all about choice. Another valuable lesson she'd learned here.

'What can *you* possibly...?'

'If you hold your tongue, I'll tell you,' she said, cutting him off.

'And you expect me to believe you?'

Pain seared her chest. 'In this, I do, yes.'

He folded his arms across his chest and stared at her.

Clasping her hands she said, 'Arthur and Blair returned at dawn, but Arthur is terribly ill.' William's arms dropped to his sides. 'His symptoms are similar to those of the Black Death.'

'What?' He looked behind her. 'Where is he? I'll discern for my...'

'No.' She stepped forward as he made to leap the low timber wall. 'Please, William. 'Tis Elspeth who described the dark lumps under his arms.'

He stilled and looked at her. 'Elspeth?'

'Yes. She awoke early and bid them welcome and stayed to help Blair care for Arthur.'

'Are you certain?'

'No, but I trust Elspeth's word. The people know and we've set measures in place, hoping to stop it spreading.'

'Bloody Christ.' He turned to the side, fists on hips, and stared off into the distance.

Lynelle wanted to give him time to absorb the shock, but time was precious. 'I don't know if other places have been stricken and I have no clue if there is a cure. All I can suggest is that once you return to the castle, lock the gates and let no one in. Confinement is most important.'

'You expect me to run and hide behind my walls? These are my people, Lynelle...'

'I know it's difficult, but it might be too late for the villagers. You have a castle full of clansmen who are unaware of the danger and in need of guidance. You are laird. They need you.'

Her chest ached at his bleak expression. He was trying to find another solution, but there was none to be had. She'd already sorted through other options. She had to sway him, somehow stop him from risking his life in the name of duty or honour.

'Edan needs you,' she said softly. 'You are his only brother, the only family he has left.'

Edan was his weakness, and she believed she'd convinced him, but she continued. 'There is naught more that can be done here, except wait. Two weeks, William. Please.'

'And if it's true, how do you plan to dispose of the dead?'

As morbid as it was, she'd thought about this too. 'The safest and cleanest way is to burn them.'

'Almighty God!'

'I must go,' she said, not daring to give him time to change his mind. There was one more thing she needed to say. 'I'm deeply sorry for not telling you who I was.'

'You should have trusted me.'

'I know.' She swallowed and blinked back threatening tears. 'Be safe, William.'

I love you.

On trembling legs, she turned and walked back to the village.

Chapter 28

William stood as if carved of stone and forced himself not to move, to do nothing but watch her walk away. His fingers bit into the wooden wall, the only outward sign of the battle raging within.

His lack of knowledge about dealing with such a foe slashed his pride, scoured his soul. How could he strike down and defeat an enemy he couldn't see?

Her reasoning made perfect sense. It seemed she'd thought of everything, including what method would be best if her predictions proved real. Christ! Though it galled him to admit it, he'd grown to trust her when it came to caring for his people's ills. How could he not, when her skills and kindness had won over his clansmen, with Edan her greatest champion?

Edan needs you.

It was true that with only a few words of reassurance from William this morning, Edan's expression had changed from wretched to joyous, giving weight to her words. Edan relied on William. Though his young brother was surprisingly mature in some respects, he lacked self-confidence in others, a deficiency William would do all in his power to correct.

Prizing his fingers from the timber, he stared at the point where Lynelle had disappeared and flexed his stiff hands. Despite his confusion and mounting anger when he'd come upon the barrier, he'd had to fight his reaction to her beauty. He'd done well, knowing she couldn't see the quickening of his blood or hear the reckless pounding of his heart.

She'd stood in her worn gown, her fiery hair tamed into a single braid. An aura of strength and determination had shimmered about her, even as she'd relayed such dire suspicions, news he needed to share with the unsuspecting castle folk.

He prayed to God she was wrong.

*** *

Giving Keita's arm a gentle squeeze, Lynelle peered into the large pot of broth she'd asked the young woman to prepare. Tear-tracks marked Keita's pale face, but she offered a tight smile and continued stirring the bubbling brew. The chore gave Keita something to do and Lynelle would make use of the nourishing liquid later.

Ian set down several clay bottles, fitted with stoppers and filled with water, on a table. Carney played with one of the older children whose family had come to share their home until...

Thank God he'd stopped asking for his mother.

Slipping outside, Lynelle visited the three cottages crammed with extra people and made sure they all had enough water and food to last them for ... however long it took. Everyone's spirits seemed high, considering the circumstances, but the air was thick with fear and false gaiety.

The sun was setting by the time she returned to Keita's home. Aware of the curious eyes watching her pack fresh vegetables and water into a sack, she was relieved no one asked why. She didn't want to explain her actions, didn't want to think too deeply about what she planned to do. In her heart she knew she was making the right decision, and that was the only thing that mattered.

She retrieved the small bundle she'd set aside earlier. 'Ian, can you bring the broth outside?'

'Aye.' He left Keita and Carney exclaiming over the carved wooden toys, lifted the pot and followed her outside.

Once they passed the third cottage, lying empty and silent, she stopped and turned to face him. 'This is far enough. Please go back to the others.'

He stared at her, and within moments his puzzled expression altered to one of disbelief. 'You mean to join them, don't you?' His head jerked toward the far end of the village.

'Yes. Please don't waste time or breath. I need to do this.' He wanted to protest. She could see it in his eyes. 'You love Keita, don't you?'

He nodded. 'Aye.'

'Elspeth asked me to tell you to take care of Keita and Carney if ... will you?'

'Aye.'

'You're a good man, Ian. They will all need your guidance and support.' She swallowed. 'Two weeks from today, the laird will return. If no one shows symptoms of illness by then, I believe all will be well. But, and this is most important,' she said, clutching his wrist, 'after two weeks, if none of us answer you when you call, you must burn the cottage.'

'Nae. I can't–'

'Yes, you can. You must.' A look of horror filled his eyes. 'It is the only way.' She loathed heaping such grievous responsibility on one so young, but there was no one else. 'Your word on this, Ian.'

His struggle flitted across his features. 'You have it.'

Relief poured through Lynelle. 'Thank you.'

Ian looked miserable.

Juggling the sack and bundle, she took the broth. 'Go back now, Ian.' She turned and walked away.

Setting all she carried on the ground between the two end cottages, she entered hers and gathered some necessary herbs. She held little faith they would provide a cure.

Dusk's dimming shadows proclaimed the end of another day as she stepped back outside. A tranquil breeze touched her face and she stopped to let it linger. Birds called to one another from the darkened trees that looked like towering giants in the distance. She drew strength from knowing Mother Earth continued as always, despite the threat of impending chaos.

She searched her heart and mind for any sign of regret and heard only a single whisper. Should she have told William she loved him? No. Doing so might have hampered her efforts to send him away. She wasn't certain if he loved her, but he did have feelings for her. He must, for how else could he touch her with burning softness? She'd seen the light in his eyes when he joined with her.

With a sense of peace and warmth filling her chest, she piled the goods in her arms and tapped on the cottage door with the toe of her boot.

A few moments passed before Elspeth's voice sounded through the wood. 'Who is it?'

'Hurry, Elspeth. My arms grow weary.'

'Dear Lord. Go away, Lynelle.'

'No. Let me in.' Her limbs truly were starting to ache.

'You are stubborn,' Elspeth said. The latch rattled and the door opened a crack. 'You shouldn't have come.'

'I'm a healer. Where my skills are needed, I will go.'

The crack widened, revealing Elspeth's expression of remorse mingled with relief.

'Please, Elspeth. Stop shaking your head and help me.'

After swift introductions to Blair, the slight, hollow-eyed woman kneeling beside her slumbering husband's pallet, Lynelle set the broth over the flames and added two pots of water to boil.

'Elspeth, we must always have water boiling,' Lynelle said softly, looking into the corner occupied by husband and wife. 'Once the water cools, we will bathe Arthur with one lot and use the other to wash our hands, before and after we touch him.'

Elspeth nodded.

Lynelle ground feverfew and added it to a small amount of broth. She carried two bowls to Blair, asking her to coax Arthur to take some of the soup containing the herbs. She then sprinkled lavender oil about his bedding, hoping the natural calming properties would help them all.

Late the same night, Blair was struck with a fever. They placed her on a pallet beside her husband and dribbled broth mixed with herbs into the their mouths. Blair seemed at peace, lying as quietly as Arthur now did. They bathed her from head to toe and found several dark masses in the crease of her upper thigh.

As they worked, Lynelle said, 'Be careful not to burst the swellings. I fear they are full of poisoned blood.'

Elspeth's hand stilled where she worked, cooling Blair's chest.

Lynelle looked up and found Elspeth staring at her with terror-stricken eyes.

'Elspeth. What's wrong?'

Elspeth peered down at her hands. 'When I first bathed Arthur, I washed beneath his arms. He groaned and jerked and my nail scored the lump under his arm. That is how I first noticed the dark swelling.'

A chill swept through Lynelle. 'I am not certain, Elspeth.'

Elspeth nodded and Lynelle heard her swallow. Then she ducked her head to hide her fear for her friend.

The ill pair suffered bouts of delirium and sleep. Lynelle and Elspeth bathed them, encouraged them to take in broth, paced and dozed wherever they sat.

Two days after her initial fever, Blair died. As if sensing his wife no longer lived, Arthur joined her in death a few hours later.

Leaving them where they lay, Lynelle covered them with linen cloths and joined a weeping Elspeth on the opposite side of the room. Lynelle did her best to remain encouraging, but it was difficult to look into

Elspeth's fearful, sunken eyes. Neither of them slept, as exhausted as they were.

Elspeth's fever started with a shiver. 'I'm glad you came,' she said to Lynelle when she knew she hadn't been spared. She fought well, calling for Keita and Carney whenever she woke. Lynelle doubled her useless efforts.

Three days later, moments before dawn, Elspeth's struggle ended.

Lynelle draped Elspeth's body with linen and knelt beside her friend. Dry-eyed, numb, her gaze roamed over the three that no longer were. Days ago she'd witnessed the miracle of birth, and now she'd experienced the cruelty of death.

Was she next? Not yet. There was one more thing she had to do.

Wresting her way to her feet, she stripped out of her gown and set a torch to flame. Shuffling to the door in shift and boots, she opened it, stepped through and closed it behind her.

Cool morning splashed her face and bare arms. She stumbled a few paces into the clearing and turned to stare at the death-ridden cottage. Sucking in huge gulps of fresh air, she sent a prayer to the heavens for the souls within and with an exhausted groan, threw the flickering torch upon the roof.

Fire caught quickly, devouring the thatched roof in moments. Red-hot flames crackled, as thick swirls of dark smoke tumbled high, marring dawn's pale sky. The scent of burning stole the sweetness from the air. Heat stretched out to meet her, drying the tears spilling down her cheeks. Guilt for not saving them almost drove her to her knees.

She removed her boots and hose with trembling hands and tossed them into the thriving blaze. Her heart ached. Her head pounded, every inch of her hurt.

No more. No more. Please, no more.

Spinning about, she staggered to her cottage and sealed herself inside. Bone weary, she slid down the wooden door, clutching her knees to her chest. She'd seen the pain the three afflicted with the pestilence had suffered, knew exactly what to expect.

But as exhausted as she was, she couldn't sleep. Resting her chin on her knees, she waited for death to come.

Chapter 29

On William's return to the castle, he and Geordie dragged the rowboat and barge from the loch, securing both onto land. They closed and barred the massive gates and while Geordie called together every clansman in the bailey, from stable hands to blacksmith and the guards on the battlements, William carried Edan from his chamber and summoned the people inside the keep.

When everyone had gathered in the great hall, William relayed Lynelle's grim suspicions and gave strict instructions for the next two weeks. Not a single person was to leave the castle grounds and absolutely no one from outside the walls was permitted entry inside, including those from the village.

Horrified stares met his, for many friendships had been struck between villagers and castle folk. None however, matched the pain in Geordie's eyes. Guilt filled William's chest, for he had sent Geordie's son Ian to the village as a form of punishment, a decision well accepted by all involved – until now.

'I'm sorry,' William said, grasping the man's slumped shoulder.

'Ian's a strong lad,' Geordie said, straightening. 'He'll do well.'

The guards resumed their posts, but many had families. With Donald's help, William reduced each man's time patrolling the walls, ordering them to inform William of any unusual activity coming from the village, no matter how small it seemed.

Having appraised the stores of grain, meat and ale, Malcolm assured William they had more than enough to see them through the allotted time, and longer if necessary. The hunt William had planned could wait.

William spent the daylight hours in the great hall with his people, Edan never far from his side and never out of his sight. Foreboding thickened the air of the crowded hall as William roamed from group to group, offering hope he didn't feel.

Mary, bless her, did the same, digging out several old chessboards and dusty knuckles, encouraging play. After supper on the second evening, she managed to coax one of the men to strum his lute and convinced a few to dance. Their steps were heavy, their laughter forced.

Meeting on their rounds one evening, William pulled the older woman aside. Low voiced, he asked Mary to tell him all she knew of the Black Death. The symptoms she described were gruesome, the outcome crushing.

Each night, William accompanied Edan back to his chamber, the climb slow, his brother refusing to be hefted about like a babe any more.

William didn't complain about the drawn-out process. He had plenty of time. Too much time to think of the hell his people in the village might be suffering. An abundance of time to worry over the woman he loved and missed, every dragging moment of every cursed day.

He'd resumed his place in the chair beside Edan's bed, finding little rest. Each night, once certain his brother slept deeply, he slipped from the room to peer at the village from the laird's chamber above, and he did the same before daybreak. He didn't doubt the sentries in their duties, but he needed to look for himself.

With the passing of each long day and even longer nights, the false hope he tried to bestow on his clan flickered to life and began to grow. But as he stood staring out the window into the darkness on the fifth night, even his burgeoning hope couldn't erase the feelings of powerlessness swamping his soul.

It wasn't a new sensation. He'd experienced it before. Using the time of enforced idleness, he'd searched for the source and discovered an undeniable link.

At the onset of illness or the moment of mishap – whichever befell his family, his loved ones – he'd suffered the same sinking, restless anger now bruising his heart. He'd paced, he'd brooded, he'd demanded that something be done, but all the while he'd done naught to help. Hadn't known what to do. Couldn't find a way to fix it, them, to make everything right. He'd been useless, as he was now.

He'd cast the blame on Jinny for their deaths, banishing her for her inept efforts. But at least she'd tried, done everything in her power to save them, while he ... he'd done nothing.

Just as Lynelle now risked all to protect his people.

Oh, God!

He drove his fist into the stone wall, relishing the pain. His claim of mistrusting healers held no truth. They were the victims of *his* helplessness.

Dragging shaking hands through his hair, William strode the length of the room as his heart twisted and his mind screamed. He wanted to do *something,* go to the village and help, but the image of Edan's frightened face loomed in his head. How could he leave his brother alone, perhaps never to return?

Two weeks, William. Please.

Lynelle's fervent plea echoed in his ears. The vision of her loveliness and her beauty from within, rushed over him in waves and stole his breath.

Did it really matter who she was? Did it truly matter that she hadn't enlightened him when she'd trusted him, gifted him, with her innocence, her passion?

No!

Could he repay her by racing to the village, ignoring her heartfelt appeal?

The least he could do was grant her the fourteen days she'd requested. The first week was almost over. He could wait another, couldn't he?

William left the chamber and re-entered Edan's. He'd been gone longer than usual and made certain his brother still slept. Assured that his absence hadn't been noted, he sank into the chair by the bedside.

The feeling of powerlessness hadn't eased; it pressed on his head and body as if the sky had fallen down around him. He prayed for strength to bear his helplessness, heavier now, since he'd defined its cause. And he hoped to God he'd made the right choice.

Rising from his seat, before the sun rose in the east, he crept up the stairs to his room and took up his place in front of the open window. Flexing his bruised hand, he searched the awakening landscape. Relief pulsed through him as a peaceful dawn heralded the beginning of the sixth day.

A puff of thick black smoke curled into the sky above the village. A stabbing pain pierced William's chest, a sickening moment before a guard's cry sounded from below.

His intention to honour Lynelle's plea for time crumbled to dust.

He ran from the chamber, flew down the steps and burst into Edan's chamber. 'Edan, I have to–'

'Go,' his brother finished for him. Edan turned away from the window and looked at William. 'I know.'

Running feet echoed on the stairs outside the room. The guards were coming to tell him what he'd already seen for himself.

'The smoke is a bad sign, isn't it?'

'Aye,' William said, crossing to Edan's side.

'You've been looking for such a sign each morning and night, haven't you?'

'Aye,' he said again, startled that his brother had been aware of his absences but hadn't said a word. 'Edan,' he said, only to be interrupted again.

'I know you love me, Will. But you can't keep holding back from what you need to do because you're scared of leaving me alone.'

Stunned, William stared at his brother and then crushed him against his chest.

A knock, then 'Laird–'

'Saddle Black, open the gate and set the barge,' he said without releasing Edan.

'Aye.' Quick steps rang back down the stairwell.

'Please be careful, Will.'

William's arms tightened and he pressed a kiss on the top of Edan's dark head. 'And you, brother.'

Letting go was the hardest thing he'd ever done. He strode to the door and turned around. 'Edan, if I don't come back, be sure to marry a pretty lass and have hundreds of bairns.'

Some of the colour leached from Edan's young face, but he rallied. 'You'll be back. I know it.'

'You seem to know a lot in your old age, lad.'

Edan nodded. 'I kept telling you how wise I was, but you wouldn't listen.'

'I won't err again,' William said softly.

'See you don't. Now go.'

William turned and raced down the steps. Donald met him at the base of the stairwell. He nodded in greeting and gazed upon the sleepy-eyed clansmen filling the hall. 'I must go,' he said loud enough for all to hear. 'While I'm gone, you must adhere to Donald's command.'

Striding out into the bailey, he stopped Donald's protest saying, 'Nae, you're not going with me. I need you to take care of Edan and guide him, if necessary.'

He slapped Donald on the back as they reached the gates and slipped through the opening. 'Ground the barge once you arrive back, and bar the gates.' Vigorous energy surged through him, replacing the gaping emptiness, as he walked the grassy slope to the pier.

'I'm coming with you,' Geordie called from the loch. 'And I'll not take nae for an answer.'

'I welcome your company, Geordie.' How could he refuse the man, knowing his son was all he had left?

Stepping onto the floating barge, he took Black's reins from Geordie, leaving the man free to see to his own mount. Donald took them across the loch and once he'd delivered them to shore, he started back the way he'd come.

With a wave, William and Geordie gained their saddles and thundered toward the village. The smell of burning timber and earth grew stronger as they neared their destination. William tried to convince himself the sickening odour of scorched flesh underlying the scent was all in his mind.

They halted at the wooden barrier and jumped to the ground. As William made to leap the barricade, he noticed Geordie falter and glanced into his ashen face.

'I need you to stay and watch the horses,' William ordered. 'The smoke will likely spook them.'

He cleared the barrier and ran to the first hut. Thumping on the door with his fist, he looked to the far end of the village, where a smouldering heap marked the place where a cottage once stood.

'It's William Kirkpatrick,' he said, pounding the wood again.

The door opened. Ian slipped outside and closed it again, but not before William glimpsed half a dozen tear-streaked faces and heard their muffled sobs.

'How many were in there?'

'Four. I tried to stop Lynelle from going, but she–'

Pain pierced William's heart. 'Name them.'

'Arthur and Blair, Elspeth and Lynelle.'

William swallowed the bile rising in his throat. 'Who burned the cottage?'

'Lynelle set the fire at dawn.'

'You saw her?'

'Aye, but not the others.'

His heart jolted and thudded in his chest. 'What happened after she set the fire?'

'She went to her cottage. She was ... stumbling.'

Lord God!

'Is anyone else ill?'

'Nae.'

'Thank Christ.'

"Tis glad I am to see you, laird.'

'Aye, lad. But there is someone waiting at the barrier who I'm sure you'd rather see.'

'My Da?'

William nodded.

'I can't risk it yet,' Ian said. 'We've still another eight days before–'

'You can wait, Ian, but I can't.' William started heading further into the village.

'But Lynelle said two weeks. I promised–'

'I promised too, Ian. But what if she's sick and needs help? I'm tired of waiting and doing nothing.' He was terrified he was already too late.

He marched to the end of the village, seeing small flames still flickering in the ruins across the way. He turned from the ugly sight and rapped on Lynelle's door. Nothing. He knocked harder. 'Lynelle. It's William. Open the door.'

No denial, no protest about him breaking his word. His hands shook as he reached for the latch and pushed the door inward. It didn't move. He pushed harder, to no avail, suddenly aware that something must be barring the door from the inside.

Bending his knees, trying to erase the agonizing image of Lynelle's body causing the obstruction, he pressed his shoulder to the wood and forced the door open.

He stepped through the gap and found Lynelle lying face down on the earthen floor, the skin of her bare legs and arms tinged blue.

Stabbing pain pierced his heart and he fell to his knees beside her. He turned her over and gathered her against his chest. Her head lolled over the back of his arm. Placing unsteady fingers on the cold flesh of her neck, he strained to feel any sign of life. A faint fluttering tickled his fingertips and a relieved groan shuddered from his lips.

He searched her body for any of the symptoms Mary had told him were common in those afflicted by the plague. Finding none, he wrapped her threadbare cloak around her and bundled her into the old woollen blanket.

Footsteps sounded from outside. The door slowly opened to reveal Ian and Geordie.

'How is she?' Ian asked.

'Lynelle lives, but barely, and there are no signs of the illness.' Father and son crept closer. 'She is as cold as a loch in winter and I need one of you to strike a fire.'

'I'll do it,' Ian said, walking straight to the stones in the centre of the cottage.

'I need you to hold her and watch her, Geordie. There is something I have to do.'

Geordie nodded and sat near the fire his son deftly kindled. William brushed stray wisps of hair from Lynelle's pale face, wishing with all his might that she would open her eyes and look at him. She remained still and lifeless.

Pressing a kiss on her cool brow, he settled her into Geordie's waiting arms and ran out the door. Leaping onto his horse, he drew Black around and raced to the bend in the path. Once there, he cut through the oak forest, the thickly leafed branches threatening to tear him from the saddle. Breaking into the meadow on the other side, he spurred Black on to the north.

They galloped over a few rolling hills and through a heather-swathed glen, eating up the single mile between Closeburn and their destination. The length of the journey didn't trouble William. He had to find the one person he trusted to heal Lynelle, and convince her to help him.

He slowed his mount to a canter as they entered the small town of Thornhill. Early morning sunlight washed over the thatched roofs of at least thirty homes. He interrupted two women talking in front of one of the cottages in the town's centre and made his enquiry. Thanking them, he whirled Black around the way they'd come and pulled to a stop at the third cottage on the right.

Leaving the reins trailing, he rushed to the door. It might have been wiser to send Ian in his place. But Ian was a good lad, or perhaps he wasn't as desperate as William, and he wouldn't dare throw the woman across his saddle and force her to come back with him.

Praying she'd forgive him, he knocked and waited, wondering if he'd notice any changes in her over the last half year.

The door opened and he stared at a sturdy woman with greying red hair.

'William,' she said in surprise.

He drew a deep breath. 'Forgive me, Jinny. I need your help.'

Chapter 30

Lynelle clawed her way up from the pit of blackness, fighting to reach the surface. Sandalwood. Lavender. The smells she'd inhaled before, though this time a brightness teased the darkness behind her heavy lids and William's deep voice rumbled through her dream. With her heart fluttering, she strained toward the light.

'Come to me, Lynelle.'

I'm coming, she wanted to tell him, but the words were trapped, her voice lost. Her skin tingled, as if she could feel the warmth of his embrace. Never had a dream seemed so real. Never had she been taken to the place she most wanted to be – cradled in William's arms.

Lynelle pushed forward, and the murky fog surrounding her thinned to a swirling mist.

'Jinny. She stirs again.'

William's low words spurred her on.

'Patience, lad. Give her time.'

A woman's lilting tone, unfamiliar yet soothing. Scratches of light flickered between her lashes, beckoning. She forced her weighted lids to open.

'Lynelle.'

Her heart clenched at the sound of William's hoarse whisper. Her pulse skittered at the sight of his beloved face. Dear God. He looked so real.

She lifted her hand, wanting to touch him, afraid he'd disappear, afraid not to try. Dark bristles scored her fingertips.

'William?' Her voice croaked.

'Welcome back, lass.'

Lynelle blinked, and stared into shimmering silver eyes.

'Here, William,' the woman with the unknown voice said. 'Encourage the lass to drink, while I assure the others all will be well.'

'Thank you, Jinny,' William said quietly. 'For everything.'

Lynelle sipped from the cup William held to her lips, savouring the cool water as it slid down her parched throat.

'You came,' Lynelle said in wonder.

'I had to see you,' William said. 'I couldn't stay away.'

'But the sickness...'

'Rest easy, Lynelle. Nae others have taken ill.' Gentle fingers caressed her brow, her cheek. 'You stopped the plague from spreading. Many more might have died if not for you.'

Memories flooded back and a chill swept through her. She clutched his shirt. 'Elspeth'

'Hush, lass.' The pad of one finger settled on her lips. 'I know you did all you could.' Sorrow filled his eyes. 'Perhaps they weren't meant to be saved.'

It hadn't been enough, but she had done everything within her power. A shuddering breath escaped her, and the guilt holding her rigid slowly drained from her body.

'The villagers constantly praise your efforts,' William said, breaking into her pain-filled thoughts. 'Jinny had to bar the door to keep them out, while they argued over who should tend you.'

'Jinny?'

'She was the only one I trusted to care for you.'

'You trust Jinny?'

'Aye. Thanks to you, I finally realized healers are people, and can die too.' He took her hand and pressed his mouth into her palm. 'I was wrong to blame Jinny for the loss of my family. My inability to aid those I love blinded me, and Jinny suffered for my helplessness.'

Warmth pooled in her belly, knowing he'd made peace with Jinny and himself.

A ghost of a smile touched his lips. 'Though I did find it difficult not to sample each potion Jinny brewed, before giving them to you.'

'You would do that ... for me?'

'I'd do anything to keep you here with me.'

Tears welled, and seeped from her eyes.

'What is it, Lynelle?'

She swallowed, relishing his touch as he wiped the moisture from her cheeks. 'I have been cursed all my life, yet you risk your life to care for me.'

'I don't believe in curses, lass.' His hand cupped her face and he looked into her eyes. 'But I believe in you.'

Lynelle's breath caught. 'But ... my father?'

'Doesn't deserve a daughter such as you.'

A wisp of pity for her father rose inside her. 'My father still grieves. He lost his wife the day I was born, and his son.' William frowned. 'I am a twin,' she said softly.

'Ah.' His brows lifted. 'You truly are special,' he said, stroking her hair. 'Blessed with strength and courage, even then. More reason your father should have cherished you.'

She searched his handsome face, struggling to believe she lay in his arms. Dark circles smudged the skin beneath his eyes.

'How long...?'

'How long have the villagers despaired of hearing you would live?' His fingers skimmed her cheek. 'Three days.'

Three days?

His eyes locked with hers. 'But it seems I have waited forever to say, I love you, Lynelle.'

Her heart soared, and a fresh bout of tears blurred her vision. She blinked them away.

'I love you, William,' she whispered.

A slow smile tilted the corners of his mouth as he gazed down at her. 'One more thing, my precious little fool.'

The endearment washed over her, warming her soul.

'Will you marry me, Lynelle?'

She stared into sparkling-grey eyes, finally discovering the place where she belonged.

'Aye, William,' she said softly, as her heart overflowed with joy.

'But first, I have a request, my handsome, brooding laird.'

'What is your wish?' William asked as his thumb traced her mouth.

'A kiss.'

William's eyes darkened and a grin stole over his face. 'I must warn you, Lynelle. Once we are wed, I won't stop at a single kiss.'

Reaching up, she curled her fingers about his nape. 'Praise Saint Jude,' she said with a smile, and pulled his mouth down to hers.

BESTSELLING TITLES BY ESCAPE PUBLISHING...

The Chieftain's Curse
Frances Housden

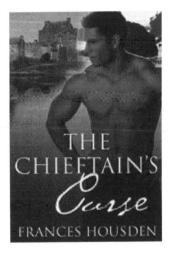

Nominated for the 2014 RITA Award for Best Historical Romance

Euan McArthur is a chieftain in need of an heir.

While still a young a warrior, Euan incites the fury of a witch. She retaliates with a curse that no wife will ever bear him an heir. As he buries his third wife and yet another bonnie stillborn son, Euan can no longer cast her words aside.

Morag Farquhar is a woman in need of sanctuary. With a young relative in tow, Morag flees the only home she has ever known to escape her brother,

Baron of Wolfsdale, and find sanctuary in the MacArthur stronghold. Pronounced barren by a midwife, Morag is of little value to her family, but a Godsend to Euan, a lover he can't kill by getting with child.

Years ago, chance drew them together, and tangled their lives in ways they could never have imagined. This time their destiny lies in their own hands, but it will take courage and strong hearts to see it through to the end.

Chieftain By Command
Frances Housden

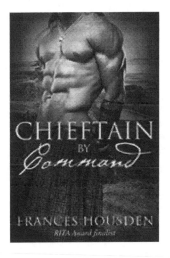

From the bestselling, RITA nominated author Frances Housden comes the gripping, sensual, suspenseful follow-up to The Chieftain's Curse...

Gavyn Farquhar's marriage is forged with a double-edged blade. Along with the Comlyn clan's lands, a reward from the King, he is blessed with an unwilling bride, Kathryn Comlyn, and an ancient fort with few defences that desperately needs to be fortified before it can act as a sufficient buffer between Scotland and the Norsemen on its northern borders.

Gavyn needs wealth to meet his king's demands, and he knows of only one way to get it—with his sword. Leaving his prickly bride behind in the hands of trusted advisors, he makes his way to the battlegrounds of France and the money that can be made there.

Two years married and Kathryn is still a virgin. A resentful virgin, certain that, like her father before her, she is perfectly capable of leading the Comlyn clan. In her usurper husband's absence, she meets the clan's needs, advising and ruling as well as any man.

But she is an intelligent woman, and she knows the only respect and power she will ever hold will be through her husband. And to wield it, she needs to make him love her. An easy task to set, but impossible to complete, when said husband has been gone for two years, and there is no word of his return. But Kathryn is undeterred. After all, a faint heart never won a Chieftain.

Jazz Baby
Téa Cooper

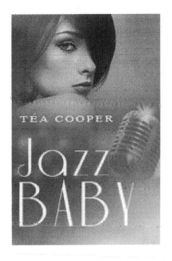

In the gritty underbelly of 1920s Sydney, a fresh-faced country girl is about to arrive in the big, dark city – and risk everything in the pursuit of her dreams.

Sydney is no place for the fainthearted – five shillings for a twist of snow, a woman for not much more, and a bullet if you look sideways at the wrong person.

Dolly Bowman is ready and willing to take on all the brash, bustling city has to offer. After all it is the 1920s, a time for a girl to become a woman and fulfil her dreams. Turning her back on her childhood, she takes up a position working as a housemaid while she searches for her future.

World War I flying ace Jack Dalton knows he's luckier than most. He's survived the war with barely a scratch, a couple of astute business decisions have paid off, and he's set for the high life. But a glimpse of a girl that he had forgotten, from a place he's tried to escape suddenly sets all his plans awry. Try as he might he can't shake the past, and money isn't enough to pay the debts he's incurred.

Connect with us for info on our new releases, access to exclusive offers, free online reads and much more!

Sign up to our newsletter

Share your reading experience on:

The Escapades Blog

Facebook

Twitter

Watch our reviews, author interviews and more on *Escape Publishing TV*